HOW TO WRITE A LOVE STORY

ublishing and the non-profit sector before

Catherine Walsh was born and raised in Ireland. She has a degree in Popular Literature and the only prize she ever won for writing was at the age of 14 in school (but she still cherishes it).

She lived in London for a few years where she worked in Publishing and the non-profit sector before returning to Dublin where she now lives between the mountains and the sea. When not writing, she is trying and failing to not kill her houseplants.

ALSO BY CATHERINE WALSH

One Night Only
The Rebound
Holiday Romance
The Matchmaker
Snowed In
Merrily Ever After

CATHERINE WALSH
HOW TO WRITE A LOVE STORY

SPHERE

SPHERE

First published in Great Britain in 2026 by Sphere

1 3 5 7 9 10 8 6 4 2

Copyright © Catherine Walsh 2026

The moral right of the author has been asserted.

*All characters and events in this publication, other than those
clearly in the public domain, are fictitious and any resemblance
to real persons, living or dead, is purely coincidental.*

All rights reserved.
No part of this publication may be reproduced, stored in a
retrieval system, or transmitted, in any form, or by any means, without
the prior permission in writing of the publisher, nor be otherwise circulated
in any form of binding or cover other than that in which it is published
and without a similar condition including this condition being
imposed on the subsequent purchaser.

A CIP catalogue record for this book
is available from the British Library.

ISBN 978-1-408-73413-1

Typeset in Fanwood by M Rules
Printed and bound in Great Britain by
Clays Ltd, Elcograf S.p.A

Papers used by Sphere are from well-managed forests
and other responsible sources.

Sphere
An imprint of
Little, Brown Book Group
Carmelite House
50 Victoria Embankment
London EC4Y 0DZ

The authorised representative
in the EEA is
Hachette Ireland
8 Castlecourt Centre
Dublin 15, D15 XTP3, Ireland
(email: info@hbgi.ie)

An Hachette UK Company
www.hachette.co.uk

www.littlebrown.co.uk

This one's for my parents.

CHAPTER ONE

Sam

NEW YORK

'He's not going to fire you.'

'He might.'

'He won't, Sam. You're basically his protégé. And also one of, like, three straight men in publishing. They need to keep numbers up.'

'Funny.'

I switch my phone to the other ear as I accept my coffee from the already exhausted-looking barista. It's not even eight a.m., and the Monday morning rush is in full swing. Behind me, a pack of finance bros in crisp white shirts and open spread collars read their emails as they wait to order, and for once I don't look completely out of place next to them. Granted, my shirt is neither as crisp nor as white as theirs, but I wanted to make an effort this morning. As if forgoing my usual uniform of dark jeans and the first sweater I find will make my boss go, *Here's a man I need on my team.* Or, at the very least, *Here's a man who owns an iron.*

I mean, it can't hurt.

'Plus, he asked you to come in early,' Lizzie continues as though reading my mind. 'If he wanted to fire you, he'd ask you to stay late.'

'How do you figure that?'

'Because that's what I'd do.'

'But you don't have a job.'

'Excuse me?' My sister's tone sharpens. 'You think looking after three boys under five isn't a job?'

'An *office* job,' I correct, clutching my laptop bag to my chest as I squeeze past the line. 'Like the one I'm about to lose.'

'Could you stop sounding so defeatist? At least save some of that self-pity for when it happens.'

'When it—'

'*If*,' she hurries on. '*If* it happens.'

'You're bad at pep talks.'

'I know.' Her voice grows faint next to the roar of traffic as I step outside, and I turn up the volume on my phone.

'Do you want to say good morning to Oliver before we hang up?' Lizzie asks.

'He's three months old.'

'Exactly. He's developing. He should learn his uncle's voice.'

'How about this: when I'm unemployed, I'll spend the whole day with him. The whole *week*.'

'You'll be fine.' The words sound sympathetic enough that I don't believe her. 'And anyway, would it be such a bad thing?'

'Would losing my job be a *bad* thing?'

'I just mean that you've been working so hard and—'

'I like my job, Liz!'

'*Okay*. Sorry. Just let me know how it goes, all right? And don't make any stupid decisions in the meantime.'

'I make no promises,' I say, and we hang up as I scan the five-word email I've read a hundred times since I got it last night.

See me in the morning.

Seriously? That could mean anything from *I'm giving you a promotion* to *pack up your stuff*. And this is what Lizzie doesn't understand. It doesn't matter how well I'm doing. Cutbacks are happening everywhere in the industry. Two of my friends were let go in the past month alone. That's the state of publishing right now. More books. Fewer staff. And those of us who remain have to pick up the slack. I can't count the number of all-nighters I've pulled recently. All the weekend work and reading on the commute. And okay, maybe it was getting to the point where I was starting to envisage a world where my entire social life didn't hinge on whether or not my authors got their drafts in on time. But I thought about it in the way someone thinks about shaving their head, or selling all their possessions to travel the world. Not seriously.

And definitely not right now.

I take a sip of coffee, dread pooling in my stomach as I force myself through the revolving doors of our building and into the elevator.

Richardson Books takes up two floors of an office in Midtown and is almost empty when I stride inside. We have flexible hours, but there are only a few early birds at their desks, and they don't give me a second glance until Amy, one of our assistants, takes one look at me and bursts out laughing.

'Oh, Sam,' she says, pretending to wipe away a tear. 'Sammy Sam Sam. Samothy.'

'What?'

'Nice shirt, boss.'

'I have a meeting today and— Shit.' I glance down, finally clocking what she means as I see the large brown stain spreading down my front.

'I think you pull it off,' she says as I set the coffee down.

'How the hell did that happen?'

'It's because your cup is leaking,' Deborah says, barely lifting her eyes from her computer. She works across from me, and I like to think she secretly enjoys my company even though she makes it very clear every day that she doesn't. 'You should have double-checked the lid.'

'Didn't you feel it?' Amy asks, pointing her phone my way.

'Obviously not.'

'I would have felt it.'

'This is why I don't drink coffee,' Deborah adds.

Amy grins. 'You are peak Monday morning right now,' she tells me. 'If you were wearing heels, they'd be broken.'

'Then thank God I'm not,' I mutter, undoing the buttons only to realise the coffee's leaked through to my undershirt. That sends Amy cackling again, and it's at that moment that my fellow editorial director, Laura, walks into the office, sipping from an extra-large, not-leaking iced latte.

'Why is Sam stripping?'

'We're starting a romance imprint,' Amy quips as I shrug the first layer off.

'I'm sure romance readers have better taste than that,' Laura says, ignoring my *ouch* look as she tosses me one of the many blankets she keeps under her desk.

'Don't listen to her,' Amy says. 'You're extremely hot. If I were poly—'

'This is a professional environment,' Deborah interrupts.

Laura kicks Amy's chair. 'Are you taking pictures?'

'Just of his arms.'

'Delete,' Laura warns. 'Now.'

'But he needs them to reel in women online.'

'No, he doesn't.'

Amy waits until her back is turned before gesturing me over, and I pause at the not-terrible photo of me on her screen.

She's right. I do need to reel. 'Send that one to me first.'

She nods, completely serious. 'If you pretend to take your shirt off again, I can get a great shot of your—'

'*Samuel*.'

As one, we turn to where my name was yelled from the next room. Right. That.

Amy snorts as I wrap the blanket around my shoulders, trying to cover myself.

'You've been summoned,' Deborah says.

'And you're telling me no one has any spare T-shirts? I helped pack three boxes of blogger swag-bags last week, and there's not a single branded T-shirt left?'

Amy bats her lashes. 'I have a little black dress in my drawer.'

'I'm giving you three hours of printing today,' I tell her, and turn with as much dignity as I can muster towards the small side office.

Laura catches up with me before I'm even halfway there. 'You're in early,' she says, sounding so casual that I laugh.

'He wants a meeting.'

'What kind of meeting?'

'Don't know yet.' I stop, turning to face her. 'Why are *you* in early?'

'Because I'm a go-getter,' she says, innocent as ever. 'You want me to sit in?'

'Nope.'

We stare at each other as she takes a slow sip of her latte.

Laura is my work nemesis. In the purely professional sense. She joined the company a few years ago, leapfrogged a whole job level and now we work side by side overseeing the editorial department. She's really good at what she does, which is great for Richardson Books and terrible for me, because I am also really good at what she does and that's been fine until now. Until the point where we're both vying for the same promotion.

All the more reason to get rid of one of us.

'It creeps me out when you do that non-blinking thing,' I say when she doesn't move.

'I know.'

'*Samuel!*'

Shit. I tug the blanket tighter. 'Your paranoia is making me late.'

'All part of the plan,' she stage-whispers, and backs away as I poke my head through the doorway to find my boss at his desk.

Casey Richardson is a self-described *relic of the publishing industry*. He rose through the ranks long before I was even born, and his eye for spotting talent is the stuff of legends. His authors love him. His staff do too, which is why many of them followed him when he set up his own publishing house thirty years ago, dedicated to bringing the best sci-fi and fantasy fiction to shelves around the world. Even now, at seventy-three, he shows no signs of slowing down. He still reads more than anyone I know. Still comes to the office every day and is usually first in and last out. He hired me as an editorial assistant ten years ago, and I can't imagine working anywhere else. I don't want to.

'You rang?' I ask, knocking on the doorframe.

'That was me shouting, actually.' He looks up from his phone, peering at me over his thin-rimmed glasses. 'You're not wearing a shirt.'

'No.'

'All right. Close the door.'

I hesitate, but he doesn't miss a beat.

'You're not being fired.'

Well, that's a relief. 'You could have mentioned that in your email.'

'My apologies.'

He gestures to the armchair in front of his desk, and I swing the door shut before gently nudging Melville out of the way. Casey's cat doesn't like me, but he doesn't like anyone (the Deborah of the cat world, if you will), so I don't take offence when he hisses at me.

'What's up?' I ask, more relaxed now we're not at doomsday scenario.

Casey puts his phone down and leans forward, steepling his fingers together. 'Ciara Sheridan.'

I wait a long moment. He doesn't go on. 'What about her?'

'What do you know of her?'

'Frank Sheridan's daughter? I know that she's Frank Sheridan's daughter.'

Casey gives me a look. 'You don't have to pretend in here, Sam. I know you're a fan. It's why I hired you.'

Right. Ciara Sheridan. 'She's an only child,' I offer. 'Somewhere near thirty. Her favourite colour is blue.'

Casey's eyebrows rise.

'He mentioned it in a *New Yorker* interview.'

'I see,' he says. 'I meant professionally.'

Yeah, that makes more sense. 'Crime author. Or at least she used to be. She had a series under a pseudonym.'

'She did. Three books. Three good books, as a matter of fact. But she got stage fright when her real name was revealed and didn't publish again.'

'I heard she moved to France.'

'Did you? And where did you hear that?'

Reddit. 'Around.'

'It was London,' he says, readjusting his glasses as he turns to his computer. 'But she moved back to Ireland just before Frank died. She lives there now.'

'In his house?'

'In his house.'

I let out a low whistle. Frank's house is famous. Almost as famous as his books. He bought it after he sold his first million copies, and it became this mythical pilgrimage site for his readers. He lived in the middle of nowhere, and locals kept tight-lipped, but it didn't stop people from travelling halfway around the world to try to find it. I'd thought about making the trip myself after college, but when I got the job here I'd figured the whole 'stalking one of our authors' vibe might be frowned upon. Especially someone like him.

Even after his death, Frank Sheridan is still our biggest name. His Ravian books, a nine-volume epic fantasy series, have sold in the tens of millions, aided by a wildly successful movie trilogy. Everything remotely to do with him turns to gold, so if Casey is bringing up his daughter...

'Is she writing something else? Under her own name?' Just the thought has me sitting straighter. The marketing plan writes itself.

But Casey's being coy.

'She is.'

'Fantasy?'

'That's the plan.'

'Finally walking in her father's footsteps.'

'You could say that. She's writing *The Last Mountain*.'

I laugh, as anyone would when their boss tells a joke. But Casey doesn't say anything more. He just continues to tap away with slow, deliberate prods of the keyboard, waiting for me to catch up.

It takes me a minute. '*The Last Mountain.*'

'Yes.'

'As in . . .'

'Yes.'

'Ciara Sheridan is writing *The Last Mountain*?'

Casey's eyes shoot to the door and I press my lips together. 'Sorry,' I say, lowering my voice. 'But . . . what?'

The Ravian series wasn't supposed to be nine books; it was supposed to be ten. And, for years, *The Last Mountain* had been the promised culmination of nearly two decades of storytelling. The ending to it all. Like everyone else, when Frank died I'd resigned myself to never knowing what was supposed to happen to the characters I'd grown up with, to this world I'd loved. So . . . *what*?

'He kept copious notes,' Casey continues.

'He said he didn't want anyone else to write it.'

'Anyone but her, though he didn't say that in public. He knew the pressure she'd face.'

'But she's writing it now?'

'Yes.'

'But she's . . .' I shake my head. 'But he didn't . . .'

'Sam?'

'I think I need to sit down.'

'You are sitting down.'

Oh.

Casey pushes a glass of water towards me.

'Frank got in touch with me a few years ago,' he explains as I take a gulp. 'He said he'd started writing it, but I never thought he'd finish.

I knew he was unwell and assumed he was just growing sentimental. But after his death his estate sent some final letters and things he wanted me to have. Among them were explicit instructions regarding his final manuscript. Chiefly, that he wanted Ciara to finish it. I waited a few months to give her space and then reached out. When I asked her if she would write it, she said yes.'

She said yes.

Ciara Sheridan said yes.

The team are going to lose their minds.

Not that we'll need to work that hard. We could charge fifty dollars a copy and people would still buy it. Hardback. Paperback. Special edition. Exclusive edition. Bonus material. *Complete box set*. We could repackage the whole series. No more talks about cutbacks. We'd probably have to double our staff just to keep up with it all.

My heart starts to race just thinking about it. Frank Sheridan's final book. Frank Sheridan's *final book*. This is it. This is the moment that makes up for every late night and every long email. This is the moment that—

Casey shuffles some papers. 'I don't think she'll be able to do it.'

And I swear there's a goddamn record-scratch in my brain.

'What do you mean?'

'The first few chapters were good,' he says. 'So good that I thought about telling you all weeks ago, but I wanted the book on my desk before we announced it. We can't afford to make any mistakes.'

'Understood,' I say slowly. 'So what's the problem?'

'She hasn't written any more. She hasn't sent me anything in five weeks. And she's barely responded to my emails in the past two.'

'Maybe she's just putting her head down,' I point out. 'Doing the work.'

'Maybe,' he agrees. 'But maybe not.'

'You think she's bailing?'

'I think she's struggling. In fact, she told me as much in her last message.'

I sit back, confused. 'So we'll get a ghostwriter. Put her name on the cover. The important thing is that we get the story right.'

Casey frowns, but I don't see the issue.

'Or we say she was a contributing writer,' I insist. 'She did some Zoom calls. Came up with the character names. It's not like every random celebrity doesn't do the same thing.'

'But this is not a random book. And Frank was clear that he wanted her and only her to write it, or no one at all. When she agreed so quickly, I hoped she was up for it, but I think we'll need to do some hand-holding.'

'You want her to come to New York?'

'I proposed that, but she refused. Says she has too much to do at home.'

'What, then?'

'That's why I wanted to speak to you,' he says as Melville hops from one stack of papers to another. 'I was hoping you'd go to Ireland for me.'

'To—' I break off with a wince as the cat lands directly on my lap, digging his claws into my thighs. 'Excuse me?'

'Ireland,' he repeats as I encourage Melville off.

'And do what?'

'Something on this scale can't be worked out over a few emails. I want you to sit with her and go through Frank's notes. I don't expect her to piece it together by herself, and no one here knows these characters better than you do.'

'Is that your way of saying I'm a giant nerd?'

'It's my way of saying that this is my solution to publishing the biggest book I'll ever work on.'

'Paul is supposed to send his draft back in a few days,' I remind him. He's my most difficult author, but he writes extremely sellable books. When he wants to, that is.

'We can move things around. I'm sure Amy will be eager for the opportunity to take on some titles.'

'And she deserves it, but—'

'Sam,' he interrupts, and I shut up. 'I'm asking if you would like to edit the final book in one of the most popular series of all time. One that you grew up reading and that, if published right, will probably define your career. Is that something you're interested in?'

'It's only my greatest dream,' I admit, and I swear his lips twitch.

'Then it's decided. Your passport's up to date?'

'I think so.' I shift in my seat as Melville stretches and settles on the windowsill. 'Does anyone else know?'

'No one. We're keeping it quiet at Ciara's request. She doesn't like publicity.'

'Please tell me she's not a recluse.' Visions of a peephole-peering, get-off-my-property figure come to mind, but Casey shakes his head.

'She just doesn't want the pressure of too much attention.'

'Then she's writing the wrong book,' I mutter.

He gives me a knowing look. 'I can ask Laura to take over if you don't—'

'No,' I say quickly. 'Sorry. It's just a lot to wrap my head around.'

'I know. And I know it's a big change to the schedule, but I want you on this, Sam. I'm trusting you to get this done.'

'But how will I—'

'I'll send you an email with the details.'

That's Casey-speak for *get to work*.

'Okay, then,' I say as his phone starts ringing. 'I guess I'll start on my handover.'

'Wonderful. And Sam?'

'Yeah?'

'Find a shirt, would you?'

CHAPTER TWO

Ciara

COUNTY KERRY, IRELAND

Three weeks later

The beach is busy today. I guess it's been busy since early April, when the weather first changed, but it's especially busy today. They must have let the schools out early. Or maybe everyone's just playing hooky.

I can't blame them if so. My father used to say that nowhere is more beautiful than Ireland in the sunshine. Probably because we never get that much of it. Especially on the west coast, where it rains fifty per cent of the year. We're used to clouds here. To dull, drab grey permeating our world. And so, when they part, when that big ball of fire shines down on us, it's a little like Dorothy stepping into Oz. The grass looks greener, the rivers sparkle and everyone walks around with bemused looks as they inform each other that for two hours the other day we were hotter than Seville.

There now, they say triumphantly. *Where else would you get it?*

Beautiful. For a week or two anyway. Because the thing is, when you're not used to much more than that, when your buildings are designed to keep *in* the heat and your entire humid-loving ecosystem has developed around the rain you so often complain about, you start to long for a breeze. For an item of clothing you haven't sweated through. And as I stand manning the tiny smoothie truck on this sweltering May afternoon, watching a mother diligently cover her toddler head to toe in sunscreen, I wonder how much longer my people, my temperate, let-me-just-grab-a-jacket people, can pretend to enjoy this.

'What the hell are you doing?'

Maddie's voice whips through the cramped space of the truck, sounding so furious that I look down to make sure I'm still peeling bananas and not, you know, murdering a small child.

'*Ciara.*'

'What!' I exclaim as she stomps inside. 'Stop yelling at me. I'm on my period.'

'No, you're not; we're synced. Where's Natalie?'

'I let her go early.'

'You can't do that. You don't work here.'

'And apparently she doesn't know that.'

Maddie plucks the banana skin from my hands, dumping it into a bin bag before pinning her glare on me. 'You're supposed to be at home. Writing.'

'I'm taking a break.'

'You're procrastinating.'

'And providing you with free labour in the process. I'm making smoothies,' I add when she goes to argue. 'I'm not heading down the mines for the day. Plus, you have air-conditioning.' I grab the small portable fan from the shelf, holding it up to my face. 'We're in the middle of a heatwave.'

'It's going to be in the late twenties for a couple of days. That's barely a heatwave.'

'They say it's going to be like this for the whole summer. The shops have run out of factor 50.'

'No, they haven't.'

'The tar is melting on the roads.'

'Get out of my truck.'

'Right after I help this gentleman.'

I nudge her out of the way, beaming at the man approaching the counter. He's cute. Got the whole surfer-boy vibe going for him. Probably a tourist. You can tell because he's one of the few people here who doesn't look as if they're dying from sunstroke.

'Hello there,' he says, smiling up at me. 'And how's your afternoon going so far?'

'Oh, I've had worse. What can I get you?'

He barely glances at the menu before picking the first thing. 'I'll take a banana crush.'

'Fabulous choice. Lucky I prepped ahead of time, huh?' I add to Maddie, who huffs as she starts scooping ice. 'Would you like some honey with that?'

'I'd love some . . .' He peers at my nametag. 'Sierra.'

'*Keer*-ah,' I correct. 'It's a hard C.'

'It's cute.'

'It's four-fifty.' Maddie leans past me, card machine in hand, and the man's attention flicks to her. His smile stays right where it is.

'And what's your—'

'No. Pay. Thank you.'

Oh, she is not in a good mood. *It's not you*, I want to tell Mr Flirty, but then I catch him checking out my boobs, so I don't.

'It's really your people skills that make this business such a success,' I say when he's gone.

She ignores me. 'Did you sleep okay last night?'

'Yes.'

'Are you sure?'

'I don't know, Mads. I was asleep, wasn't I?'

For an hour or two, anyway.

I woke up this morning with a ball of anxiety in my stomach so tight that all I could do was lie there until I needed to pee badly enough that I got up. And I tried after that. I did. I showered and dressed and turned on my computer and opened up all the things I needed to, but the room was too warm and my mind was too empty and when I went down to the kitchen it was to find the sink leaking and the freezer not freezing and one of the pictures I'd hung last week fallen to the floor and smashed, scattering glass all over the tiles. On top of that, John, my postman, rocked up to the house with the usual bundle of seven fan letters addressed to my father, and I had to find a new box for them because the others were already full.

I like John, but he always brings me seven letters, a number so exact that I'm starting to think he's lying to me about them. As if he's hoarding a lot more but thinks *seven's enough. She'll be able to handle seven.*

Well, joke's on him.

I can't handle anything.

And the way Maddie's looking at me right now, I think she knows it.

'I didn't send Natalie home,' I say. 'She's taking a break. She'll be back in five.'

Maddie just shakes her head.

She does that a lot these days, but I understand why. Her

frustration comes from worry, which comes from love because she's been my best friend since we were kids, which means she's stuck with me. And ever since I moved back to look after Dad, she stops by the house every other day to pop in and check up. Real *I was just in the neighbourhood* vibes for someone who lives an hour in the other direction. But she continues to do it anyway. Because that's what she does. She was there throughout my father's sickness and then his funeral. She let me mourn and grieve and stay in bed for days on end, and now, slowly but surely, she's doing her best to make sure I don't stay that way forever.

Which is why I'm not entirely unconvinced I won't wake up chained to my laptop one of these days.

'Where were you anyway?' I ask. 'I've been here unsupervised for a whole twenty minutes.'

'I went to see the café,' she says, checking her stock of strawberries. 'One of the boards across the window came loose and I found I can see inside if I squint hard enough.'

'That is ...' I shake my head. 'You have a problem, you know that?'

Her expression turns wistful. 'I know.'

Maddie is the proud owner of this smoothie truck, but it's not exactly her dream. That would be the long-abandoned, dilapidated unit ten minutes up the road. She wants to open a café there some day, but that involves a lot of money she doesn't have, and the banks aren't exactly lining up to hand out loans to seasonal businesses that are shutting up shop everywhere else.

Still, she works and she saves and she keeps that dream alive, so really she should be accepting all the free help she can get.

I give her a hopeful smile. 'Do you want me to man the ice-cream machine?'

'I want you to go home and write,' she says. 'Or at least get some sleep. You look exhausted.'

'Rude.'

'But true. Did you read that article about insomnia I sent you?'

Last time I checked, there were a thousand and twelve unread emails in my inbox, so . . . no.

'I'll be grand,' I tell her as I try to catch the eye of two teenage girls walking past. They're in a fast-food mood, though, and head straight for the burger joint parked next to us. Our neighbours are a bit of sore spot for Maddie, seeing as how she was supposed to be the only food truck this summer, and sure enough, she follows my gaze with a scowl as they join the queue.

'I keep getting his deliveries.'

'Whose?'

'*Shane's*,' she says, as though his mere name is enough to put her in a bad mood.

'Burger Boy's?'

'They never put his name on the order form, so they give everything to me because I'm the only one here in the mornings. Which means I have to sort through it all and deliver it myself.'

'Travelling a whole three metres to the left.'

'It's the principle of the thing,' she mutters, holding a chilled water bottle to her cheek.

'Just go and talk to him. Tell him you're going to stop minding his stuff.'

'I've tried! He's never there, is he? He probably manages the whole thing from some penthouse apartment. I bet you he has a business on every beach in the country.'

I nod, though I've listened to the same spiel from her a hundred times already. I get it. She's worried about the competition. But it's not as though she'll be short on customers for the next few months. That sun isn't going anywhere.

'Maybe we should start table service,' I say. 'We could make up a batch of juices.'

'Didn't I tell you to leave?'

'And I'll find a tray to—'

'Ciara.' Maddie's hands land on my shoulders, her eye contact almost unnerving in its directness. 'You are the most beautiful, talented, wonderful friend I could possibly have, I love you with my whole heart and thank the universe every day that we grew up in the same place at the same time, but if you don't go home in the next five minutes and write your book, I will, without hesitation, dump a carton of yoghurt all over your head.'

'That's food waste.'

'Get out of my truck.'

And, with a firm hold on my elbow, she escorts me out.

Thirty minutes later, I turn off the radio and pull up outside my house, already missing the distraction of other people. The air-conditioning in my car is weak at best, and I can feel a headache coming on, a dull pounding at the base of my neck that's been threatening me all day. I always seem to have a headache these days, but I guess only getting three or four hours of sleep a night will do that to a person. I don't need a doctor to tell me that.

This one feels especially dramatic, though, so I grab my bag from the passenger seat and root around for a painkiller as my phone lights up with a text from Maddie.

I probably shouldn't have told her about the publisher's offer to write *The Last Mountain*. If I'm honest, I'd hoped she'd talk me out of it. But no. She thought the book was a *great* idea. That writing it would take me on some magical journey through grief and out the other side. Now, I realise I should have kept it from her as I'm doing with everyone else; but I tell Maddie everything, and so here we are.

With a link to yet another article.

> *I think you should look at this one. It's on writer's block.*

At that, I scoff.

Writer's block.

I don't have writer's block. I have a dead father and a mountain of bills to pay. I have life block.

Besides, Dad would never dream of having something like that. He always said he didn't have time to. One look at his bibliography and you can see why. He wrote twenty-four novels in his lifetime. Twenty-four novels, eleven short stories and a library of scribbles and notes and thoughts. He spent years working as a teacher during the day and telling stories at night – raising me as a single parent all the while. And if he hadn't come up with the world of Ravian, that's how it might have stayed.

I was seven when it happened. When his dream became a reality. The first book in a new series was published to small but overwhelming praise. Most fantasy books weren't mainstream back then. They were at the back of the bookshop, hidden away. But this one kept going, the word of mouth strong and passionate, and by the time the second one came out eighteen months later it was tipped as the most anticipated novel of the decade.

And then he did a magical thing.

He did it again.

And again and again and again.

I didn't get it at first. I was used to seeing his face in the local paper. I understood it. We were from a small town. Of course everyone knew my dad. Everyone knew everyone.

It was only when I got older, when I started travelling, that I got a real sense of it. Germany on a school trip. France on a summer exchange. Translated versions with unfamiliar covers on Spanish bus stops. A woman reading one on the plane with a spine so creased I was surprised it didn't fall apart when she turned the page.

But despite his newfound fame, our lives didn't change. Dad didn't have much use for money. In fact, he spent most of his career giving it away. Scholarships, grants, prizes. There isn't a university in Ireland that doesn't have a plaque with his name on it. And it wasn't just the literary world. Dog shelters, cat shelters. A stranger needing medical care. He sponsored shirts for the local football team. He bought a school bus for the village down the road. Money was for spending, and life was for living. He wasn't irresponsible. He just didn't believe in keeping it for himself.

But he did make one purchase just for us. One very large, ill-advised purchase, the kind that everyone should make at least once when their life and fortune changes so dramatically for the better.

He bought the house I'm sitting in front of right now.

Four acres, three floors, two rooms hidden behind bookcases, and no architectural style to speak of.

He was obsessed with it. His readers were, too. Maybe because he only ever showed them hints of it. Snaps in the background of author photos. Brief descriptions in articles he wrote.

I think he loved it even more than his books.

And when he died, he left it to me.

And now it's ruining my life.

The thing about big houses is that you need an equally big fund to maintain them. Especially if they're falling down. And even if they're not falling down, there's still property tax and land tax and a million different ways to take money that I don't have.

I know what the smart thing to do is. The simplest thing. Sell it on for a small fortune and set myself free. It's not as if there wouldn't be any takers.

But I can't sell it.

I won't.

Dad wanted me to have this house because it was his favourite place in the world. He didn't want it to go to anyone else. And privately, selfishly, I know that to give it up would be like saying a final goodbye to him. And I'm not ready to do that yet.

So when, a few months ago, I got an email from his old editor, I sent a reply. And after a few days of talking, when Casey Richardson offered me enough money to solve all my problems, I said yes.

All I had to do was the impossible. Write Ravian's final book.

At the time, I figured, why not? I've written books before. And what Casey said to me in that first email was true. No one knows that world better than me. They couldn't, even if they tried. Even if they read all the books a hundred times over. Even if they debated on forums and wrote fan fiction and spent their whole lives growing up loving it. They didn't have an ounce of the information I have access to. The notebooks filled with my dad's neat handwriting. The rough maps scrawled on napkins. All the snippets of all the stories he never had the chance to explore.

I did my research and wrote the first few chapters in a daze, focused on the money and nothing else. But as soon as Casey gave me the thumbs-up, as soon as this became reality, it was as though a curtain came down over my brain, stopping everything in its tracks.

I've been stuck ever since.

Another text arrives from Maddie, another link to another article, and I pop the headache pills into my mouth, swallowing them dry as I tilt my seat back.

As though I've just given my body permission, exhaustion hits me, and I reach out blindly, turning on the radio and letting the quiet voices discussing the hot weather tune out everything else.

Rest.

Just for a few minutes, anyway.

Just a few minutes and then I'll fix it all.

CHAPTER THREE

Sam

There are times in your life when you know the choices you make will change your trajectory forever. Pick a college. Choose a career. Swipe right.

But what these choices can't predict, what you'll never foresee, are all the little moments that occur because of them. Learning you're allergic to hamsters because your roommate insists on keeping one. Almost getting frostbite sleeping out for concert tickets because you're twenty-one and an idiot.

Or finding yourself three thousand miles from home, trying to get more than one bar of signal, because at thirteen you read a certain book and never looked back.

'Hold on,' I say as Amy's voice drops in and out. It's just gone ten a.m. in New York and she's already tried to call me twice. 'I can't hear you.'

I give up on the closed storefront I'd been trying to peer into and jog across the road to a pub, stopping beneath a sign that says *Guinness is good for you.*

'What did you say?' I ask as her voice crackles in my ear.

'I *said*, do you remember in my job interview when I told you it was my dream to become an editor?'

'I do.'

'Well, I take it back,' she says abruptly. 'I don't want to be an editor. I want to work in production with the cool kids.'

I swat a fly from my face and lean back against the wall. I'd dressed for mixed weather as the guidebook said, but the sun is beating down today, and I'm already sweating from the heat of it.

'Has the sheen finally worn off? What's it been – two days without me?'

'I'm not built to work with authors.'

'You asked to work on Paul's book.'

'I reached too high, Sam. I don't know what to tell you. I am Icarus and Paul is the sun and my wings are my ambition, fraying into nothing. It's a real bonus trait of mine that I can admit when I'm wrong. So here I am, admitting that I'm not ready to step up. I would like a demotion, please.'

'Just email the—'

'I did!' she exclaims, and I crack a smile. Amy's good at her job. She's just very theatrical about it. 'I emailed him with my friendliest of tones, and when he didn't reply I emailed his agent, and his agent replied and said he'd get on it, but he did not, Sam. He did not get on it. That man is now a month late sending in the draft, and I'm *this* close to losing it.'

'Be nice,' I warn her. 'We have to stay on their good side.'

'Do we? Or can we send them both into the jungle?'

'Email again and cc me,' I tell her. 'That's all we can do. If they complain down the line when we have to change the publication schedule, then we'll have the receipts.'

'I'm not paid enough for this. I want to work on estate stuff like you.'

'Oh, yeah, I'm having a whale of a time.'

My cover story for the rest of the office is Casey's idea. Apparently I'm here to rustle up some bonus material we can use in future editions. He didn't exactly give me a choice in the matter, but it still makes me uneasy to lie to my team. Especially since Laura looked suspicious as hell when she heard the news.

'At least you get to travel,' Amy continues now, just short of grumbling.

'It's not exactly Paris.' I glance around for some sign of life, wondering what I'm supposed to do. I booked what looked like the only inn around the village, but I'm starting to think I got scammed. The street I'm on is completely deserted. I only know I'm in the right place because of the sign I passed saying *Carrigwest*, but otherwise, it's as if I've stumbled on to an abandoned movie set. Casey had warned me I'd be isolated out here, but, beyond a few houses and one tiny convenience store with a faded *Closed for Lunch* sign, this truly is the middle of nowhere.

'What if I show up at his house?'

'Huh?' I turn around, distracted, as I hear the faint sound of an engine.

'What if I just show up at Paul's house like *Hey, where's that book we paid you six figures for?*' She sounds worryingly serious. 'I'd be polite about it.'

'I'm sure,' I say as a beat-up Ford comes rumbling around the corner. 'But also, no. Don't do that.'

'But—'

'Look, I've got to go. Signal's pretty bad out here. We'll probably get cut off.'

'Don't you da—'

I hang up as the car wheezes to a stop beside me and a man steps out. He looks to be in his late fifties, thin and balding with an easy smile on his face.

'You're the lad taking the room, then?' His accent is so thick it takes me a moment to parse through it.

'That's me. Sam Avery.'

'Ronan Delaney.' His hands go to his hips as he looks me up and down. 'There's no smoking, now. Or drugs.'

'No problem.'

'Or pets.'

'It's just me.'

'Or cheese.'

'I... excuse me?'

'We had an incident a few years ago.'

Right. 'No cheese. Got it.'

'Great! Well, let's get you settled.' He takes my case and gestures at the building beside us. 'You're above the pub here. Don't worry,' he adds, catching my expression. 'It's not a rowdy crowd. But you should pop in later. Meet the locals. New York, is it? I had a brother working in construction there back in the day. Might have outstayed the old visa but he's a good lad. He's in Brisbane now with the wife. Have you ever been to Brisbane?'

'No. I—'

'Never been myself. A bit too far, but he likes it well enough. They have sharks in the water there, apparently. You ever seen a shark?'

I shake my head as Ronan leads me around the side of the building, where right beside the dumpsters is a flimsy-looking door that I hope we're going to walk past, but no.

'It's nothing special,' he warns as he opens it. 'But we haven't had any complaints.'

That I find hard to believe. It's not that I was expecting the Ritz, but...

Huh.

Behind another door at the top of a narrow staircase is a small room that is as bare as bare can be. A single bed made up with a thin floral sheet, a dresser with a mirror, and... that's it. Besides the curtains hanging limply on either side of the window. And, I guess, the faded picture of John F. Kennedy next to one of the popes with a random dog. The walls are white. The furniture is pine. It smells overwhelmingly of chemical air-freshener.

'Here,' Ronan says, passing me a small scrap of paper. 'For the wifi. Do you want a chair?'

I hesitate. There's no desk or anything that needs a chair, so...
'That's okay.'

'Are you sure? I can bring one up from downstairs.'

'Positive. Thank you.'

He spends another minute showing me around. How to open the window (with effort). How to lock the door (also with effort). I'm told that parking outside is free and that the shower in the minuscule ensuite is new and instant, and then he hands me the keys, shakes my hand and off he goes.

It doesn't take long to unpack. I dump my clothes in the dresser, set my laptop on top and shove my suitcase under the bed. The bed that I then check for bugs, Googling for the telltale signs. I find nothing: the room is bad, but clean. So, with nowhere else to stay in this town, I take some pictures because no one back home will believe me, and call my sister because I promised her I would.

She picks up after only a few seconds and switches to a video call, where I get a close-up shot of her nostrils.

'Hi. Hold on.'

'Who's that?' one of my nephews screeches.

'Santa Claus,' Lizzie says. 'He wants to discuss the bad word you said yesterday.'

'Billy *told* me to—'

The door clicks shut behind her, cutting off his outrage.

'Hey,' she says to me. 'Guess who figured out the child locks on the kitchen cabinets?'

'Oh, no.'

'Oh, yes. So that's been fun.'

She finally brings the phone to her face, and I blink at the sight that greets me. 'What are you wearing?'

'It's a face mask. My skin needs moisture.'

'Then drink some water.'

'Never. Are you there? Are you alive?'

'I'm here and alive. My knee hurts, though.'

'Because you're old. And cheap. I thought work trips were supposed to shell out for business class?'

'I work in the arts,' I say, rotating to show her the room. 'This is about as fancy as they can manage.'

'As if you care,' she says with a snort. 'They'd put you in a tent and you'd still fall to your knees thanking them. You're *editing Frank Sheridan's book.*'

'That's not what I sound like.'

'That's exactly what you sound like. Don't act as if this isn't the greatest thing that will ever happen to you.'

'I feel like you could have phrased that differently.' I sit on the bed, wincing as the springs dig into me. 'How are you?'

'I bought yoga pants online, and they accidentally delivered two pairs. It's literally made my week. What's Ireland like? Green?'

'Not really,' I say, glancing outside. 'Kind of brown. They're going through a heatwave.'

'I'm still jealous. Invite me over.'

'I'm working.'

'With the mysterious author,' she taunts.

'She's not mysterious.'

'She's very mysterious. I looked her up and couldn't find anything. It's like she disappeared off the face of the planet. Have you met her yet?'

'No.'

'Are you going to?'

The questions come at me rapidly, but I'm used to it. Lizzie loves raising her boys full-time, but I know she gets desperate for adult conversation.

'Are you going to meet her now?' she continues as I hear the faint yells of a tantrum in the background.

'Maybe,' I say, checking the time. Past three p.m. 'She hasn't responded to my email, but Casey said he sent over the introductions.'

'She hasn't responded because she's *mysterious*.' Something crashes at her end, and I fight a yawn as she yells at one of my nephews. 'Just remember, you need to eventually befriend her so I can befriend her, and then I can know a famous person. So be cool, okay? Don't be you.'

I let the phone fall to the side as I lie back on the bed with a thump. 'What's that supposed to mean?'

'I think you know,' she says as I rub my eyes. And then, 'Is that a picture of the Pope with a dog?'

*

An hour later, when I've had a shower and an ill-advised nap, I push open the door of the pub below, a piece of paper clenched in my hand. Casey sent me an email with all the details I'd need, but the address is confusingly simple.

Ciara Sheridan, Carrigwest.

Helpful.

The pub itself is like something on a postcard. Painted a deep red with a green sign saying *Delaney's* over the entrance, it has barrels of wilted flowers outside and old-fashioned lampposts bracketing the door. It takes a moment for my eyes to adjust to the gloomy interior, but, when they do, I find the place cosy but empty, except for Ronan, who stands behind the bar doing a stock-check.

'How are you getting on?' he asks when he sees me. 'Thirsty?'

'Parched. A Diet Coke if you have it.' I perch on one of the stools, feeling too warm in my fresh shirt. 'Do you think you could help me with some directions?'

'I'll do my best,' he says, passing me a small glass bottle followed by a card machine. 'Researching your family, is it?'

'No. I'm looking for Ciara Sheridan's place?'

The way his smile drops, you'd swear I'd added *so I can egg it*. The mood in the pub changes instantly, all of Ronan's previous friendliness vanishing.

'I'm here to help with her father's estate,' I continue after a lengthy silence. 'She knows I'm coming.'

'Is that right?' he asks slowly. 'But you don't have her address.'

'I do, but it's not ... ' I trail off as his eyes narrow. 'She's not responding to her emails,' I finish lamely.

'I can't be giving out private information, now. We get all sorts around here, you understand?'

I don't. But, knowing that's probably as much as I'll get out of the suddenly suspicious bartender, I drink the most awkward soda of my life and head back outside.

She's got to live around here somewhere. Carrigwest only takes up a few miles and I've seen ... five, maybe six houses so far? Granted, none are anywhere near as impressive as what Frank's place is supposed to look like, but it shouldn't be that hard to find if I drive around.

In the end, that's exactly what I do. With the windows down and my GPS on, I travel slowly through the one-street town and out the other side, moving through woodlands and back out to open fields. The roads are narrower here and lined with grey stone walls, but besides a few tourist coaches that I manage not to crash into, I meet little traffic on the way.

I also find nothing. Every side road I come across leads only to small bungalows or old cottages, and I'm weighing up the option of calling Casey and asking him why he hates me when I spy a man resting against a gate up ahead, a sheepdog sitting next to him. When I slow down, he raises his walking stick in acknowledgment.

'Lost, are you?' He has to be nearing ninety but is steady on his feet as he shuffles over to me.

'Only by a lot,' I say as he nears. 'I'm looking for Ciara Sheridan. Am I in the right area?'

'Ciara?' His smile falls momentarily, and with it my hope, before a sly look passes over his face. 'Are you the new boyfriend, then?'

I don't pause. I don't even think. I'm tired and I'm hungry and I keep almost driving on the wrong side of the road. 'Yes,' I say. 'Yes, I am.'

And I feel no guilt when he laughs, looking delighted. 'It's about time you showed your face around here,' he says, pointing a gnarled finger back the way I came. 'You're not far now, but I wouldn't be starting from where we are if I were you. I would have come from the main road, but I'll see you right.'

And he does, in his own way at least, directing me back to the woods I'd passed through earlier.

'If you hit the red house, you've gone too far. But if you see a horse, you haven't gone far enough. You understand?'

Again, not really. But I smile anyway. He makes me repeat it back to him before he's happy, and then he slaps the car roof and waves me goodbye.

But while his instructions may be unorthodox, they also work, and fifteen minutes later I pull up to an unmarked dirt road surrounded by thick trees. I missed it completely when I passed earlier, but now I know what I'm looking for, it seems obvious.

It isn't until I turn up it that I start to get nervous, anticipation making me slow to a crawl. Ever since Casey told me about the book, I've been so focused on getting here and meeting Ciara that I haven't even considered the fact that I'd be seeing her house as well. Frank's house.

The house.

Just the thought of it has me pulling over, and I get out and walk a few steps to shake off the excess energy. I consider myself a grown man and I'm here to do an important job, but I think even Casey would understand my spark of excitement as I realise I'm about to see what so many of Frank's readers dream of. I mean, I've got to take *some* pictures. For Lizzie, at least. And my old college roommate who was as obsessed with the books as I was. Plus, a couple of my friends who—

Yeah. Screw it.

There's a well-trodden path through the trees, and I head into the bright forest, thinking I can circle the place before introducing myself. Turns out it's the right move, and it isn't long before I spy a break through the leaves, a glimpse of hazy sunlight on uncut grass. I pick up my pace, taking out my phone, but I don't make it another step.

At first I think I've slipped on some mud, and I fling my hands out to catch my balance, but when I place my foot forward it meets nothing but air. It happens so fast that I don't realise I'm falling until I stop, my phone still clutched in my hand and my ass firmly in the dirt, as I land at the bottom of what appears, at both first and second glance, to be a giant hole in the ground.

CHAPTER FOUR

Ciara

A shout wakes me so abruptly that I jerk upright, momentarily forgetting where I am. My heart races. My brain screams *danger*. But all I've got is a sore neck and a dry mouth from napping.

At least it's still daylight, the sun blazing high in the sky as I stumble out and scan my surroundings. It might have been just a dream, but it sounded too real for that, and as I stand there, listening, I hear it again.

From the direction of the noise, I have only one guess as to what's happened, mostly because a very drunk Maddie did the same thing a few years ago. And sure enough, when I head into the trees and peek over the large hole in the clearing, my suspicions are confirmed.

There is a man in my pit.

He hasn't heard me approach, he's too busy trying to climb out the other side, so I get a good look at the back of his head and then the rest of him without him noticing. If he were dressed all in black with a balaclava I might have backed away, but instead he's in stained jeans and a filthy white T-shirt that probably weren't stained or filthy five minutes ago.

I watch as he makes another admirable attempt to climb out before giving up. 'Hello?' he calls, clasping his hands around his mouth.

'Hi.'

He spins around to face me, his expression almost comical in its surprise. 'How long have you been there?'

His tone is pretty demanding for someone who's stuck in a hole, but that might just be because he's American, so I let it go.

'About ten seconds,' I say. 'Need some help?'

'Please.' He lifts a hand to wipe his brow, and I hesitate as he does, catching a glimpse of his underarm. Now, I'm not so single that the mere sight of toned triceps renders me speechless. But the simple black tattoo inked there does. The small but unmistakable swirling mark that Finn, the hero of the Ravian series, has.

'Do you have a rope?' the stranger asks, but my concern has morphed into suspicion.

'What are you doing down there?'

He looks confused. 'I fell?'

'No, I mean—' Christ. 'Why are you here? This is private property.' Not that it's ever stopped anyone before. They may not all fall into the pit, but it wouldn't be the first time one of Dad's fans has gone creeping around the house. It got so bad after he died that they had to send a local Garda down for a few days to patrol. The guy wasn't even on the job for a few hours when he caught someone peering in through the window.

But the man gazing up at me doesn't act guilty. He just frowns. As though I'm the one in the wrong here.

I clear my throat, trying to sound authoritative. 'You're trespassing on this land and—'

'Are you Ciara?' he asks, and I break off, startled. 'Ciara Sheridan?' he continues as I take out my phone.

'You're trespassing on this land, and you're an—'

'Editor,' he interrupts. 'I'm your editor.'

Eh?

'Casey sent me,' he continues when I don't say anything.

'You know Casey?'

'You didn't get the emails?'

'I get a lot of emails.' But, even as I speak, something tugs at the back of my mind. Me telling Casey I can't go to New York. Casey saying we could work here instead. But then the builders came back with a quote for the insulation and the gardeners said they'd be delayed until August and a donkey sanctuary in England rang because Dad apparently donated a ridiculous amount of money before he died and they wanted to name a new donkey after him and would that be okay and would I like to come and see the donkey, so no, I don't remember an email telling me about whatever the hell is happening now.

'My name's Sam Avery,' he continues, speaking slowly as though he wants to make sure I understand. 'I'm an editor with Richardson Books. Casey put me in charge of *The Last Mountain*. I'm here to help you with the story.'

As he speaks, I pull up the publisher's website. It takes me two clicks to find him. A few lines of biography accompanied by a photo of a much neater and cleaner version of him smiling in front of some bookshelves.

He is not smiling now.

Shit.

Sam's brows rise and I realise I've spoken out loud.

'Sorry,' I say. 'Sorry. I— don't move!'

'Not a problem,' he mutters, but I don't have time to worry about sarcasm as I race over to the shed at the bottom of the garden and pull out the old ladder. It's too heavy to carry, so I end up dragging it through the grass and then whacking it off every tree in my path; but I manage to get it back to where the guy is, predictably, still in the hole.

'Okay, back up,' I call. 'I'm going to lower it down.'

This turns out to be the easy part. The ground is dry, so there's no slipping as Sam helps me lead the ladder into the pit. He climbs up so quickly that I have to scramble back so we don't knock foreheads, and, when I do, he rises to his full height, all six feet something of him.

He doesn't look like an editor. At least not like the ones I've met before. Old-school, Caseyesque figures who reminded me of my dad and maybe wore some sort of a smoking jacket. This guy looks to be in his early thirties. Short dark hair. Hooded brown eyes. His nose is straight; his face is tired. There's a faint blush of razor burn along his jaw and a smartwatch on his wrist.

'You booby-trapped your house?'

'What?'

He gestures at the pit.

'Oh. No.' Though that's not a bad idea. 'It's old,' I add, growing defensive. 'I forgot it was there. I dug it when I was a teenager.'

His lips part as if he's about to speak, but no sound comes out.

'It sounds worse than it is,' I continue, starting to get embarrassed. 'I wanted to see how deep I had to go to hide a body.'

Jesus, Ciara.

'I used to write crime,' I hurry on before he can say anything. 'I was writing a book about this accidental hitman, and I wanted to be as accurate as possible, so I dug a hole to see how long it would take. It was research.'

'How do you become an accidental hitman?'

'Bad luck.'

Sam stares at me for a long moment before he glances back at the hole. The one I wish I could now jump into. But, when he turns back to me, he seems curious.

'How long?'

'What?'

'How long did it take?'

I hesitate, but he looks serious enough. 'Two days. Or at least I dug it over two days. I probably should have stopped, but my cousin said I couldn't do it, and then it became like an *I'll show you* thing, so . . . ' I'm babbling. 'Sorry. Are you hurt?'

'Not mortally.'

'There's a first-aid kit in the house,' I offer, and his eyes dart to mine with such obvious interest that it's almost laughable.

Almost.

Because I know that look. I've spent most of my adult life dealing with that look, learning to recognise it so I could keep far, far away.

Casey sent a fanboy.

My guilt about the pit dissipates.

I've dealt with men like him my whole life. People who got close to me just because they wanted to get close to my father. It took me two crappy boyfriends before I spotted the trend, too flattered by their interest to see through them. And it wasn't just romantic interest, it was friends too. Classmates, colleagues – I've lost count of the people in my life who saw me only as an extension of him and never just me.

I was halfway through college when I made the rule I still live by.

Don't make friends with people who read.

And certainly not with people who have Ravian tattoos on their arms.

'Is that okay?' he asks when I don't move.

No. 'Sure.' I force a smile on to my face. Professional. Be professional. 'Let's get you patched up.' I make a weird *follow me* motion that I instantly regret, and we leave the ladder where it is as we start the short journey to the house.

'Sorry again,' I say when he limps a little. 'I should put a sign up or something. Did you walk here?'

'I . . . no. I drove.'

'But the woods—'

'Yeah.' The base of his throat goes pink. 'I parked on the road. I just thought I'd— What?'

My arm shoots out to stop him from taking a step further, and I put a finger to my lips as I see a familiar car parked next to mine. One with no one inside.

I drop instantly to the ground.

'Get down,' I hiss.

Sam looks at me as if I've lost my mind. 'Excuse me?'

'Get. Down.' I tug on his jeans to emphasise my point, and he slowly lowers himself to the dirt beside me until he's hidden in the long grass.

As soon as he does, a figure emerges around the side of the house, and Mary Macken calls my name.

'Dare I ask?' Sam murmurs as she places two bottles of milk on my porch.

'She's my sworn enemy.'

'Your sworn enemy is the milk lady?'

'She's not the milk lady. She just brings me milk sometimes.'

He falls silent as she starts knocking on the door.

'Don't take this the wrong way,' he begins, 'but this is the weirdest twenty minutes of my life.'

I glance over to find his eyes on me and forget what we're even doing.

'Why does she bring you gifts?' he asks.

'Mary? She feels beholden to me.'

'Beholden.'

'Her husband lost his job during the recession, and Dad used to fake-employ her to give them some extra cash. Errands, light housework, that kind of thing. It was just an excuse to give her some money, but she's fine now. Civil servant for forty years – she's got a killer pension. But she's kept bringing me stuff like this ever since he died.'

'That sounds nice to me.'

'It's not.'

'Why?'

'Because what am I going to do with two pints of milk?' I whisper. 'Or a box of chocolates that went off five Christmases ago? She doesn't do it to be nice. She does it to get inside. And, if I invite her inside, she'll never leave. And you're still looking at me like I'm an awful person because I didn't explain this well. I've made her seem like a kind, generous figure down on her luck, but she's not; she's the village gossip, and no one likes her. She'll just walk around pointing out all the things I'm doing wrong and telling me all the rumours she's heard. All the while she's gathering rumours about *me*, so trust me when I say we need to stay here until she—'

I jerk, breaking off as Sam flicks my arm.

'Spider,' he explains, and my heart gives this weird thump. 'So she brings you gifts, but only so you have to talk to her.'

'It's a known tactic.'

'How long does she usually hang around?'

'A couple of minutes.'

Sam doesn't respond, hopefully absorbing the importance of what I've just told him as he eases himself into a more natural position. The grass shifts around him as he does, but thankfully Mary isn't looking our way.

'So how's it going?' he asks.

'With what?'

'The book. How's it going?'

'You want to talk about the book?'

'Is it a bad time?'

I bat a dandelion out of my face before it makes me sneeze. We're both still whispering, which only makes this even more ridiculous. 'We're crouching in a field.'

'And from what you've told me, we'll be doing it for a while.' He looks completely earnest, so earnest that I wouldn't be surprised if he whipped out a pen and paper from his pocket. 'I read the chapters you sent to Casey. We both think they're great.'

'Uh-huh,' I say, distracted as Mary scans the treeline.

'And I can tell you know your stuff. The suspense in the first few pages is incredible.'

'But?' This isn't my first rodeo. He's doing that editor thing of easing me in before ripping me apart. *Amazing job! Just a suggestion, but what about rewriting the entire plot? Let's discuss!*

'But,' he continues, 'we've got a long way to go and I'm only here for a few weeks. I was hoping you could send me some more pages tonight so I can see where you're at. Just whatever you've been working on.'

'I can't do that.'

'It doesn't matter if they're rough. Believe me, I've seen it all.'

'It's not that the pages are rough. It's that they're not written. And I— *Finally.*' I blow out a breath as Mary gives up and heads to her car. My leg started cramping thirty seconds ago. 'One more minute, I promise,' I say as she gets inside. 'Just until the coast is clear.'

'What do you mean?'

'Sometimes she hangs around in her car until she—'

'About the book,' Sam interrupts, and I drag my gaze back to him.

'What do you mean, what do I mean?'

'You haven't written anything more?'

'I told Casey that,' I say, growing defensive.

'You told him you were struggling, not that you'd stopped writing.'

'That's what struggling means.'

'No, it means – it *means*,' he says, lowering his voice when I shoot him a look, 'that you're struggling. You're saying you haven't written anything else? It's been months since you sent him something.'

'I've been busy.'

'Doing what? Digging more holes?'

'I'm—'

I duck my head as Mary's car starts. To my surprise, Sam joins me. 'This is ridiculous,' he says, but he doesn't get up. If anything, he sinks down further. 'And it's worrying me that you're not more worried.'

'Why would I be worried?'

'Because a 250,000-word novel is due by the end of the year, and you don't seem concerned. In fact, you're—' He scowls as I motion him to hush again.

It's the wrong move. His lips thin until they're practically non-existent and he gives his head a firm shake. 'I think I should come back tomorrow.'

'But the first-aid kit is—'

'I'm fine. I just need a shower.'

I hesitate, suddenly aware that his mood is no longer a good one. 'Look—' I start, but he doesn't want to hear it.

'You signed a contract. And I know it's hard, but there are a lot of people waiting for this book. A lot of things riding on it, and you need to take it seriously.'

'I am!'

'You ignore Casey's calls. You didn't even know I was coming. And now you're telling me you haven't written a single word in two months?'

'I've written *some*thing.'

'Prove it,' he says, pushing himself to his feet. 'I'll come back in the morning.' He starts forward, only to turn around at the last second as Mary's car drives off. 'It was nice meeting you,' he says stiffly, and I can only gape after him as he strides across the field.

CHAPTER FIVE

Sam

Okay, so bad first day on the job.

Scolding-your-author bad.

Your now-biggest author who lost her father less than a year ago and who your boss sent you across an ocean to help.

I adjust my laptop bag over my shoulder and stare at Ciara's front door as though if I look at it hard enough it will magically open.

Jetlag is kicking my ass this morning. I didn't sleep last night, the surroundings too unfamiliar for me to settle. That, and the heat. There's no air-conditioning in my room. There's no air-conditioning in any room, and when I got up early to drive to the nearest town in search of a portable fan I was laughed out of the store and told I should have come in three weeks ago.

As a result, my patience is not at its highest as I stand here on her porch like a sucker.

I shouldn't have been so short with her. I should have stayed and discussed everything, because that's what an editor does. Contrary to what my family and friends might think, it's not just about reading.

It's about being an ego-manager and a therapist rolled into one. It's knowing when to pull back and when to push hard, and remaining calm when someone is sobbing down the phone about not hitting the *New York Times* bestseller list or writing you a six-page email about how they couldn't possibly cut five thousand words and I would know that too if I understood anything about craft.

This kind of stuff comes with the job, but, for the first time in my career, I snapped. I don't know why. I've dealt with worse than her before. Paul is perpetually late with his books, and he doesn't have a tenth of the sales she's going to get for us. But I lost it.

Maybe it was the flight. Or the whole falling-into-a-pit thing. In any case, it doesn't matter. That was yesterday and today is today, and Casey said she needed hand-holding and that's what I'm going to do.

It's just that, in order *to* do that, I need her to at least be home.

I don't have her number to call, and I know now she doesn't look at her emails, but still, I take out my phone to check she hasn't sent anything in the last few minutes. That movement alone makes my shoulder twinge, and I let my bag fall to the ground as I stretch it out. It's not the only part of my body hurting this morning. I woke up to bruises in the weirdest places. All because she dug a grave for research.

I'd hate to see what her search history looks like.

Distracted, I open Google, trying to find the hitman book she mentioned yesterday, but, if she wrote it, it was never published. A quick scroll shows nothing with that description, but it does pull up a bunch of articles from when she was revealed as Frank Sheridan's kid. A lot of *like father, like daughter* headlines and a scramble for old photos. The most used one is of them together at some signing event. She can't be more than fifteen and looks agonisingly shy, her waist-length blonde hair covering half her face, her shoulders slumped, her smile wary.

She didn't look like that yesterday. The woman I met was all long, tanned limbs, with a sparking energy I could almost feel. She held herself straight and strong, with no hint of the awkwardness so painfully obvious in the photo. Not to mention that the blonde is gone. Her hair is brown now. Cut short in a choppy bob that flew around her face with every movement.

No wonder Lizzie couldn't find a trace of her. She looks like a completely different person.

I keep hunting for mentions of her and am halfway through a fan site interview with Frank from ten years ago when I hear a car approach. A second later, a small blue convertible glides up the driveway before rolling to a stop by the house. A woman steps out, a bag of groceries in her hand. She's tall and beautiful and wearing a navy jumpsuit with bright pink Crocs. Her blonde curls are pulled up into a scrunchie, and she pushes her sunglasses into them as she examines me from head to toe.

'Can I help you?' she asks, and I brace myself for more suspicion.

'I'm here to see Ciara Sheridan,' I begin. 'I'm an editor from—'

'An editor?'

I pause, surprised, as she bounds up the steps.

'*Her* editor? Are you here about the book?' She stops before me, looking confused. 'Sorry. Aren't you supposed to be ninety or something?'

'That's my boss,' I explain. 'And I didn't think anyone was supposed to know about—'

'Oh, I'm not just anyone,' she corrects. 'I'm her best friend. And I know everything. Maddie Buckley. Sagittarius.'

'Sam Avery. I . . . June twentieth?'

'Gemini.' She tilts her head, her gaze assessing. 'You don't know your star sign?'

'I don't believe in astrology.'

'How manly of you.' She takes a step back. 'Ciara's not in trouble, is she? She's been working really hard; she's just going through a lot and—'

'There's no trouble,' I interrupt. 'I'm here to help.'

'Oh. Okay, then.' We watch each other for a beat before she smiles. 'You want to come inside?'

'I—'

'Don't worry,' she says, rummaging through her bag. 'I've got a key.'

'You sound like you shouldn't.'

'She doesn't know I have one. But what am I going to do, let you stand out here all day? You'll melt.'

'I don't think she's even in.'

'She is,' Maddie says, unlocking the door. 'She's just asleep. Ciara's a night owl."

'Seriously,' she adds at my obvious reluctance. 'Come in.'

She ushers me past her, practically pushing me over the threshold, and before I can so much as blink I'm inside Frank Sheridan's house.

It's not exactly the massive moment I thought it'd be. My first impression is of dark wallpaper and cool air, but I barely get a chance to look around as Maddie crowds me from behind. As she shuts the door, there's the subtle beep of an alarm, one she deftly turns off as she meets my curious look. 'I also know her code.'

I say nothing, following her into an adjoining kitchen. This room is stuffier, with the sun streaming in through the windows, but it's inviting and warm, with white cabinets and wooden counters. Mugs of every shape and size take up the open shelves, along with trailing plants and herbs, giving the space a wild feel despite the modern appliances, like a cottage in a picture book.

'Frank was a big cook,' Maddie says as she gestures to a stool. 'Ciara, not so much, though she makes a mean lemonade.' As she speaks, she dumps her bag on the counter and opens the fridge, pouring two glasses of said lemonade before sliding one my way. She waits until I take a sip before she unloads her shopping, taking out fruit and vegetables and what looks like a tub of smoothie mixture.

'So you knew Frank?' I ask as she washes and dices a bell pepper. She's not being quiet, but there's no sign of Ciara.

Maddie hums, not taking her eyes off her admittedly impressive knife skills. 'I used to come here after school while my parents were at work. Did you?'

'Know him?' I shake my head. 'I wish.'

'A fan, then? What's your favourite book?'

'*The Winding Path*,' I say, growing more comfortable now we're on familiar territory. 'What's yours?'

'Oh, I only read the first one.'

I smile, thinking she's joking. She's not.

'What?'

'I don't really read,' she says. 'Like I know *how* to read, but I just . . . ' She flicks the air by her head. 'You know?'

'Not really.'

'Yeah, guess you wouldn't. I bet you have to read a lot if you're an editor, huh?'

'It's part of the job.'

'Lucky I'm in catering, then. Pepper?' She holds out a slice, which I dutifully take. 'Christ, it's hot in here. Are you hot? I'm roasting.'

Before I can answer, she spins on her heel, heading to a side door by the refrigerator, where she undoes three locks before throwing it open.

'She has a lot of security,' I say, stating the obvious.

'Yeah. It's a bit much, but it makes her feel safe. She gets a lot of people showing up at the house.'

I think back to the woman I saw yesterday. 'You mean like Mary?'

Maddie rolls her eyes as she returns to her vegetable. 'Of course, you've been here for, like, an hour and you know about Mary. She's fine,' she adds. 'Don't get me wrong, the woman could run her own gossip column, but she's harmless.'

'Then who?'

'Readers mostly. I mean, people came by over the years, but they just wanted a peek at the house and off they'd go. Like if they actually saw Frank, their heads would explode. But when he died ...' Her forehead creases, and she starts on another pepper. 'It started out innocent enough. People left flowers by the road. Cards. Drawings. But then they got braver, and now she can't go a week without strangers knocking on the door or leaving stuff around the garden. She got the alarms installed after someone came inside.'

Shock makes me straighten. 'Someone came into the house?'

'I don't think they expected to be able to just walk in,' she says, unfazed. 'But what do I know? Basically, Ciara and I were in the front room watching TV, and then the door opened, and this man and woman are just *there*. We all stared at each other, and then I screamed, and then they ran. Ciara put in all this stuff the next day. Cost her a fortune.'

Shit. No wonder the bartender was suspicious of me. No wonder Ciara was too.

'Sounds like a lot,' I say eventually.

'Frank meant a lot to them,' Maddie says. 'So I get it. People are sad, and they want to pay tribute. But he's not here any more. It's Ciara who has to sort through all the things people leave, and worry about them breaking in. And maybe it would be different if she got on with his fans, but she does *not* and—' She breaks off, her eyes shooting to mine. 'Not that she's a grump or anything,' she adds hurriedly. 'She can be grumpy, but we all get a little grumpy. It's just that they can be intense sometimes.'

'Sure.'

'She's a professional otherwise. And a really good writer. She just needs some bolstering.'

As if on cue, a floorboard creaks above us, and Maddie throws her head back, yelling at the top of her lungs, 'It's me! I brought food!'

There's nothing for a moment, and then sudden, rapid footsteps. I can practically track her movement across the floor as they grow louder until they're thudding down the stairs.

'Morning, sleeping beauty,' Maddie calls, and I twist on my stool to see Ciara appear in the doorway.

She's in pyjama bottoms and a short, baggy white T-shirt that shows off a sliver of her stomach. Her feet are bare and her toenails are painted blue. She looks furious.

'What the fuck, Mads?'

'What? You can show up to my place of work unannounced, but I can't show up to yours?'

'How did you even get in?'

'I took a key for emergencies.'

'This is not an emergency.'

'Lunch is always an emergency. Plus, your editor was waiting.'

'I can come back,' I say, rising and focusing on the space above her left shoulder. I'm not sure why. She was wearing less clothing the other day, but pyjamas are . . . pyjamas.

Not that Ciara seems to care. There's a long pause as she and Maddie have some sort of silent conversation with their eyebrows before they both huff.

'No,' Ciara finally says to me. 'I slept in. Give me two minutes. And *you* can go.'

'*Moi?*' Maddie asks.

'You.' She turns and heads back up the stairs. 'And leave the key on the counter!'

Maddie dumps the peppers into a bowl and the bowl into the fridge as she grabs her empty shopping bag. 'Good luck,' she whispers exaggeratedly to me and, slipping the key pointedly into her pocket, vanishes through the porch door she just opened.

Leaving me alone in Frank Sheridan's kitchen.

Somewhere upstairs a door slams, and I stare at the pile of mail on the counter and the clock on the wall and the corkboard filled with printed-out recipes and *be cool, Sam*.

Be. Cool.

No matter how much you want to log back into the fan forum you moderated when you were fifteen and tell them where you are.

I move silently as I turn in a circle, taking in the room. Outside the window, I spy the corner of a large oak tree and know instantly it's the one Frank included a drawing of in his fifth book. The one that made him buy the property in the first place. He spoke at length in an interview once about how it inspired him. How he used to read under it. And now I'm looking right at it.

Another slammed door. This time followed by footsteps, and I sit and then stand again as Ciara reappears.

She's brushed her hair and changed into a tank top and a pair of loose cotton shorts. Her face looks damp, as though she just splashed water on it, and for the first time in a long time I have absolutely no idea what to say. It's as if someone's taken an eraser to my brain, and for a moment all I can do is stare at her.

'I usually work at night.' Her voice cuts through the silence, defensive and unsure. 'I sleep in because I work at night,' she tries again, and this time I feel myself nod.

I open my mouth to apologise for yesterday, to blame my attitude on any number of things, but instead all that comes out is, 'I thought we could start looking at what Frank left you. Casey said he was in the middle of outlining when he ...' *Died.*

Yeah. Good start, Sam.

Ciara just frowns. 'There's not much,' she says. 'That's part of the problem.'

'Whatever you've got is great.'

'Okay.'

A pause as the tap drips once behind me. 'So do you want to do it here or—'

'Right. No. This way.' She turns stiffly and leads me back into the hall, the one that I take in properly for the first time. I do my best not to be obvious about it, only letting myself glance at the wood panelling and the faded gold mirror, the antique lampshades hanging from the ceiling. Dark green wallpaper covers the walls, as if we're stepping into the oak tree itself, and—

'You've already seen the kitchen,' Ciara says, almost hitting me in the face as she points a finger to my right. 'Living room's over there. I work up here.' And with that she starts up a large winding staircase, taking it two steps at a time.

'It's not haunted,' she says as I follow.

'What?'

'The house. It's not haunted, if that's what you're thinking. It's just falling down.'

'I didn't think that at all,' I say, confused. 'And it doesn't look as if it's falling down.'

Without stopping, she whacks her hand lightly against the wall. As she does so, somewhere below, something thuds to the floor. 'It's falling down,' she says grimly, and swivels to a stop at the top of the stairs. I almost walk straight into her.

'This is my dad's old office,' she says when I'm done stumbling. My breath catches in my throat, and I glance at the plain door next to us, trying not to react. Instinct tells me this is a test. One I'm determined to pass.

'Great,' I say. 'Where's yours?'

Her brows rise in a *nice try* move, and she jerks her head to the left before leading me two doors down. Sunlight streams through the crack at the bottom, and when she places her hand on the polished brass handle, anticipation thrums through my veins.

'Where the magic happens,' she says and twists it with a firm jerk, letting us into a bright, airy room that faces out on to the oak tree and the woods beyond. Inside, though, it's simple – sparse, even. Nothing like the chaos of other writers' spaces I've seen. There's a low couch pushed against the wall, a rug laid down in the centre and a desk placed under one of the windows. It's a heavy-looking thing: dark, polished wood that dwarfs the slim laptop on it. The only other objects are a chair and a bookcase. A quick scan of the shelves shows a random assortment of Frank's books, one chunky thesaurus and a collection of stones that look as if they've been taken from the beach.

And that's it.

I hover in the doorway as she walks over to the desk and produces a manila folder from one of the drawers. It's stuffed to the brim, and, as soon as she takes it out, a few pages flutter to the floor, each one filled with blue ink in a tiny, neat scrawl.

I know instantly it's not her writing. And with that knowledge, something in my brain short-circuits.

'This is what Dad left me,' she says, picking up the papers.

My fingers twitch when she dumps them on the desk. I feel as if they should be in a museum. Where you can only look at them in low lighting behind a glass box and surrounded by lasers. Instead, she just riffles through them like an old magazine.

'I know it seems like a lot,' she says, unaware of my internal freak-out. 'But it's mostly a list of characters and him trying out different settings. There's nothing helpful plotwise.'

'Nothing?'

She gives me a wry look. 'No one reads Dad's books for the twists.'

That, I can't argue with. His magic was in the smaller moments. The characters, the language. Frank Sheridan never did the shock death. He'd tug your heart out and stomp on it, but he would do it slowly. Which made it all the more painful.

'I've been over these a dozen times,' Ciara continues. She sounds terse now. As though she doesn't expect me to believe her. 'But there's nothing. Here.' She snatches the folder up, thrusting it my way. 'Maybe you can make sense of it.'

And then it's in my hands.

She perches on the chair in front of the desk, and, with nowhere else to sit, I take the couch. I immediately wish I hadn't. It's one of those *once you're in it, you're never getting out of it* ones, and my normal act of sitting turns into an abnormal act of falling as I sink into the cushions and lose my balance.

Ciara just watches me. Waits.

Her body is rigid, her shoulders almost to her ears, and just like that I can see how the next few weeks are going to go. How difficult this is going to be.

Ciara Sheridan does not want me here. And, even more than that, I don't think *she* wants to be here either.

I glance down at the bundle of papers in my lap, stalling as I rethink my opening spiel. My little speech about all the authors I've worked with before and how safe she'll be in my hands seems moot. Casey's right. This is the biggest book of the decade. The one that will follow me around for the rest of my career. That could *make* my career. And she's not even pretending to try. She's already given up.

The realisation rankles more than I thought it would, and I rub my thumb over the corner of the first page, smoothing out a crease. Maybe she thinks she can coast by on her father's name, or that, because of who she is, we'll let her run rings around us. But this is clearly not going to work, and I didn't spend the last ten years climbing the ladder to crash and burn on the final rung.

Yesterday's annoyance with her resurges, and I take a moment before I meet her wary gaze.

Fuck it.

'We can give this to someone else.'

Ciara startles, her blue eyes going wide, but I push on.

'We can get a ghostwriter,' I say, rehashing the same proposal I ran by Casey. 'Or a collaborator. You don't have to write this book if you don't want to.'

'I do want to.'

'You would still be involved,' I say as her face pales. 'We could work up a list of names. Audition a shortlist. You would have the final say. Oversee the entire process.'

'No.'

The word is firm. Unbreachable. I try a different tactic.

'These books are loved by millions of people.'

'I'm aware.'

'I just mean—'

'I know what you mean,' she interrupts coolly. 'But thank you for trying to explain my father's legacy to me. Maybe you could remind me who shared this house with him while he wrote them? Or who made his dinners every night because he'd get so lost in the story, he'd forget to eat if you didn't feed him. Maybe you also know what it's like to receive threatening messages from people who didn't like the movie casting or who accuse you of being ungrateful because you dared to publish your own work under a pen name.' She slips one leg over the other, her back now ramrod-straight. 'I know what this book means to people,' she continues. 'I know how big it is. Even if I didn't, the money you're giving me would tip me off. But I didn't spend a lifetime with these characters just to see a stranger finish their story. My dad wanted me to write this book and, while I admit I need some help, what I don't need is some stranger waltzing in here with a Moleskine notebook and a fan club membership thinking he can do it better.'

She finishes with a sharp exhale, and I gawk at her before my eyes drop to the notebook poking out my bag. Then I wonder, did she guess about the membership or does she actually have the records?

'So,' Ciara says, dragging my attention back to her. 'Where do you want to start?'

CHAPTER SIX

Ciara

How did it go?

The text from Maddie comes later that night as I'm wiping down my kitchen table. I think about not replying and then send her a thumbs-up emoji because I'm a liar.

It did not go thumbs-up. It did not go anywhere near thumbs-up, but I'm too tired to get into that with her. After I more or less told Sam where to shove it, we spent three long hours together in that room as I tried to explain the mess that was my father's creative process. My head was pounding by the end of it, my eyes dry and tired, but Sam kept going, treating each scrap of paper as if he were reading the Rosetta Stone. Eventually, though, even he seemed to accept we weren't going to intricately plot a 250,000-word book in one afternoon and took everything with him to read overnight.

Then he tried to give me homework.

Or at least that was what it felt like.

'Try a writing sprint,' he'd said. 'Just push through it. Twenty minutes. No distractions. Just type.'

Just type. Says the man who probably never wrote anything longer than an email in his life. But I got worried if I said no he would never leave, so I ended up agreeing to send him fifteen hundred words by tomorrow.

It shouldn't be a problem. It's not as if I haven't been punching out that same number every day for weeks now. I know Sam thinks I haven't been writing, but I've been writing more than I ever have in my life. That's not what's wrong. What's wrong is that it's all *bad*. The prose is forced. The dialogue stilted. I don't sound like my dad, and I'm also starting not to sound like me, and it's freaking me out.

But it's not like I'm going to sit and explain all of that to a stranger who has made it crystal clear he already has his doubts about me.

I Googled him extensively when he left, looking up everything I could find on my hotshot New York editor. Because he *is* a hotshot New York editor. I found three announcements of his various promotions, all within Richardson Books, and page after page of high-profile deals and industry awards. There's even an article about him in *Publishers Weekly* from four years ago. Seven hundred words about how great he is next to a picture of him leaning against his desk with the same haircut he has now.

He doesn't seem to have taken a breath in the past decade.

And now he's here.

I scroll absently through a list of his other authors, picking out the ones I know as I finish cleaning the kitchen. Every night, it feels too hot to cook and I end up eating what amounts to half a baguette and some kind of cheese, along with whatever vegetables Maddie puts in my fridge. Yet even without any cooking, the kitchen is always a mess by the time I'm done. The whole house is a mess. Even though

I got rid of most of the stuff in it. Even though I feel I barely *exist* in it. There's always something to do. Something to fix. Laundry to wash. Floors to sweep, carpets to hoover. There's dust everywhere and fruit flies constantly banging on the windows and *how* can a place so empty feel so dirty?

I wonder what Sam thought of it. If he was disappointed when he saw the peeling wallpaper and scuffed floorboards. He must have been. He's probably one of those readers who grew up dreaming about this house. And now he sees the reality.

But it's not like I'm not trying. I read two books on grief when my father died. In both of them, there was a chapter about clearing the dead person's house and how it can be an important part of the mourning process. That it's tough but cathartic. Tear-inducing, yet therapeutic. There were tips and advice and a link to a podcast.

It took me two weeks, with some help from Maddie and others. We went by object size instead of room, but I was methodical and ruthless through it all. I sold what furniture I could and threw the rest into a skip. I got rid of all the ancient electronics and the twenty-year-old cutlery. I tackled the Closet of Towels. I dumped the Drawer of Cables. I polished the floors and washed the curtains and took a power hose to the porch.

The only things I didn't touch were to do with Dad's books. His notebooks and his sketches and his boxes of fan letters and old contracts and mementos from over the years. Mostly because I didn't know what to do with them. Weirdly, they were the only things in the house that felt as though they didn't belong to me. But I didn't dwell. I stored them away and closed the door and that was that.

I was excited at first. I got some new furniture, which seemed like a lot when I ordered it and nothing at all once it was in the house. I bought a colourful throw rug and an essential oil diffuser and daydreamed about what paintings I would buy and where I would put them. I thought I had beaten the system. Bucked the trend.

And then, one day, I woke up and realised that my father wasn't here any more. That I had scrubbed the place clean of him.

None of the books told me how I was supposed to feel when the house-clearing was complete. I think they assume you're going to sell it. Or maybe move in with your loving partner and two-point-four children. Life moves on, they all seemed to say. There wasn't a chapter for twenty-nine-year-old orphan daughters with a tiny social circle and no consistent sleep schedule.

No footnote on what to do with the emptiness I didn't know how to fill.

And now here I am almost a year later and the house I grew up in still doesn't feel like home.

I move on from Sam's professional life to his personal one, looking up his social media as I turn off all the lights and double-check the doors are locked. The extra security is new, but the rest is more out of routine than concern. Even as a kid, the night-time wind-downs often fell to me, though back then I set my own bedtimes too. Sometimes it would be nearly three a.m. by the time I finally got to sleep. It's not as if I was abandoned or anything, but Dad was the kind of writer who would disappear into his work, which meant I had free run of the place most of the time.

How did it really go?

I smirk as Maddie messages back, debating calling her. But it's late and she's probably in bed.

I think I've forgotten how to write books.

Isn't he here to help with that?

I hate it when she's logical, so I tell her this as I finish downstairs before heading back up to my office. It's another sticky night and I push the window open, keeping the lights off so I don't become a moth magnet, but the soft glow of my laptop screen only highlights the emptiness around me. I'd meant to do something with this room. Some proper bookshelves, some pictures, maybe one of those desk things with the pendulums. But, like most things in my life right now, it's been pushed down the list, so it just looks as unlived-in as the rest of the house.

Maybe I'll get a fern.

I collapse into my chair, spinning once before opening my email.

My inbox is both horrifying and impressive in equal measure, but I manage to find something from Casey easily enough and pull out his number.

It rings for five seconds before he picks up.

'Ciara. How are you?' He sounds delighted that I called, and I feel calmer just hearing his voice. Dad used to refer to him as 'one of the good guys', and I picture his lined face and hunched shoulders, sitting behind some messy desk thousands of miles away. He was with my dad from the beginning and is one of the people I trust most in this world, so I get right to it.

'Please tell me you sent that man with the shoulder bag to my door and it's not an elaborate plot cooked up by one of the superfans?'

'That depends,' he says. 'What does he look like?'

I groan, dropping my head back to the ceiling. 'When we talked about it, I thought you meant it was going to be *you*.'

'And I thought Sam would be better.'

'Why?'

'Because I'm seventy-three years old and have a business to run. How's it going?'

'Badly.'

Casey pauses. 'Did something happen?'

'No,' I say quickly. I'm not about to get somebody into trouble because I'm an insecure mess. 'I was being flippant. He's fine. Or at least I presume he is. He's just trying to do his job. I'm the problem. I'm the one who—'

'Ciara,' he interrupts, as gentle and firm as always, and it's because of that tone that I stop talking.

Because, in that moment, he sounds like my dad. And the thought hits me in the chest so hard it's like I've been punched.

'Sam's one of the best in the business,' he continues. 'He knows what he's doing, and he cares deeply about these characters. More than anyone I know.'

'But—'

'You need help with this,' he says bluntly. 'You're stuck.'

'Yeah,' I say, and there's a beat where I wait for an exhale. For something to click in my brain. That's what's supposed to happen, isn't it? You confess something and the weight on your shoulders feels lighter? Your mind calmer?

I feel none of that. Just the same.

Like crap.

'Massively, shittily stuck,' I continue.

'You're a good writer. I wouldn't have brought this to you if I didn't think you could do it.'

'I guess,' I mumble. 'I'm sorry I've been AWOL. Time is kind of running away from me.'

'You're going through a lot.'

I actually feel like I'm going through a perfectly normal amount and I just can't deal with any of it, but I don't tell him that.

'I don't want anyone else to write this book.'

'That never occurred to me,' Casey says. 'Frank wanted you to write it and I'm not going against his wishes. But you don't have to do this alone. You have to give us a chance to help you. And you have to give *you* a chance as well.'

'I'm trying. Admittedly, not very hard, but—'

'Just show Sam what you have,' Casey says. 'And let him do his thing.'

'You make it sound like he's going to wave a magic wand and make everything better.'

'Sometimes all you need is a different perspective. Your father used to always say that when he was asked for writing advice.'

'Yeah, but that was also the man who'd eat a peanut butter and pickle sandwich every night, so I'm not sure we can trust him.'

'You know, he brought me over to his side on that one. Though I did once see him pair half a tomato with a bar of chocolate, which is where I drew the line.'

I smile even as an ache shoots through me. He did have the grossest food habits. I used to have to leave the room sometimes when he was creating a snack. Of course, now, I'd give anything to have one more meal with him.

'I miss him,' I say, and Casey sighs.

'I do too,' he admits. 'I wish I'd spent more time with him towards the end. He invited me out many times, but . . .'

'You couldn't have known.'

'No.' And now it's his turn to sound sad. 'Did I ever tell you about the time we got stranded by a storm in Miami?'

'No.'

'Must have been the first tour,' he muses. 'Or maybe the third. No, it wasn't the third, we didn't go to Miami for the third. It was before the first film, anyway. He wanted to spend a day sightseeing. You'd apparently demanded a picture of your father with an alligator, so off we went on one of those tourist trap tours. And it was all going fine until Frank realised he'd left his reading glasses on the boat. So he turned around and headed back . . . '

Casey's voice grows warmer and more animated as he talks, as soothing as listening to the waves on a beach, and as he goes on I close my eyes and listen. Just listen. And if I feel a tear at the corner of my eye, I do nothing with it but let it fall.

CHAPTER SEVEN

Sam

'It could have gone better.'

Lizzie stares at me through the screen, her eyebrows rising so high they disappear into her bangs. 'You think?'

'We'll get through it.' I shove at the double-hung window next to my bed, using all my weight in an attempt to push it open further, but give up as it threatens to shut on my fingers. 'I just need to gain her trust.'

'She's not a stray cat, Sam.'

'All I'm saying is, we got off on the wrong foot.'

'Because you threatened to take her off the book.'

'I didn't threaten. I offered.'

'Uh-huh.'

'It'll be a lot of work,' I say. 'But I can do it. I'll be here all summer if I have to.'

'All of it?' Lizzie doesn't look convinced. 'I thought you were only there for a few weeks.'

'Casey said I could stay as long as I need to.'

'But it's not even June! You can't just—'

'Is that Sam?'

A voice interrupts my sister's argument, and a second later her husband, Ben, shoves half his face into view of the camera. They've been married for seven years and still act as if they're on their honeymoon. It would be sickening with anyone else, but they pull it off. Amy met them at the company barbecue last summer and informed me Ben had 'golden retriever energy'. The phrase has stuck with me ever since.

'How's Scotland?' he asks now.

'Ireland.'

'Sam's thinking about staying for the *whole* summer,' Lizzie says disapprovingly.

Ben just grins. 'That's awesome! Have fun.'

'Thanks, man.'

'Send us some more pictures,' he says, and he waves at the camera before disappearing out of sight.

'Your husband likes me more than he likes you,' I say to Lizzie's scowl.

'False. He's obsessed with me. And while he might not have said so in as many words, he also thinks you have no business staying away for so long. You're getting too involved again, and— *Sam*,' she snaps as I check my email.

'What? I'm listening.'

'No, you're not. Eyes on me. Eldest sibling speaking.' And she waits until she has my full attention before saying, in the gravest tone imaginable, 'You're being you again.'

'Some people might argue that's a good thing.'

'You need a work-life balance. You work way too hard at your job.'

'I'm taking that as a compliment.'

'You shouldn't. What about your birthday? We were supposed to go to that new pasta place.'

'Are you worried about not seeing me on my birthday or not eating pasta?'

'The pasta.'

'Lizzie—'

'But that's not the point,' she continues. 'You've practically disappeared since Casey said he was thinking of retiring. You're working so much I feel like we barely see you any more.'

'That's not true.'

'You literally bailed on my last dinner party with an hour's notice.'

'And I took all of you guys to the zoo to make up for it,' I remind her. 'I told you I had a twenty-four-hour exclusive submission, and I had to read it before—'

'You bailed,' she interrupts. 'And I made a lobster bisque. A *bisque*, Sam. It was freaking delicious.'

'I'm sure it was. And again, I'm sorry about that. But this is my life.'

'I know,' she says, sounding tired. 'That's the problem.'

The conversation moves on to her ongoing grudge with some new woman at her book club, but it's early morning in New York and Lizzie soon hangs up as everyone gets ready to leave the house. What she said digs at me, but I don't know what she expects me to do about it.

I won't lie and say I'm not ambitious. In this business, a love of books pairs well with a love of competition, and this industry is all about competition. For shelf space and sales rank. For finding the next big thing. For keeping it once you do.

If I didn't get distracted by the books I work on, I wouldn't be where I am today. And while that's meant some sacrifice – and some burnout – I wouldn't change any of it. I went into this career with my eyes wide open. The job is the job.

And, right now, I've got a hell of a one to do.

I spent all night reading Frank's notes, only to discover that Ciara was right. There isn't much there. A skeleton synopsis at most. But that's because he focused on the two characters who mattered most. The ones the entire series hinges on.

Finn and Maeve weren't always the heart of Ravian. But they became it. And Frank was a smart enough writer to know it.

Finn was just a kid when he was first introduced. A weedy twelve-year-old orphan who accompanied the original hero on his journey. Maeve only appeared in mentions, not making her on-page debut until halfway through the second book. Their romance didn't begin until the third. But once it started, it was everything.

They were the real story. Not the war. Not the politics. Woven through it all was Maeve and Finn. Finn and Maeve. And yesterday, when I sat on that dusty couch in that dusty room in Frank Sheridan's house, I read through his final notes and learned their fate.

It was a happy one.

I won't lie and say I wasn't relieved. Not that there's a rule that says we have to stick with what Frank wanted, but I wouldn't put it past any author to try to go out with a shock. It would have been easy to kill one of them off. Create the big dramatic moment. Instead, he chose a quieter end, and, if done right, a much more satisfying one.

But we still have to work out everything else. The broad strokes of the book are there, but everything else is a puzzle to be solved. We've got at least three characters whose timelines need to be completely reworked. Two who need to come together despite starting the book on different continents. And one Frank seems to have completely forgotten about. We've got to decide where everyone starts and where they end. We've got to figure out how to finish twenty years of storytelling in six hundred pages.

And then there's the small matter of her writing the thing.

I sit on the bed, refreshing my inbox.

Ciara was supposed to send me something this morning. That was the plan we agreed on, anyway: she'd spend the evening writing however much she could and send it to me first thing, before we regrouped. It might be throwing her in at the deep end, but I wanted to see how well she could do under pressure.

Turns out, not well at all.

Frustration pricks at me, and I re-read the extra-polite *just checking in* email I sent her an hour ago as a car pulls up outside. Footsteps sound a second later, but I ignore them as I've ignored the others. I'm still getting used to the noises of the building. Of people coming in and out of the pub. I was woken abruptly this morning by a drinks delivery, and I don't know if they have raccoons in this country, but some sort of animal definitely likes to scurry around on the roof.

It's only when the steps get louder that I realise someone is coming up the stairs, and I get to my feet just as there's a knock on the door.

I open it cautiously, half-hoping that it's Ciara, but instead I find the woman I saw at her house the first day. Mary. Though the first thing that comes to my mind is *Milk Lady*.

She stands on the landing in a linen dress and an anorak that looks too heavy for this weather. There is a clingfilm-wrapped plate of smoked salmon in her hands.

So, I guess I'm dealing with this now.

'Hello,' I say when she doesn't. She's much smaller up close, no taller than five feet, and has to crane her neck to look me up and down.

'I own this building,' she says finally.

'I thought Ronan—'

'I'm his landlord.'

Okay. 'Well, nice to meet you. I'm Sam.'

'Divorced, are you?'

'I . . . no.'

'The last man here was divorced. He was from Waterford.'

I can't tell from her tone if that's a good thing or a bad thing, so I just nod. 'I've never been,' I say, shuffling to the left as she tries to look at my bed and all of Frank's notes on top of it.

She scowls when I do and offers me the plate. 'Salmon?'

'I . . . there's no fridge, so I don't know if I should—'

'Better eat it quick, then.' She shakes it, proffering it at me until I'm forced to take it. 'I also run a laundry service in the village,' she says. 'For whoever needs it. You'll find my number on the noticeboard below.'

'Great.'

'Or we can discuss a rate now.'

The town gossip wants to do my dirty laundry.

Yeah. That's not happening.

'I'll be sure to keep you in mind,' I say as politely as I can. 'Thank you for the welcome. But I should get back to work.'

Her lips thin at the dismissal, but she's out of excuses to stay, and, with one final glance at the room behind me, she turns and lumbers back down the stairs. I wait for her footsteps to fade before I shut the door.

Now what?

Thankfully, as soon as I think it, I hear the faint sounds of movement below and, not wanting to keep a plate of fish in an already overly warm room for much longer, I shove my shoes on and head outside.

The pub's front door is shut and locked when I try the handle, but, when I go to knock, it swings open, revealing Ronan. He looks less than pleased to see me.

'If you're trying to break in, you should make less noise. We're not open until three.'

'I know. Sorry. I . . . ' I have no idea how to explain any of it, so I just hold up the plate of salmon wordlessly.

To my surprise, it does the trick, and some of the wariness fades from his expression. 'Oh, for the love of Jesus. That woman.' He takes it from me with a sigh. 'Ah, come on, then. Don't just stand there. You're letting in the heat.'

I slip inside after him, though I'm unsure if it's warmer out than in.

'She's not great with newcomers,' Ronan says. 'But she's harmless.'

'So I've been told.' I linger in the centre of the room as he heads back to the bar. 'I found Ciara, by the way. And spoke to her friend. Maddie? She explained about the people intruding on her property. So, I wanted to apologise if I didn't introduce myself properly the other day. I understand why you might not have trusted me at first.'

'Oh, you do, do you?'

'Yes,' I say as he slides the plate into one of the beer fridges. 'I think it's great that you look out for each other.'

Ronan clears his throat, looking abashed. 'Well. That's what we do here,' he says firmly. 'We're a community.' He pauses. 'Sorry. You didn't want to eat the salmon, did you?'

'No,' I say quickly. 'You can keep it.'

'It's not poisoned,' he says, amused. 'Or at least it won't be on purpose.' He points at a stool. 'Have a seat. You can keep me company while I open up. Do you like hot chocolate?'

'Hot chocolate?'

'I've heard it can be very refreshing,' he says, scratching the back of his neck. 'And we're also trying to get rid of the stuff. The weather isn't helping. You'd be doing me a favour.'

And as much as I'd like to do that, I'd also like to not die of heat exhaustion. 'I'll stick to the Diet Coke.'

He throws up his hands in an *I tried* gesture and starts scooping ice. As he does, my eyes drift over the framed photos of various black and white figures smiling for the camera, including one of Frank and Ronan in what looks to be this very pub.

'Fan of his?' Ronan asks, noticing my interest. 'He used to write in here, you know.'

'He did?'

'Well, no. He drank in here. But he used to tell me all about what he was working on. Went over my head most of the time, I've never been much of a dragon man myself – but he had a way with words.' His chest puffs out a bit. 'I've got some more photos somewhere, if you'd like to see them. Been meaning to pass them on to Ciara when the time's right.'

'I'd love to see them,' I say honestly, and Ronan beams at me, all suspicions seemingly forgotten as he puts my drink in front of me and disappears into another room. As he does, I take out my phone, my good mood dimming even before I check my email. Still nothing from Ciara.

Yeah. This is going to be a problem.

CHAPTER EIGHT

Ciara

It took me two years to write my first novel. The first one that got me published, anyway. Two years on and off, mainly because I didn't know what the hell I was doing, and I kept giving up and coming back to it because I couldn't stay away. I didn't tell anyone about it. Not even Dad. When it was finished, I saved it in a folder on my desktop labelled NEVER MIND and pretended it didn't exist.

Four months later, I reread it, decided it wasn't terrible and sent it off to a handful of literary agents under a pseudonym before I could change my mind. I only got one rejection, but that's because the rest didn't reply.

I completely rewrote the opening chapters. I added a new scene to the ending and cut out a character who didn't do anything. I sent it out again, and this time I got an email back from a junior agent in London who looked as if she wasn't old enough to buy alcohol yet. But she liked the book, and she was the only one who did.

We edited it some more, and then she sold it in a three-book deal to a major publisher for an incredibly modest sum. It was barely enough to cover my rent for a few weeks. I was bottom of the barrel. What the industry calls *low list*.

And I was over the moon.

I was in my early twenties and working in an advertising firm in Dublin. I got news of the sale in the afternoon, told my boss I was sick and drove all the way home to Kerry so I could tell my dad in person.

You don't think about your memories of people until they're gone. You never go out with a friend and think, *This is fun. I must remember this in case you die before me, and I need loving thoughts of you.*

So even if it was one of the proudest, biggest moments of my life, I can't remember my dad's expression when I told him that I had not only written a book, but sold it too. I have a picture in my head, of course. One of his surprise followed by his delight. But I can't tell for certain whether I made it up or not. A false memory from that blur of a year.

I do remember being in the kitchen with him later. Remember him calling everyone in his contacts list to tell them the news. Drinking beer at the table I sit at now.

'I saw someone taking pictures of your driveway yesterday.'

I look up from my laptop as Maddie jerks the pan, flipping a perfect pancake. She came over this morning because she *wanted to make me breakfast*. Which turned out to be code for *starving her friend*, because she keeps looking disappointed after each one and doesn't give me any.

'They were wearing a Ravian T-shirt,' she adds, and I groan.

'They didn't leave anything, did they?' I swear half my time these days is spent cleaning up the notes and gifts left by fans. They used to keep the location of the house a secret among themselves, but ever since Dad died, it's like they decided there's no need for privacy any more.

'Not that I could see,' Maddie says. 'But who knows? You might need to put up another Private Property sign or something.'

'Yes, because the ones I already have work *wonders*.'

'Well, you know what they say,' she sings, pouring more mixture into the pan. 'If you can't beat 'em—'

'No.'

'I'm just saying that if they insist on coming here, no one would judge you if you wanted to take advantage of that.'

'You mean take advantage of *them*.'

'Your words. Not mine.'

'Maddie—'

'You can let them into the house,' she continues, as if she's been thinking about this for a while. 'Give them a tour of a few rooms. Let them take some pictures. Sign a big guest book.'

'My home is not a tourist attraction.'

'It will get them on your side,' she finishes, and some of my annoyance fades. Because I know, deep down, she thinks she's looking out for me. Even if the idea does make me squirm.

'I'll think about it,' I say to get her off my back. 'But in the meantime, no letting readers into the house.'

'Does John count?' she asks, peering out of the window. A second later, heavy footsteps stomp on the porch.

'Good morning!' a booming voice calls, and my postman strides into the room. He's in his summer uniform and has added a large sunhat that leaves a red indent on his forehead when he takes it off, but he makes it work. 'I'll tell you what, ladies, it's getting a bit much for me out there,' he says, wiping his face with a handkerchief. 'Don't shoot the messenger,' he adds. 'I thought about hiding the bills, but they tell us that's illegal these days.'

'I appreciate the thought, though,' I say as he passes me my usual bundle. Fan letters, some newspapers addressed to my father and . . .

Ravicon.

I sigh as I pull out the bright yellow invitation. The fifth one in two months. The world's largest annual Frank Sheridan convention is happening in Dublin later this summer and my lord, do they want me to know about it. As if spending two days listening to people who never met my father talk about him ad nauseam would be something I'd like to experience.

'You can start recycling these,' I say, holding it up to John.

'Not a problem,' he says cheerfully. 'But I should probably give you a heads-up. There was a bit of a backlog at the depot, so I have some more stuff coming your way soon.'

'How much of a backlog?'

His lips purse. 'Well, now, a pretty big one by the looks of things.'

Oh, God.

'John, please don't tell me you have a truck of fan mail for my dead father outside.'

'Not a truck,' he says. 'And not with me. But there's a sack. Or two.'

'A sack?'

'Or three. It's like Christmas Day down at the sorting office.'

'You're not serious,' I say as Maddie finally wanders over with a single pancake. She swaps out the post for the plate, a trade I happily accept.

'I can start sending them back,' John says.

'No. Don't do that. I just . . . give me a few days, yeah? No problem. Three sacks of letters.'

'Maybe four.'

'I am going to *murder* him.'

We both freeze as Maddie stares at a copy of the local newspaper, her expression furious.

There's a long, weighted pause, and then John smiles.

'Okay! That's me, then. Busy day. Lots to do. Ciara. Maddie. I didn't hear nothing.'

He leaves, giving her an exaggeratedly wide berth that she doesn't notice as she slams the paper on to the table.

'Can we mind the pancake, please?' I ask, trying to eat the thing before she throws it at the wall or something.

'Can you believe this guy?'

'What guy?' I peer down at the grainy picture she's showing me. A hulking, bearded man smiles pleasantly back. 'The hot guy?'

'Shane McCauley,' Maddie says. 'And he is not hot.'

'Agree to disagree. And *this* is Shane? Burger Boy? The man who's trying to put you out of business?'

'The man who's now doing press.'

'Ups?'

'Ciara—'

'Sorry, sorry.' I look at the article properly as she sits opposite me, dropping her head into her hands. **PLANS FOR A NEW SEAFRONT CAFÉ TO OPEN IN CARRIGWEST**, reads the headline.

> Dubliner Shane McCauley may still feel like a visitor in this part of the country, but the trained chef is determined to set down roots, with plans to launch a new dining spot right next to one of Ireland's best-loved beaches. Locals will already be familiar with his Burger Boy truck located at the entrance of the North Strand beach. Owing to its success, Mr McCauley plans to expand on his current hot food selection to include a range of pastries and cakes available—

'I have never seen this man in my life.' I picture the two teenagers who usually work in the truck. 'I've definitely never seen him. I'd remember.'

'Because he doesn't live here! He barely comes by and now he's *putting down roots*.' She grabs the paper from me, twisting it her way. 'How the hell did he make the front page when he's barely spent a week here? I've tried to get them to write about me dozens of times, but Uncle Pat says it would be nepotism.'

'He *is* your uncle.'

'Everyone's related to everyone here! Everything is nepotism! Just because he's a blow-in means he makes front page news?'

'I mean, again,' I say, putting a forkful of pancake into my mouth, 'he's also really hot.'

Her mouth drops open. '*I'm* hot.'

'You are. I'm sorry.'

'Two years,' she says. 'I've been working in that truck for two years, come rain or shine, and this guy thinks he can just rock up and do everything I've been saving up for in a matter of weeks?'

'It's a big beach, Mads.'

'Exactly! He can go to any other part of it. There is a whole south car park, and no reason he can't go there, and I've wanted to open a bricks-and-mortar store for *years*.' She sits back with a huff, glaring at the paper. 'You know what I think happened? I think he broke into my house and looked at my plans.'

'I think that's what happened too.'

'He's going to start selling pastries.'

'Your pastries are better.'

'They are.'

'And they won't have burger grease all over them.'

That gets a smile from her, and she half-sighs, half-groans as the last of her anger releases. 'I'm going to try the bank again,' she says. 'See where my loan application is. I should have more than enough to get started by now.' Her eyes flick to me, confidence faltering. 'Right? What do you think?'

'I think you need some time off.'

'Whatever,' she mumbles, slumping in her chair. 'Are you going to tell me about yesterday or what?'

'There's not much to tell.' I shrug. 'We talked. It went badly. He wants me off the book. I want to lie on the floor and cry. I think it's going to be a great working relationship.'

'You *have* done this before,' she reminds me. 'I loved your books.'

'You have to like my books; you're my friend.'

'And as your friend, I would tell you if they were shite.'

She probably would.

But still.

'This is different,' I say. 'I've never written fantasy before. I can't write like my dad could.'

'Because you're not him. You're you. Casey knows that. And Sam will too, eventually. Get out of your head and stop trying to make it perfect.'

'Oh, says you.' I twist in my chair as she returns to the stove. 'You've literally been here thirty minutes and have fed me *one* pancake.'

'That's different.'

'How?'

'Just is,' she says, and spins the whisk in her hand before starting on a new batter.

CHAPTER NINE

Sam

'Right. Try this one.'

I just about hide my grimace as Ronan places another glass before me, this one filled with two inches of cloudy amber liquid. Not as murky as the last one, but not exactly appetising either.

'Your honest opinion, now,' he says, folding his arms. 'I can take it.'

'All right.'

'Seriously. Whatever you think. First words that spring to mind.'

'I—'

'Your gut reaction.'

I turn my book over to keep the page and clear my throat like it might clear me of my tastebuds.

Deep breath. Knock it back.

Immediately cough.

'Not bad, right?' He seems encouraged. 'Packs a punch?'

'It's . . .' Like vinegar. 'Something,' I say. 'Not as bitter as the last one. And should beer pack a punch?'

It turns out that Ronan is an amateur brewer as well as a bartender. One who's made me his latest guinea pig.

'I suppose it's a bit strong,' he says, sounding as if he doesn't suppose that at all. 'How's the aftertaste?'

'Definitely there.'

'I'll take that on board,' he says, and swaps the empty glass for a fresh pint. 'You're a good lad, Sam. None of these gobshites will even try a sip any more.'

Because they're all smarter than me.

'Happy to help,' I say, and pick up my book as he welcomes in another customer. I ended up staying in the pub for the rest of the afternoon, knowing I'd go stir-crazy in my room otherwise. Ronan is easy company, and, when the sun started to set and people trickled in, the place lost its gloomy, desolate feel.

It's definitely basic. There's no television or food or anything beyond a simple menu of ales, stouts and spirits. But I guess all you need is a chair and a drink, and everyone who stops by is offered both. Their chatter is a pleasant hum in the background, as is the alcohol buzzing through my body, and it could be a pretty good Friday night if I didn't feel the need to check my phone every five minutes for an email that never arrives.

Frustration gnaws at me, and I'm wondering if Amy was on to something with the whole rocking up to an author's house with a 'where's my book' idea when the door opens after ten and Ciara Sheridan strolls inside.

She's alone and dressed in denim shorts and a T-shirt, a light-blue rain jacket slung over her arm. Her hair looks freshly washed, and she must have spent time outside today because her nose is sunburned, the faint blush along the bridge giving her an otherworldly look as she glances around before spotting me.

For a moment we just stare at each other, and a flush of heat crawls up the back of my neck. Probably some kind of survival instinct.

'Ciara!'

We both jump, and Ciara tears her gaze away, focusing on Ronan.

'Where the feck have you been?' he says with more fondness than you'd expect to accompany those words.

Ciara shrugs. 'I was doing Dry January.'

'It's almost June.'

'I was really good at it.'

'Sit down,' he orders, mumbling, 'Dry fecking January,' as he continues pulling a pint for a man three stools down.

Still Ciara hesitates, her gaze drifting again around the room before swinging my way.

I don't think a woman has ever looked so resigned while walking towards me.

'You're in my seat,' she says when she reaches my side, and I realise I'm still staring at her.

'Sorry. I'm—'

'Kidding. That's the bad seat. I never sit there.' Her eyes drop to the book, and I whip it back into the bag.

Then she looks at that. 'Nice tote.'

'Thanks,' I say, shoving it in the space under my stool. 'I have three hundred of them.'

'Sounds like overkill.'

'They're like cocaine to publishing people.'

'So I've heard,' she says. 'Tell me, do you usually read at the bar?'

'Actually, I—' I tense as she hops on to the stool beside mine. 'Do. Sometimes.'

'And do you usually read alone at the bar on a Friday night?'

'No,' I admit.

'Then I hope you don't mind my company.' She stares straight ahead, then swivels to face me so fast that our knees bump. 'I talked to Casey,' she says abruptly. 'He says you're cool and not a con artist.'

'Casey Richardson said I'm cool?'

'Well, not in so many words, but that's the vibe I got. Apparently you're the best editor in the whole wide world, and you're going to fix everything.' Her smile is quick. Forced. 'But I'm not spending my Friday night talking about work.'

I want to spend my Friday night talking about work. I want her to tell me the exact cadence and tone in which my boss implied that I was good at my job. But I've got more important things to discuss right now.

'How did your writing go?'

It's the wrong thing to ask. And her gaze slides from me once more as she turns back to the bar. 'Fine.'

'Do you have anything to share?'

'I will Monday,' she says. 'I promise.'

'You agreed to send me something this morning.'

'That was to make you leave.'

My patience snaps. 'Are you usually this blunt?'

'Are you usually this anal?' she counters, matching my tone. 'I can't work the way you work, okay? I'm not a computer. I would have churned out the novel by now if it was that easy.'

'I didn't say it was easy, but, at the pace you're going, you're not going to meet your deadline.'

'I'm *trying*,' she says tersely. 'There's no point in sending what I have if I'm just going to change it anyway. Monday morning, I swear.'

'But you—'

'Can we please not talk about the book?' she interrupts. 'I just want a drink and I can sit back there if you want. We don't have to chat. We don't have to do anything.'

And she leans away as if she's going to do just that.

'Wait,' I blurt out, visions of Casey taking this away from me making me panic. All it would take is one email from her asking to switch editors and then where would I be? Finished before I barely started. 'Monday, then. Morning,' I add. 'Seeing as how you work nights.'

A soft noise comes out of her, a little like a scoff. But she settles back down.

'Monday,' she echoes, and that's that.

An awkward silence stretches between us, and Ciara shifts beside me, drawing one leg over the other before scratching her cheek. Her fingers are stacked with silver rings, each one glinting in the low light, and I'm momentarily distracted when she drums them against the polished wood.

'I'm staying in the room above the pub,' I say, because I can't think of anything else.

She just hums in response, scooching her stool closer to the bar. Her entire body is angled away from me and I'm pretty sure anyone looking at us would think we were on the worst first date in the world.

Don't be you, Lizzie told me. But the problem is, I don't know how to be anyone else.

Restlessness fills me. I've always hated not knowing what to do. And, with this woman beside me, I feel completely lost. 'Look—' I begin, scrambling to fix this, but that's all I get to say before someone calls from behind.

'Well, now! He exists.'

The farmer I spoke with the other day, the one who directed me to her house, steps inside the pub. He's still wearing the flat cap, and his dog trots in behind him, tail wagging as it heads to the spot in front of the unlit fireplace.

Ciara smiles warmly, twisting to face him. 'Evening, Bernard.'

'Don't *evening Bernard* me. When were you going to introduce me?'

'To who?' she asks, startled as he shakes my hand. 'Sam?'

'Is that your name, young man?' His grip is surprisingly firm. 'The boyfriend.'

Ciara's brow furrows. 'The what?'

'How long have you been keeping him a secret?'

'Ah, you didn't tell me you were seeing someone,' Ronan says, moving back our way. 'I'm sorry, lad. You should have said something.'

'I'm not seeing anyone,' Ciara says firmly.

'We've barely seen her the past few weeks,' Ronan tells me. 'We were starting to worry. Thought maybe she was getting into that whole – ah, what did you call it again, Bernard?'

'Cryptocurrency,' the ninety-year-old says grimly.

Ronan nods. 'Wouldn't know much about it myself now, but you hear things.'

Ciara looks as though she's barely holding on to her patience. 'I'm not trading cryptocurrency. And he's not my boyfriend.'

'I'm not going to say anything,' Ronan says, holding up his hands. 'I know you like your privacy.'

'But—'

'My lips are sealed.' And then he winks at her. Or at least he tries to. It's more like he brings one side of his mouth up and half-closes his right eye.

'I hoped there might be someone when you disappeared on us,' Bernard says happily. 'But you're right to. Live your life while you're young.'

'I was just busy.'

'Of course.' He pats me once on the shoulder. 'Bring him up to the farm one day. Let me see what he's made of.'

'I'm not going to . . . ' She breaks off when he wanders away, and Ronan gives her one final smile before he does the same. She turns back to me, bewildered for half a second before she sees the look on my face.

'This is on you?'

My smile is nervous. 'Maybe.'

'*Maybe?*'

'No one would give me your address.'

'So you lied.'

'No, Bernard assumed.' I pause. '*Then* I lied.'

'Oh, for the love of—'

'Found it!' Ronan reappears, thumping an old cardboard box on the bar. 'I knew I still had them. And to think you wanted me to throw everything out,' he says to Ciara.

She just looks at him warily. 'What are you talking about?'

'Sam was looking for some photographs of Frank earlier,' he says, digging a bundle out. 'I'd put them away for safe keeping but turns out they were too safe. Couldn't find them for the life of me, but here we are. Spick and span.' He taps the first one proudly. 'Well. Spickish. That's me in my better years.' He passes me a faded one of himself behind the bar, and then another of him and Frank outside. 'You're in some of these too,' he adds to Ciara, who's gone deathly silent. Ronan doesn't seem to notice. 'I think Sam here knows even more than you do about your dad,' he continues. 'How many times did you say you read the series?'

'Uh, six,' I say as he delves back into the box. 'You know, I can look at these another time.'

'Think I've got some bookmarks down here,' he mutters. 'You all right, Ciara? You're looking a little pale.'

'I'm . . . ' A line appears on her forehead as she trails off. 'You know, I'm not great.'

'Fancy some medicinal brandy?'

'Actually, I think I'd better go home.'

Ronan looks up in surprise. 'But you didn't even have a pint.'

'Sorry.' She slides off her stool with a wide, false smile. 'I'll swing by next week.'

'But—'

But nothing, as it turns out. She avoids my eye as she grabs her jacket and hurries to the door, nodding at the few people who call out hello to her.

'Must be something she ate,' Ronan says, sounding put out, but I don't think that's it. One by one, every tense interaction we've had speeds through my mind, and I glance back at the photos, knowing that if I let her go now, I might as well get on a plane tonight.

'Ah, here,' Ronan complains as I drain the last of my drink, 'not you, too.'

'I'll be back,' I promise, leaving my bag on the bar. 'Could you mind this? I've gotta—'

'Fine, fine,' he says as he waves me off. 'This is why I stayed single,' he adds, and I don't bother to correct him as I chase after her.

CHAPTER TEN

Ciara

Well. That's what I get for leaving the house.

I step outside, the warm night no fresher than the stuffy air of the pub. But it smells different from the way it did earlier. Earthier and more alive.

The weather forecast said it wouldn't rain for a few hours, but my spidey sense tells me otherwise, so I tug on my jacket as I head down the road, annoyed with myself.

I knew Sam had taken the room above Delaney's. I knew this. First of all, it was a reasonable assumption because there's nowhere else to stay nearby, and second of all, it was a confirmed fact because I finally read the emails he sent me. I knew this, yet when I walked into the pub to get a drink, and talk nonsense to Ronan because I didn't want to spend another night alone, I was still thrown to find him there. And still didn't have a clue how to talk to the guy, either.

I should have just left him be. Should have but didn't. And now look at my Friday night.

Pintless.

Pintless and pointless and—

'Hey!'

Gravel crunches behind me as the man himself appears, and I just about check my groan. Doesn't he ever take a break?

'You should head back in,' I call over my shoulder. 'It's going to rain soon.'

'I think we've gotten off on the wrong foot,' he says, catching up with me, and I'm suddenly so tired I could lie down and fall asleep right here and now. 'This book is—'

'I told you I don't *want* to talk about the book.'

'Tough shit,' he says, and I blink, swinging around to face him.

'Excuse me?'

He doesn't back down. 'Why did you agree to write *The Last Mountain* if you didn't want to?'

'I don't know? Because you offered me a lot of money and I've got a house that's falling apart? And I never said I didn't want to,' I add. 'I'm struggling, that's all.'

'And what? You think I came all this way for kicks? A paid-for vacation? I'm here to help you.'

'*Help* me?' I gape at him. 'You're the one who wants me off the thing!'

'Because I thought you didn't want to do it!' he exclaims. 'I thought I was doing you a favour, offering you a way out. Obviously I was wrong, and I apologise for it.'

He steps closer and I glance back at the pub to make sure no one's watching us. Guess we're just going to have this out in the middle of the road, then.

'You were right,' Sam says. 'What you said back in your house? I didn't know your father. I have no clue what it was like growing up with him. But the reason I'm pushing you is because you need to be pushed. And I think, deep down, you agree.'

I do. But it's still hard to hear him say it.

'You don't like your dad's readers,' he continues, and I bristle.

'They don't like *me*,' I correct, only to immediately wish I hadn't. I sound as though I'm twelve. 'And I saw your tattoo.'

It comes out like an accusation. But I don't know how to explain it. A lifetime of living in the shadow of this series. Of these characters. I've learned to be wary.

'You're not just a fan,' I say. 'You're a *fan*.'

'And I'm not going to apologise for that,' he replies. 'It's why Casey sent me here in the first place. Would you want to work with someone who doesn't know the first thing about Ravian?'

'Of course not.'

'Then give me another chance. I understand you don't know me, but I'm here for one reason and one reason only. I want to publish the biggest books in the world, and it'll never get bigger than this. Than you. I can help. But I can't edit a blank page. Nobody can.'

I shift on my feet as Sam stares at me as if he's trying to do some mind tricks or something. He's completely serious. And honestly, I thought it was what I wanted to hear. This sit-up-straight, rip-off-the-band-aid, get-the-job-done attitude. I didn't want him to be just another fanboy.

So it's weird that I'm a little disappointed by his words. Strange that instead of them making me feel better, I just feel kind of empty.

'We don't have to be best friends,' he says when I don't respond. 'But for this to work, you've got to give me something.'

'I'm not . . .' I break off, frustrated. 'It's not that I haven't been trying,' I tell him. 'I've been trying harder at this than anything I've ever done.'

'And you can do it. You know you can. I read your first pages. You're a good writer.'

'And you're a good editor, is that it?'

His eyebrows rise. 'I'm a great one.'

I huff, but there's no annoyance in it. Can't be annoyed when he's looking all sincere again. There's a boyishness to him when he talks about his job. A kind of unabashed passion that makes me believe him. Or want to, anyway.

'This probably isn't what you expected when Casey asked you to come here, huh?'

'It's not so bad,' he says lightly. 'I met Mary.'

'Oh, yeah?'

'She gave me a plate of salmon.'

My bark of laughter is so sudden, I almost choke on it.

'She also wants to do my laundry,' he continues when I've got a hold of myself.

'You should have hidden,' I tell him, still coughing slightly. 'That was, like, the first thing I taught you.'

'I'll know for next time.' The strained tension between us begins to fade, and he must realise he has me because he smiles a wide, pleased smile. One that lights up his whole face. It's weird how much I like it.

'Come back in,' he says, as if he's the local here. 'I'll buy you a drink.'

But I shake my head. 'I should get home,' I say, taking a few steps backwards. 'Do some *work*.'

He seems surprised. 'You're walking?'

'I can't really run in these shoes.'

'Can't you call a taxi?' He grows defensive when I just look at him. 'You have taxis here.'

'Not *here* here. On the island of Ireland, yes. In the village of Carrigwest, no.'

'So you're going to walk home alone. At night. In a storm.'

'I didn't say anything about a storm,' I say. 'It's rain. If you can't handle a bit of rain, you shouldn't be visiting the west coast of Ireland. I'll talk to you tomorrow.' I waggle my fingers. 'Goodnight.'

'But it's pitch black,' Sam calls.

When I don't respond, he starts after me, matching my pace as I hit the road.

Nu-uh. 'Are you seriously following me?'

'I'm going to see you home,' he says before hesitating. 'If that's okay with you.'

And they say chivalry is dead. 'Knock yourself out,' I sigh. 'Just don't talk to me or make direct eye contact.'

'I can't tell if you're joking or not.'

'My biggest curse.'

It gets even darker as soon as we're out of sight of the pub. No streetlights out here. It doesn't bother me – I know the way like the back of my hand – but, once we leave the last building behind, Sam brings up the flashlight on his phone, lighting a small circle around us.

'Checking for snakes?' I ask.

'I know you don't have those.'

'The dark can't hurt you,' I murmur, quoting one of my father's books.

'That character gets eaten by a dragon.'

'Potayto, potahto. And the dragons are all in Wales.' I crane my neck, looking up at the sky. I usually love the stars out here, so much brighter than they are in the city, but I can't see a single one tonight. Nothing but inky, cloudy night.

A night completely ruined by the sweeping white glow behind me.

'Seriously,' I say as Sam trains his beam ahead of us. 'I know where I'm going. You just need to let your eyes adjust.'

'To complete and total darkness?'

'See, you New Yorkers think you're so tough, but put you on a country road and you have whatever the opposite of claustrophobia is.'

'Agoraphobia.'

'Now you're just making words up.'

'I broke my ankle once.'

'Eh?'

'When I was a kid,' he explains. 'My dad and I were hiking, and my ankle caught on a rock. I tripped and broke it.' His eyes meet mine. 'Do you know how inconvenient it is to break your ankle half-way through a ten-mile hike?'

'Extremely?'

He refocuses on the road. 'There are a few potholes around here.'

'But if I break *my* ankle on one, I'll be forced to stay inside and write.'

'That, I didn't think of.'

I watch the beam for a few seconds, and then take out my phone to join his.

'I've never broken anything,' I say. 'Not even sprained. Gave myself a nasty cut once, though. Maddie and I were at the beach, and I slashed my hand on a shell. It was really gross. I had this massive gouge right down my palm, and it bled like crazy and—' I stop when I realise he's staring at me. 'What?'

'Is this how you do small talk?'

'I've got a scar,' I say, showing him the white sliver of raised skin. 'I think it's cool.'

'Very,' he agrees, even though he's not even looking at it.

'So did your bone pop out?'

He makes a strange, strangled noise, and I smile. 'Don't tell me you're squeamish.'

'I'm not squeamish, I'm just . . . did my *bone* pop out?'

'Fine. No more injury talk.'

'Appreciate that,' he says, and I swing my light up and down the tarmac just as something sharp and wet lands on my forehead. A raindrop.

Sam flinches a moment later and follows my gaze.

Called it.

'It's just a shower.' I put my hood up, about to tell him to turn back, but another drop falls before I can even open my mouth. And then another and another in rapid succession until it is definitely, one hundred per cent raining.

Sam hustles me off the main road and under the shelter of a tree, but as the downpour grows heavier it provides only minimal cover. We've got a minute or two at most before we're soaked to the skin, and, while I might have my coat, Sam's only in a T-shirt.

'Just a shower?' he asks, and I look back down the road as he steps closer to me, away from the danger zone.

Ten minutes from the pub. Ten minutes from the house. We need shelter and we need it now, and luckily I know where to find it.

I shine my phone into the woods, gauging the distance, and then grab Sam's hand before I know what I'm doing. 'Do you trust me?' I ask as his head whips towards me in surprise.

'No.'

'Then let's—' I stop short and glare at him. 'You're supposed to say yes.'

'I met you three days ago.'

'Yeah, but you said we're . . . whatever. Come on.' I tug him sharply, pulling him deeper into the forest. He could resist me, but he comes easily, letting me drag him through the trees.

'Where are we going?' He has to yell the words over the noise, but

I don't even try to answer him. The world seems so much louder in here as the water bounces off the leaves, creating a cacophony that drowns out everything else.

I'm drenched within seconds, and our progress slows as we navigate between the dark trunks and uneven forest floor. But my feet know where they're going. I grew up in these woods. And so, when I bring us to a stop a minute later, all I do is point in triumph at the looming structure above us.

Sam peers up, panting. 'Is that a tree house?'

It is.

The rain still falls, but I ignore it as I let him go and climb, my dripping sneakers finding the sturdy planks of wood as they always do. It doesn't matter that years have passed. I used to spend every day up here. I could find these rungs blindfolded in a hurricane.

I reach the top in record time and haul myself up before turning back to help Sam, only to find him right on my tail. Our eyes meet briefly and I clamber back so we can both fit, a little embarrassed and not knowing why.

He climbs in more slowly, taking it all in.

'Did your dad build this?'

I shake my head. 'It was here when we bought it. The house is only a few minutes away. We're right on the edge of the estate.'

It seemed so magical when I was younger, so huge, but as Sam pulls himself fully inside, sitting with a thud against the wall, the space seems to shrink until I feel as if there's no room at all.

'It's cool,' he says, wiping his hand across his face. As he does, a raindrop runs from his hairline down his cheek, and I track it for a full five seconds before I drag my gaze away.

'Are you sure it's safe in here?' he asks.

'No.'

Kind of feels like it, though. Whoever made this thing made it well. It's dry and warm, as though we're cocooned in our own little world, and I relax back, bringing my knees to my chest. But the feeling doesn't last long.

Now that we're no longer in the deluge, my clothes start sticking uncomfortably to my skin, and I have to peel the jacket off me. I also hadn't thought to zip it up, so, while my arms are dry, I am supremely aware that I'm rocking the wet T-shirt look. Not that Sam seems to notice. He's not even looking at me, his attention on the rain outside.

There's no dramatic lightning to give me glimpses of him, but he's kept his phone on, and the flashlight beams up between us, casting his face in a harsh light that he somehow pulls off but probably makes me look like a ghost.

'I'm pretty good with feedback,' I say abruptly, and get a little buzz when he turns back to me. 'At least, I think I am. If you can just reassure me with a "not shit" every now and then, that would be great.'

'Noted.'

'And I'm great at procrastinating.'

His lips quirk up. 'All writers are.'

'I'm also not used to this,' I say, gesturing at the space between us. 'That's why I've been a bit . . . I usually go at it alone until I'm ready to show something to someone.'

'And that's fine,' he says gently. 'But that wasn't working.'

'No.' Not working at all. 'Dad always said he didn't know what would happen in a book until he finished writing it. I mean, he'd outline it to death. He'd plan it down to the sentence sometimes. But he wasn't afraid to change it. He wasn't afraid to try new things until it was perfect. So I have what he planned, but I don't know which bits he would have changed, because *he* wouldn't until he started it.'

'It doesn't matter what he would have done,' Sam says. 'We need to follow his pattern of storytelling, sure. But, while it may be his world, it's your book.'

My book.

It doesn't feel like it is right now.

But I appreciate the sentiment.

Another blast of rain hammers the side of the tree house and I comb my fingers through my hair, shaking it out.

'I think we're going to be stuck here for a bit longer,' I say, stating the obvious. 'Do you have any other life problems you need to talk about? Some more childhood trauma, perhaps?'

'Let's leave that to Week Two.'

'Suit yourself.' I stretch a leg out until it's flat next to his. 'Have you got any other super-cool injury stories?'

I'm joking, but he responds immediately. 'A kid in my class broke his arm falling off a swing.'

'Tell me everything.'

And, to be fair to the guy, he does.

CHAPTER ELEVEN

Sam

When I wake the next morning, it's to the sound of bird song and a fresh breeze drifting through my shoved-open window. I know it won't last for long. *Heatwave set to continue*, reads every article I can find, and I make it my new priority to find some sort of air-conditioning, even if I have to resort to making paper fans.

When the rain finally stopped, I insisted on walking Ciara the rest of the way home, but declined the invitation to crash on her couch. The journey back to Delaney's was pretty miserable in wet clothes, but I felt I had to claw back some professionalism now that we've reached an understanding.

She was pretty talkative once she decided I wasn't the enemy. Pretty funny, too. Humour wasn't exactly in Frank's repertoire, but with Ciara . . .

I shuffle into my tiny bathroom as I go over our conversation from last night. It was a risk going after her like that but turned out all we needed was a little brutal honesty to cut through the bullshit.

She's nervous.

Nervous is good. Nervous means she wants to do a good job. I can deal with nervous.

In fact, right here, right now, I feel as if I can deal with anything, and when I get a text from her an hour later, my confidence soars to record heights.

How do you feel about creepy churches?

I love them, I respond, and by the time I'm showered and dressed she's pulled up outside.

'This must feel like the crack of dawn to you,' I say as I get into her car.

'I'm fine,' she dismisses. 'Wide awake.'

'You just yawned.'

'That was me inhaling air to better fill my lungs.'

'That's literally what a yawn ... you know what, never mind. Sure.'

She waits until I've got my seatbelt on and then expertly navigates the winding, narrow roads at a speed that shouldn't be legal. After about fifteen minutes of this near-death experience, we pull up to the church. It's surprisingly large for a small area, with forbidding grey stone and stained-glass windows. These might not necessarily be considered creepy themselves, but the overgrown graveyard next to it certainly would.

'Right?' she asks, catching me looking at it. 'Maddie and I used to dare each other to go in there when we were kids.'

I follow her out, half-expecting tumbleweed to drift across our path. 'Is it always this ... vacant?' I ask, struggling to find the right word. *Desolate* seems harsh.

'Yep. Last time we had a priest full-time was in the nineties. Now we share one with five other parishes.'

'So what are we doing here?'

'Patience, grasshopper.' She takes out her phone, her thumb flying across the screen before she leans against the church wall, tilting her face to the sky. 'This is the best kind of sunlight,' she says, closing her eyes. 'Weak.'

'Not enjoying the heatwave?'

'Not when it lasts for four months. I'm a seasonal girl at heart.' She pats the stone beside her. 'Come bask with me.'

I do, though the wall is still damp from the rain last night, and I rest my hands behind my back so the moss doesn't rub off on my clothes. Ciara keeps her eyes shut. I keep mine on her. She's dressed in more or less the same outfit I've seen her in every day. Denim shorts. A plain T-shirt. A pair of scuffed tennis shoes. I remember staring at the bottom of them as she climbed the tree ahead of me. The curve of her calf and flash of bare thigh beneath her rain jacket.

I clear my throat, looking away. 'Can I ask you a question?'

'Nothing good ever followed those words.'

'How did you get into crime?'

'As a writer or in general?' She cracks open an eye to peer at me. 'I liked to read it, so it seemed natural to write it.'

'But you stopped writing it,' I point out. 'Ever since you were—'

'Outed?' She grimaces. 'Sorry. If I sound bitter, it's because I am. I chose a pen name *because* I didn't want that type of attention. But the journalist didn't care. She wanted to write an article and go viral for a few hours.'

'How did she even find out?'

'I don't know,' Ciara sighs. 'I doubt it was a big conspiracy. It wasn't a secret here. All my family and friends knew, so somebody probably said something and it kept travelling. It's why I've only told Maddie this time around. I know she won't breathe a word.'

'And you really just stopped?'

'I did. Didn't sign another contract. Parted ways with my agent. That was that. The whole thing was ruined for me.'

'But your reviews were great.'

Her focus shifts sharply to me, and I shrug. 'I looked them up.'

'Yeah. Well.' She kicks at the ground, unearthing a daffodil. 'That didn't matter so much in the end. The fandom turned on me. Or part of it, anyway. The very vocal part.'

'They didn't like that you hid your name?'

'They didn't like me full stop. And before you ask, I don't know why. Misogyny. Jealousy.' She purses her lips. 'Comparison. I stopped trying to find a reason when someone sent me a thirty-minute YouTube video blasting my writing.'

I wince, and she turns her attention to the moss, picking small clumps off the wall.

'Eventually, I decided to just step away from it all. It was easier that way. That's why I want this book to just be mine for as long as possible. At least until I know we're on the right track with it.'

'We can do that,' I say firmly. 'And if you're worried about reaction to the announcement, we can deal with that too. You were taken by surprise last time, but we can manage this.'

'You make it sound like you have a war room.'

'You obviously haven't met our publicity department.'

Her smile is faint. 'Can I ask *you* a question?'

'Always.'

'Why'd you get into publishing? You don't seem like the type.'

'There's a type?'

'There is definitely a type, and don't you dare pretend there isn't.'

At that, I laugh. 'Real answer or fake answer?'

'Fake answer.'

'The money.'

'Real answer.'

'Probably your dad,' I admit, and she falls quiet. 'Neither of my parents read that much, but my sister used to go to dance class after school, and I'd be dumped at the library to wait for her. When I was done with homework, I'd read. One of the librarians gave me the first Ravian book when I was thirteen, and I loved it. But I didn't know working in publishing was an actual job until I left college. And here I am.'

'Here you are,' she echoes, her gaze unfocused as she stares straight ahead. 'You should have gone into finance,' she says after a beat. 'Lots of money in finance.'

'So I've heard.'

'And do you have a real girlfriend back in New York? Boyfriend? Bedfriend?'

'You caught me reading alone in a bar on a Friday night,' I say drily. 'Does that answer your question?'

'It tells me you're a man comfortable with his own company.'

'And with his own company he does stay.'

She scoffs. 'Now *that* I understand.'

'You're single?'

'In my tiny rural community where I'm related to half the population? Only by choice. Plus, there's no way you could date properly here. Everybody knows everybody. But I'm not really looking to . . .' She trails off, pushing away from the wall as she pulls out her phone.

'Looking to what?' I ask, trying and failing to hide the curiosity in my voice.

'Nothing. Come on. Ronan told me where the key is.'

'To what?'

'The church,' she says as if it's obvious, and starts towards the cemetery.

Oh, God. 'Please tell me it's not in one of the graves.'

'Of course not. It's in the bird house.'

'You keep saying things like they're reasonable, but they're not. You know that, right?'

'Where else would you keep a spare key?' She stops beneath a sycamore tree, and I follow her gaze to a small brown bird house hidden in the leaves.

'How are you— No, of course. You'll climb.' I step back as she shakes out her hands and grabs hold of the nearest branch, lifting herself effortlessly as if she's done it a thousand times before. Then again, growing up in a place like this, she probably has.

'What?' she asks, catching my expression as she glances down.

'Just thinking about your idyllic childhood,' I say as she peers into the box before digging out a rusty silver key. 'Climbing trees. Digging holes. Summers must have been great here.'

'You haven't been here in a normal summer,' she reminds me, landing on the ground. 'And not really. Dad was usually writing so I was left alone. Practically feral for a few years.'

'Alone?'

She flashes me a quick smile. 'Don't worry, Child Services. He was a good dad. Just busy. Not like he could shut off his brain as easily as everyone else.'

'Right,' I say, feeling there's more she's not saying, but I drop it as she leads me back to the church. She lets us in with the bird house key, and we bypass rows of old wooden pews until we reach a small room at the back. This door is unlocked, but, when she opens it, we're hit by a blast of stale air.

Ciara's nose wrinkles. 'Smells old.'

It does. And not in a nice way. It smells as if no one's been in here for a while. But, other than that, it's not exactly what I expected.

It looks like a storage room. Low ceiling, cheap wooden floors. It's lined with tall filing cabinets and ancient-looking bureaux. Several tables are pushed together in the centre of the room, and a handful of chairs are stacked in the corner.

'Welcome to the crypt,' Ciara says as we step inside. 'Or, by its official title, the room where we keep the village archives.'

'Feel like it could have a snappier name.'

'Hence the crypt.'

Our voices have dropped considerably, and I wonder if she was as well trained by librarians as I was as a child.

'Dad used to spend a lot of time in here when he wrote the first few books,' she explains, pulling out one of the drawers. 'He got half his character names from here. Most of his locations too.'

She opens a bulky ledger, revealing a handwritten spreadsheet filled with names and ages.

'It's a census?' I ask, leaning over to read it.

'It's a cheat sheet.'

'Is . . . everyone a farmer?'

'Or a farmer's son. Or look. A farmer's daughter.'

I move nearer and get a sudden whiff of her shampoo, a hint of fruit and florals in the musty air.

'How were there six people called Thomas in this village alone?' she asks. 'And four Ellens!'

She runs a finger down the columns and my focus strays from the ledger to her hands. No rings today. But there's a bracelet of white beads around her wrist and two words written in faded red ink on the back of her hand. *Call plumber.*

'That's too many Ellens,' she continues and our arms brush as she turns the page. Ciara falters, and I spy goose bumps rising on her skin. 'Cold in here,' she mumbles, and I nod, even though I don't feel cold at all. I actually feel a little warm, and I don't stop even when I step back and move to the other end of the room.

'So is that why we're here?' I ask. 'Inspiration?'

'And to steal names and occupations.' She starts taking pictures of each page with her phone. 'For a writer, I'm bad at making stuff up.'

'One of my authors gets his names from movie credits. Whatever works.'

'Hmm.' She falls quiet. It doesn't last long. 'Who's the worst author you've ever worked with?'

I grin, saying nothing.

'Come on.'

'Nope.'

'Tell me.'

'I don't gossip.'

'Bullshit. Everyone in publishing loves to gossip. It's me, isn't it?'

'By a mile.'

She mock-glares at me and goes back to the book as I peek into boxes to find something useful. I'm rifling through a pile of white candles when she calls me back to her side.

'All right, Number One Fan,' she says, showing me an old set of blueprints. 'What's that?'

'A city plan?' I guess, glancing at them. 'Or a village plan or whatever?' It must be over a hundred years old, and I look closer, recognising the crop of buildings that make up Carrigwest and, further on, the church we're in now. 'It's interesting that the main road has more or less stayed the same this whole— No way.'

She smirks as I take it from her.

'He based Ravian on Carrigwest?'

'An older version of it,' she says as I turn it on its side to get a different view.

'He never said that anywhere.'

'There's a lot he never said. But you're special, so you get to see it.'

I don't mind her teasing, mentally reviewing the maps featured at the back of his first six books and comparing them with the one I'm looking at now. Instead of the church, we've got Finn's house. Instead of the parking lot, the keep.

I get a sudden shot of adrenaline that I don't bother to hide. 'I can't believe no one's figured this out before.'

'Unless you knew where to look, how would you know? And the artist based all the drawings on Dad's original sketch, which wasn't great to begin with.'

'So you're telling me that we're where Maeve had her first meeting with the Druid?'

'No, because that happened in a book, and this is real life.'

'You're not taking this from me.'

'I wouldn't dream of it,' she says, watching me closely. 'You really get a kick out of this stuff, don't you?'

'Well, yeah. You grow up with something for so long and think you know everything; it's nice to realise you don't.'

'So, the hot-shot has a soft side.'

'There aren't a lot of authors that make me feel this way,' I admit.

'And the rest of us are just money bags to you, are we?'

Her voice is light. But I wonder if I accidentally hit a nerve yesterday and put the blueprints down, meeting her eye.

'I'm here to help you write the best book possible. You know that, right?'

'Sure.'

'And you also know that finding inspiration isn't getting you out of writing me fifteen hundred words by Monday morning.'

She clicks her tongue off the roof of her mouth, but she looks pleased as she turns her back on me, pulling out another book.

'It's all part of the process,' she says, setting it down with a thump. 'Sometimes you'll just have to trust me.'

CHAPTER TWELVE

Ciara

It's almost time for lunch before I'm happy I've got enough. I'm still not exactly sure why I invited Sam to come. Maybe to make up for our first meetings. Or maybe because I've spent so long trying to write this book alone that I don't think I realised how on edge it was making me until I had someone else to bounce ideas off. And while on paper it should be a pretty boring way to spend a Saturday morning, I don't think he minds so much. He spends the entire time poring over a bunch of old maps, and I have to say his name twice to get his attention.

When I'm finally done, he heads out to the car while I put everything back. He's talking on the phone when I exit the church but catches sight of me before I can give him some privacy and holds up a hand, telling me to wait.

'All right,' he says. 'Gotta go. Yeah. Yes. Okay. Love you too.'

The last three words barrel through me, and I get very busy pretending to make sure the door is locked tight. Weird. I thought he didn't have a girlfriend. Didn't he say he didn't have a girlfriend? I could have sworn he—

'Sorry,' he says as he approaches.

'You're grand,' I chirp. 'Who was that?'

'Lizzie. My sister.'

'Oh.' *Oh*. Oh. 'Is she okay?'

'She's fine. We're close. We talk a lot.'

'That's nice.' I give the handle another tug even though it is definitely locked, but my brain is still doing this weird *everything's fine!* adrenaline thing, like when you miss a step while walking and think you're going to fall, but no, you're in a shopping centre buying socks, not wandering around a cliff edge. 'Any other siblings?'

He shakes his head.

'Two's a good number,' I hear myself say. 'What's she like?'

'Loud,' he says before pausing. 'Loving. She has three boys under five and a husband who worships the ground she walks on. He's a big insurance guy, so she's able to stay at home and look after the kids. It's hard work, but she loves it.'

'She sounds great.'

'She is.' He smiles. 'You ever wanted a sibling?'

I start to nod before stopping. 'Well, kind of. I had Maddie. Have. We were forced together as children. Her parents helped out a lot when Mam died. Dad and I lived with them for a year before the books took off.'

Sam goes quiet, and it doesn't take a genius to figure out what he's wondering.

'Cancer,' I tell him as we walk to the car. 'It was quick.'

'I'm sorry.'

'Thanks. People seemed to like her, but I was too young to have any real memories.'

'It's good you had Maddie.'

'She's my best friend,' I say simply. 'I'm pretty sure she'd help me bury a body.'

'I think that's where Lizzie might draw the line.'

'Really?'

'Nah. She'd be squeamish, but she'd do it.'

'Being closer to Mads was one of the few good things about coming back here,' I tell him as we get in. 'I never intended to stay before Dad left me the house, and she was a huge help. That being said, if she ever moves away, I'm fucked.'

His eyes dart to mine. 'You didn't want to stay here?'

'It wasn't the plan. I moved to London for a reason. I'm a seasonal *and* a city girl.'

'Wait,' Sam says. 'You mean if you didn't have the house, you'd leave?'

He sounds so surprised that I laugh. 'Would you want to live here?'

'I didn't grow up here.'

'And do you live where you grew up?'

'No,' he admits, and I nod.

'I rest my case.'

'But do you think your dad knew that?' Sam asks, only to frown before I can answer. 'And that's none of my business.'

'Don't worry.' I smile as I pull away from the church. 'I think he loved the house, and he wanted me to have it. I don't think he thought about much more than that.'

We both fall silent, and I peer ahead as a turn comes into view. One where if I go left it will lead me home, and if I head right ... Restlessness fills me; the thought of returning to the house is the worst thing in the world. The empty rooms, the still air.

I sit up straighter. 'You want to go to the beach?'

'The beach?'

'Yeah, Sam, the beach. It's a sunny day and you just reminded me that you are a visitor to this little island of mine. Let's do some sightseeing. For the craic.'

'The—'

'It means fun,' I say, full-on teasing him now. 'You know what fun means, don't you? Come on. I'll buy you a smoothie.'

He still looks reluctant, as though half of him wants to order me back to the house to work, but when he doesn't protest further I speed up, my mood brightening as I turn right and head towards the coast. It doesn't take long to get there, but it does take an age to find a parking spot, as it's the weekend.

'Watch out for seagulls,' I warn him as we weave between the cars. The place is packed with children and families, their laughter and voices filling the air. 'The key is not to look them in the eye. Now, may I suggest a Strawberry Sunrise? Which I would controversially recommend *without* honey because—'

'Ciara!'

I pause as Maddie appears around the back of her truck, looking more frazzled than normal. Her blonde curls are stuck to her forehead with the heat, and her apron is stained from grape juice.

Or at least I hope it's grape juice.

'Thank God you're here,' she says. 'Come on.' And she disappears before I can so much as say hello.

Sam and I share a glance, and I give him a reassuring smile before leading him around the generator to where Maddie waits.

'Where's your car?' she asks as soon as she sees us.

'By the dunes. I thought I'd show Sam the—'

'I need you to take these home with you.' She slaps her hand on a tall stack of unmarked boxes, looking suspiciously proud of herself.

'And are these drugs or weapons?' I ask. 'Because I'd like to know what I'm getting into.'

'It's ketchup. I think. There might be other condiments inside.'

'And why do you have—'

'You,' she interrupts, her eyes latching on to Sam. 'Put those hard-back arms to good use. Come on.'

'Nope.' I shoot a hand out, stopping him in his tracks. 'What's going on?'

But Maddie ignores me, plucking the keys from my hand and grabbing the top box before heading off towards the dunes.

'Is she okay?' Sam asks.

'She's . . . ' I knock on the side of the truck. 'Natalie?'

Maddie's only employee, a first-year college student helping out for the summer, appears in the doorway, chewing on some gum.

'What's with the ketchup?'

'The burger guy got a smoothie machine,' she explains, and I gasp.

'Why is that bad?' Sam asks me, looking supremely confused.

'He's Maddie's sworn enemy.'

He blinks. 'How many sworn enemies do you two have?'

'I only have one!' I protest. 'Well—'

'The sunglasses guy,' Natalie says.

'I really don't like that sunglasses guy,' I admit. 'And I guess there's the— Maddie!' I step in front of the boxes as she comes striding back, stopping her before she can take another. 'Is this the burger guy's ketchup?'

'I have no idea,' she says, as if she's been practising. 'It was delivered here without an order form attached. It just said to the North Beach. I have business premises on the North Beach, so I am claiming it.'

Oh, my God. 'It's obviously his.'

'It's not *obviously* anything,' she says. 'Now, are you going to help me hide the evidence or not?'

'That is not the question of an innocent woman!'

'Can someone tell me what's going on?' Sam asks mildly, and Maddie grabs another box while I'm distracted.

'He's trying to put her out of business,' I explain as she vanishes again. 'Or actually I don't think he's *trying* to.'

'Why else would he be making smoothies?' Natalie asks. 'They started opening earlier for breakfast. Exact same time as us.' She crosses her arm, looking stubborn. 'He wants to take our customers.'

'And he won't succeed,' Maddie says as she rejoins us. Her face is flushed pink, but whether that's from the sun or annoyance, I don't know. 'He's a city blow-in. I'm a beloved local. I know how this story ends.'

I gape at her. 'With you stealing his stuff?'

'With me *protecting* my business. I'm—'

'Give me back my ketchup, Madeline,' a deep voice calls behind us, and I turn as a man appears in the gap between the two trucks. The four of us fall silent and for all her earlier bluster Natalie straight-up blushes. But it's not that I don't understand why. The guy's got such a pair of baby blues, it's like he's weaving a spell on me just by standing there.

Shane McCauley is as handsome as he appeared in the newspaper, though the amiable smile is replaced with a grim scowl as he sets his sights on my friend. In fact, he'd probably look pretty intimidating because of his size, if he weren't wearing a T-shirt with a cartoon burger applying mustard to itself. I think it's supposed to be sunscreen.

Maddie's hands go to her hips. 'What ketchup? An order was

delivered to the truck at the North Beach. I signed for it and therefore, it is mine.'

'It was meant for me, and you know it. What are you even going to use it for?'

'What are *you* going to use a smoothie machine for, beyond trying to piss me off?'

'Who said anything about trying?' he quips, and Maddie goes *bright* red.

'Okay!' I say, stepping between them, but, before I can come up with some genius plan to calm everyone down, a shrill whistle cuts through the air, and Mary appears between the trucks, wearing a large straw hat and a bright green bathing suit. An old copy of the community newsletter is clutched in her hands.

'I'm trying to read,' she admonishes, brandishing the paper as if we're all a fly she'd like to swat.

Maddie looks at her, exasperated. 'You can't be back here.'

'Says who?'

'Me! This is a private—'

'It is a *public* matter,' Mary says sharply. 'The beach is getting clogged because cars can't get in and people can't get out because, if you haven't noticed, you are drawing an audience.'

We hadn't noticed. And it's only then that I spy the curious faces peering at us from around the front of the trucks.

Natalie makes a *yikes* face and scampers back inside.

'Now what's going on?' Mary asks, and Maddie and Shane speak at the same time.

'He's *stealing* my—'

'She stole my—'

The whistle blows, cutting them off. 'Enough,' Mary says. 'I don't care. If you're going to behave like disobedient children, you should be treated as such.' She points to the opposite end of the car park. 'One of you needs to go over there. I suggest the smoothie truck, as I like the smell of the onion rings.'

'You don't own the beach,' Maddie tells her through clenched teeth. 'You can't make us do anything.'

'I can and I will. And you'll do what you're told if you know what's good for you. What I know about you, Maddie Buckley, could make a sinner blush.'

Maddie's eyes go wide as Shane's gaze swings her way.

'Well?' Mary presses, gesturing at the other end of the parking lot.

Her jaw tightens. 'I can't move. My truck doesn't have wheels. Make him go.'

Shane just shakes his head. 'Look, lady, you can't tell us where to park. The county council has designated—'

Mary blows her whistle again, and Maddie slaps her hands over her ears as Shane's expression darkens.

'Why do you even have that?'

Mary looks affronted. 'To assist the lifeguards.'

'Oh, for— Fine,' he bites out. 'Anything to stop this conversation.'

'You'll move?'

'It's nearer the entrance anyway. I'll go tomorrow.'

'See that you do,' Mary says as she sends a final glare to all of us. 'All right, move along!' she adds to the curious onlookers. Another whistle-screech and she starts corralling them back until we're left alone once more.

Shane stares hard at them before he turns stiffly back to Maddie. 'Can I have my—'

'I'll keep an eye out for your box,' she says, looking purposefully at anything but him. 'Now, if you excuse me, I have to get back to work.'

Shane opens his mouth, looking as if he wants to say *exactly* what's on his mind, but stops when Maddie turns towards him, her eyes narrowed. The two share a brief, heated stare before he turns on his heel and disappears into his own truck.

Huh.

'I thought you didn't like him,' I say when he's gone.

'I don't.'

'So why were you making sex eyes at him?'

Her mouth drops open. 'I was *not* making sex eyes. Those were hate eyes. Because I *hate* him.'

Oh, boy. 'Whatever you say. Are you going to give him back his ketchup?'

'No.'

'Well, I'm taking it out of my car,' I tell her. 'And you realise you're still working in the same area together? He's just going to take it back when you're not looking.'

'I'd like to see him try,' she says darkly as Natalie calls from the truck for back-up. 'Thanks for helping,' she adds, tossing me my keys.

'Any time!' I call after her, and turn to Sam, who's still looking lost.

'We're usually very normal,' I say as I lead him back to the front. 'We're just really not used to the sun.'

CHAPTER THIRTEEN

Sam

On Monday, I wake at seven a.m. to find an email from Ciara with nothing but an attached file named *Sam FINAL final_3 (1)* and two words in the subject heading.

As promised.

It's rough, but it's something. I can tell she's anxious. Some phrases jump out at me where she's trying too hard to emulate her father, but I'm not worried. That'll fade as she gets more comfortable with the material. If anything, I'm relieved to see the hints of what she can do *now*. There's a dark scene towards the start with a trial and a dungeon that is one of the most menacing things I've ever read, and for the first time since I got here I'm excited about what's to come. All I can think about is that she might actually pull this off. I didn't realise how much I was doubting it until now.

We settle into a routine over the next few days without formally agreeing to. In the mornings, I read what Ciara sent the night before and try to keep up with an increasingly full inbox. In the afternoons, I go to her house to help plot out the stickier parts of the story and sometimes stay there until ten or eleven at night, which is when she starts to write, before I head back to Delaney's to sleep.

There's a lot to get through. I start dreaming about timelines and plot holes and it doesn't help that she isn't a linear writer. Some authors can't move on to the next chapter without perfecting the first, but Ciara likes to hop around, more than once sending me a scene that I have no idea what to do with.

By the end of that first week, she has ten thousand new words and a solid outline for Act One. By the end of the second, she gets more comfortable sharing her own ideas. She's had a lot more time than me with Frank's notes, and it's clear she's been mulling them over. She's got the brain of a thriller writer, and leans more towards action, towards the dark instincts of the characters. Some of her proposed changes are brilliant.

Others, not so much.

'You look so horrified right now, you know that? It's kind of funny.' Ciara sets the jug of fresh lemonade on the kitchen counter, smiling widely at me.

It's a Thursday afternoon, and she is in a very good mood. Meanwhile, I'm already regretting my choice to wear jeans. The temperature climbed another degree higher today, and I swear I can feel the difference, my brain unusually hazy as it tries to make sense of what she's proposing.

'What reaction were you expecting?' I ask flatly. 'You can't just gloss over a major character.'

'Why not? He's boring. No one likes him.'

'High Lord Aengus is not boring.'

'He's *so* boring.' Ciara's voice is strained as she reaches up on her toes, trying to get a glass from the top shelf. 'Don't lie to me. I know you skim over every one of his speeches. Everyone does.'

'I—' I break off, because all right, maybe I did, and she glances over her shoulder, victorious.

'Boring,' she repeats. 'I can't write pages of moral teachings like Dad could. That's not in me. I'm sorry, I'm not that smart. So instead of wasting my time trying to do something that we both know won't be any good, why don't we just kill—'

'We can't kill him off,' I say, frustrated. 'At least not just because you don't like him.'

'It can be a noble death. Respectfully done. Bye bye, High Lord Aengus. Thank you for your devotion to the future of Ravian, but no one cares.'

Her fingers skim the glass as she swipes it again, and the shelf rattles ominously. Visions of the whole thing falling down make me move behind her, and before I know what I'm doing I lean up and over.

For a moment, our bodies align, her back pressed against my front, her hair tickling my chin. The heat of her is unexpected, as is the brief brush of our hands as I reach over her head and pluck the glass from the shelf.

I step back, feeling as though I've been given a jolt to the heart as I hold it out to her, but Ciara just takes it, her attention on the jug of lemonade she left on the counter.

She gets us our drinks, speaking so quickly that I have trouble understanding her accent as she details all the ways in which I am wrong and she is right, and then I follow her up the stairs on autopilot.

'He was blocking me,' she says, tapping her head as she sits in front of her laptop. 'Killing him will help me unblock.'

'And if this is your solution for every time you encounter this problem?'

'If it is, we won't have a problem sticking to the word count, will we? I'm doing it,' she adds, spinning her chair back to face the computer. 'I'm going to write one peaceful death and one stabby death, and you can pick whichever one you like, but either way, he's dying.'

'A stabby death?'

'I'm thinking by an assassin.' She looks up when I step back. 'Are you sulking?'

'I'm peeing,' I say, and her laughter echoes after me as I head into the hallway, only to pause at what I see.

I'm used to the layout of her house now. Or at least to the rooms she uses most. But for the first time, the door opposite the stairs, the one she pointed out the first day I was here, sits partly open in the middle of the landing.

This is my dad's office, she'd said. As though daring me to ask more.

It's usually closed, and to be honest I'd forgotten all about it, but I have to pass it to get to the bathroom and it's just . . . there. Ajar.

For a long second, I do nothing but stare at it. Anticipation makes me weirdly nervous, and, with a final glance back to make sure she's still typing, I crack it open further, holding my breath as I peer inside.

He had a purple armchair. That much I remember from the one photo he ever allowed of where he wrote. A purple armchair and walls of books and . . .

A bucket and mop.

A dustpan.

A broom closet.

This is a broom closet.

It takes me only a second to realise it, and as soon as I do, it all comes tumbling down around me. A folding ironing board crashes to the floor, narrowly missing my head, followed by some perilously stored cleaning products. One whacks me in the shoulder before I can get out of the way, and I wince as a can of odour spray rolls down the hallway, stopped only by Ciara's foot where she stands in the doorway to her office.

'I knew it,' she says, folding her arms. 'You just couldn't help yourself, could you?'

'I admit it. I wanted to see his office.'

'He didn't have one.'

I keep my gaze on the ironing board I'm straightening so I don't show my surprise at her lie. Her pretty obvious one at that. 'You need to organise this,' I say instead.

'I need to do a lot of stuff.' She kicks the spray can, rolling it back to me, and I put it back with the others before closing the door with a firm snap. As soon as I do, something falls again on the other side.

A heavy expression crosses her face at the sound. Something tired and sad that vanishes as quickly as it came.

'I'm done,' she announces. 'My brain is fried, and there's no point in working through the dead time anyway.'

'The dead time?'

'Two to five p.m. is the dead time. Everyone knows this. Let's go out.'

'You need to write some—'

'I'll do it tonight,' she promises. 'When it's not so hot and I can think. Besides, I've been meaning to show you something.' She pushes away from the wall, stretching her arms above her head. Her stomach flashes, a stretch of bare, tanned skin. I force my gaze away.

'Show me what?' I ask, distracted.

And she smiles a luminous smile. 'A surprise.'

'And where exactly is this surprise?'

I look away from the rows of drab, uniform houses passing by outside to find Ciara smirking.

'Did you think I was going to take you on some beautiful mountain hike with a rainbow overhead? Green fields filled with sheep?'

'After I told you my dark hiking trauma?'

She makes a turn, and the houses turn into store fronts.

'Seriously,' I ask. 'Where are we?'

'*This*,' she says dramatically, 'is Rathcross city.'

'This is a city?'

'It has a cathedral,' she says. 'Therefore it's a city.'

'I see.'

She side-eyes me. 'I can tell by your tone that you're not impressed by the glittering metropolis around you. You don't feel at home? You're not getting New York vibes right now?'

'I was wondering what that smell was.'

She parks the car off a small square that looks vaguely familiar, but only because I'm starting to realise that every town and village in Ireland has one. The streets are otherwise mostly deserted in the late afternoon heat, but the place is clean and the cafés are busy, and the locals have made an effort with a few well-watered hanging baskets. Nothing at first glance explains why we drove an hour to get here, but my strange sense of *déjà vu* only grows stronger as we sit there.

It's not until I look closer at the square that the penny drops.

'Wait . . .'

Ciara sighs dramatically, but she's smiling.

'Is this the—'

'Statue city. Yes.'

I undo my seat belt so quickly it practically whips off me, and she just laughs as I scramble out.

'You're welcome in advance,' she calls as she follows me across the road. I don't answer, my gaze fixed on the tall bronze statue straight ahead.

'Oh, my God.'

'I know.'

'It's even worse in person.'

I stop in front of the weird bronze lump that is supposed to be Frank Sheridan but is really just ... a weird bronze lump.

It was a meme for a whole month when they unveiled it, and for good reason. The eyes are too far apart, the face contorted into this weird smile. It's uncanny valley to a tee, and everyone was obsessed with it when it was first revealed.

'How did I forget this existed?'

'You mean you didn't need a year of therapy to do it?' She tilts her head, examining it. 'Dad liked it. Or at least that's what he said to everyone.'

'It looks nothing like him.'

'I think he liked the idea of someone creating something.'

'I feel like if I look at it for too long it will trap me inside.'

Ciara snorts. 'Well, if I ever dip into horror, I know what I'm going to write about.' She shoves her hands into her pockets, squinting in the sunshine. 'Did you ever meet him? I don't think I asked.'

'Your dad?' I shake my head.

'He went to New York a lot for meetings.'

'He did, but that was before my time. And my home town wasn't exactly a hotbed for book signings when I was a teenager.' I give her a rueful smile. 'I was a hardcore follower, though. My parents used to take me to the midnight launches. *And* made me Hallowe'en costumes. I wrote a letter to him when I was fourteen and made them spellcheck it twice.'

'Your poor folks,' she says, but there's only amusement in her tone as I follow her over to a nearby bench. 'They sound nice.'

'They are. You'd like them.'

'I don't know. I'm very picky.'

'I'll tell them not to take it personally.'

She kicks one leg over the other, her sandalled foot bobbing. 'Dad and I never did Hallowe'en.'

'It's not a thing over here?'

'Uh, the Irish basically *invented* it, thank you very much. But . . . no. He was usually away. Always brought me back treats, though. From all over the world.' She shrugs. 'But sometimes you just want a normal one, right? Like everyone else.'

'Right,' I agree, wondering if I'm imagining the hint of jealousy in her voice.

'Do you have any pictures?'

'Of the costumes? No.'

'You're lying.'

'Yes. But you're not seeing them.'

'You were definitely Finn.'

'And a dragon twice.'

'No wonder you went into fantasy publishing,' she grins. 'Do you think you'll ever publish crime?'

'It's not my area of expertise,' I admit. 'At least, not the non-fantastical kind. Why – you thinking of writing some again?'

'Maybe.' She stretches her arms out in front of her, flexing her fingers. 'I've got a series I've been working on.'

'Oh, come on, you've got to give me more than that.'

'Nah,' she says. 'Too crimey for you. I'll have to go straight to the man in charge.'

'You're bruising my ego here. That'll be me some day.'

'You want to run your own publishing house?'

'I want to run Richardson Books.'

She gasps. 'You want to *murder* Casey Richardson?'

'That's exactly what I said, yes.'

'I'm just reading between the lines.'

'He says he's going to retire soon,' I explain. 'He wants to give it to someone internal.'

'And you're the top dog.'

'I'm one of them.'

'Oh, I *see*.' She pokes me in the leg. 'You have competition?'

'There's two of us who could take it. Laura's on the same level as me, and she's managed to bring in some big authors.'

'None as big as me, though, right?'

'Actually, no,' I tell her, and her smile falters. 'You're the biggest.'

Ciara doesn't respond and I raise a brow.

'You're going to have to get used to—'

'I know, I know.' But she still looks queasy. 'You must be feeling pretty confident, then, if Casey sent you here instead of her.'

'Not really. I think it's less about my editorial skills and more because—'

'You used to dress up as Finn for Hallowe'en?'

'Something like that.'

'Well, I'm Team Sam,' she says. 'Even if I am just a rung on the ladder for you.'

'You're not—'

'I *know*,' she says. 'But seriously, do you want me to push her out of a window?'

'Do you ever go a day without thinking about killing people?'

'Never.' And she winks at me before yawning. It starts off as a small one before morphing into something that takes over her whole mouth, and she brings both hands to her face to cover it. 'Sorry,' she says, the word distorted. 'I'm crashing. I didn't sleep much last night.'

'Do you sleep much any nights?'

'No. But it's not my fault society only caters to daytime people.'

She slumps on the bench, her arm pressing against mine. She's a little burned today, and there's a particularly obvious spot on her shoulder where she missed her sunscreen, but what catches my attention are the three freckles just below it, dotted in a line.

'Is it bad?' She reaches up, sliding a finger under her neon-green bra strap to reveal more of the burn. I freeze, but it's not like I was being subtle about looking.

'Not too bad,' I say, pleased with how normal my voice sounds.

'I covered it in aloe vera,' she mutters, and twists her head, trying to look at it in vain. Her hair tickles my nose as she does, and I sit back, clearing my throat.

'Is it sore?'

'It's itchy.' She scratches it once as if to prove her point and then, thankfully, puts her clothes back in order. 'Can I ask you another question?'

'Of course.'

'Do you really think I should let him live?'

It takes me a second. 'Aengus?'

'Do you think people will get mad?' She looks genuinely worried, and I wish I hadn't brought up the whole *biggest author* thing.

'They won't get mad if we do it right,' I tell her. 'And it's a major fan theory.'

'But it isn't in any of Dad's notes.'

'So?'

'*So*,' she says, 'I don't know if he'd want me to do it. Dad believed in happy endings.'

'It doesn't mean we won't have one. Just don't kill off Finn or Maeve and you'll be fine. But it can't be too close to the end. Then it will look like you're killing him for kicks.'

'Which is why I was thinking the start.'

'The start?'

'Not like the opening line. *Welcome back, everybody; look, Aengus is dead*. But yeah. Fifth chapter or so. It's not like he has much to say from then on.'

She has a point.

'Try it,' I say simply. 'I trust you. You've done good work so far.'

'Yeah?'

'It's not shit,' I say, echoing her own words, and she smiles, looking back at the statue.

A comfortable silence falls between us and I don't know how much time passes as we sit there, side by side. It's only when the sweat starts to gather at my temples that I think about moving, and my attention strays back to the corner store. To where a row of refrigerated drinks surely awaits.

The heat is suddenly sweltering, and I'm about to suggest we go and splurge on something icy and cold when I feel a soft weight on my shoulder. I stiffen, tilting my chin to see Ciara's head resting there, wisps of her brown hair fluttering against my cheek.

She's fallen asleep.

She's actually fallen asleep.

I open my mouth to wake her, but no sound comes out. It's as though the words are stuck in my throat.

Suddenly, the most important thing in the world is to leave her alone. To give her this rest.

So I do.

CHAPTER FOURTEEN

Ciara

I spend the next few weeks writing. Actual, proper writing. And probably in an extremely unhealthy, *please set some boundaries for yourself* way. But the nine-to-five model never worked for me. I just try to jump on my moods when I can. So, instead of staring at the ceiling and contemplating all the bad things in the world first thing in the morning, I reach for my laptop and write. Likewise, instead of spending every night in bed convincing myself I could solve decades-long mysteries by watching a few YouTube videos, I set myself targets for the next day. Targets I never reach, but pretending to be organised is weirdly calming and chips away at the fear that used to stop me from even starting.

My breaks are reserved for work around the house. I tear down the rotting shelves in the back room and write two thousand words. I clean all the curtains on the ground floor and replan a chapter at which Sam made his *it's good that you're trying* face before ripping it apart line by line.

I never asked about his work hours, but he always responds

whenever I send him anything or ask him over. Every email. Every instant message. He tells me to explore an idea. To ignore it. He points out when I'm lost in the plot and praises me when I do well. I like those messages most of all, but they're pretty sparse. He's kind of a tough guy when it comes to this stuff. But I guess that's important. I trust him because of it. He wouldn't take it so seriously if he didn't think I could do it.

It's been so long since I've been in a daze like this. Where all I wanted to do was think about the book. I don't know when it happened, but it finally feels as if a door has opened. Not fully open. Not thrown wide, *step right through, Ciara!* But cracked. Ajar. Enough that I can finally see a way through the tangle of characters and storylines Dad left behind.

Enough that I'm starting to think I might be able to do this.

'I'm going to start that detective series next year.'

Maddie glances up from the chicken salad she's working through. Even with Sam here every day now, she still makes a habit of coming over, as though she knows I'm desperate for the company. To not be alone for too long.

'You mean the one you've been talking about for five years without writing a word?' she asks. 'That detective series?'

'I've been subconsciously mulling over it.'

'Uh-huh.'

'It's just nice to be creative again,' I say, and her expression softens.

'I know. I just don't want you getting ahead of yourself and getting overwhelmed again. You've got to finish this one first.'

'Sam says I'm doing great.'

'Does he?' she murmurs, and I frown as her gaze turns assessing.

'What?'

'Nothing,' she says. 'How's it going with him?'

'Fine.'

'Just fine?'

'Good?' I try, but she just groans.

'Ciara, come on. You're in the best mood you've been in for months.'

'Because he's a really good editor!'

'And you're getting a crush on him.'

'I am *not*,' I protest, my voice climbing an entire octave higher than usual. 'Don't be weird.'

'You don't be weird. When you're not spending all your time with him, you don't stop talking about him, and when you *do* talk about him, you can't go two minutes without blushing.'

'I don't blush.'

'You're blushing now.'

'Because we're in a *heatwave*,' I say, pressing a hand to my cheek. 'And my fragile Irish skin can't take it. Anyway, shut up. What's going on with the truck?'

Maddie makes a face. It's an obvious change of conversation, but it's one I know will get her off the topic of *me*.

She met with the bank manager earlier this week. The same one who gave her the money to start up her business in the first place. And, while they're encouraging of her plans, it's a big step up.

'I need six more months of regular payments to get the loan I need,' she says. 'They won't sign off on anything less.'

'Six months?'

'I've got my savings.'

'Maddie.'

'I'm just saying that they're there and they're mine.'

'It could wipe you out.'

'Or give me a start.' She leans forward. 'Even if Shane doesn't open a café, someone else will come along. More and more people have been coming to this area every year, and, if I don't act soon, I might never get to.'

'Just give it a few weeks, okay? Don't do anything stupid.'

'When have I ever done anything stupid? Don't answer that.' She plants her hand on the table, all business. 'I've got to get back to the truck and give Natalie a break. Try not to make googly eyes at Sam in the meantime.'

She dumps her empty Tupperware into her bag and gives me a one-armed hug before letting herself out. The silence when she goes is as notable as it always is. But it doesn't seem so oppressive any more. Especially since, a few minutes later, I hear another engine sound in the drive.

A spark of anticipation rushes through me, one I immediately get mad about. *Crush.* I do not have a crush. I have an artistic purpose. A creative process. A—

I jump as the front door opens and quickly pretend to type as Sam enters the kitchen.

'Email it to me first,' he says, his phone to his ear. 'Because you . . . no, I . . . You can go to Laura if you want, but she's going to say the same thing I am. Okay. Yeah. Thanks.' He hangs up, sitting in the chair Maddie was in. 'Sorry.'

'No worries. Your sister?'

'My assistant. Our assistant,' he corrects. 'She's the assistant for the whole department, but she mainly works on my books.'

'Because you're so bad at your job?'

'Because I'm the only one who'll give her actual work and not just meeting minutes and coffee runs.'

'That's nice of you.'

'How else is she going to learn?'

I glance at my laptop. 'I never thought about how many people are going to work on this book,' I say. Surprisingly, I don't feel nervous at the thought. 'I only ever think about the editor.'

'Because I'm the most important one,' he jokes. 'Can I grab a drink?'

'I made lemonade last night,' I say, and he pushes himself up to get a glass from the shelf. His sleeve rises as he does, revealing the muscles of his arms, the edge of his tattoo. A bead of sweat drips down the back of his neck and for a moment I'm hypnotised, watching it disappear beneath his T-shirt.

'You want some of this?' he asks, and my heart frigging *leaps* before I realise he's opening the fridge.

'I'm good,' I say, clearing my throat. Just cursing Maddie to the depths of hell for warping my innocent mind.

Sam pours himself a drink, drains half of it and then, as if I weren't flustered enough, tilts his head back and holds the glass to the base of his throat. Condensation quickly forms along the side, and he blows out a breath as if he's finally got some relief.

He looks as though he's in some racy lemonade photoshoot.

'Why am I so hot?'

'*What?*' The word comes out like a squeak.

'I've had worse summers than this,' Sam continues, oblivious to my ridiculousness. 'I shouldn't feel this warm.'

It takes a second before I can trust myself to speak normally. 'It's called humidity,' I say. 'Warm feels warmer and cold feels colder. And we're further north than people think. Our sun burns.'

'I've noticed,' he says drily, and thankfully finishes his drink. 'Did you look at the notes I sent you?'

'Huh?'

'In my email.'

Email. Right. Work.

Or at least, work for him. He wasn't wrong before. It's a disgustingly humid day, the kind that has you zapped of energy just by breathing, and Sam doesn't help my already distracted thoughts once we head up to the office. I find myself sneaking glances at him while I pretend to type, noting the furrow of his brow when he reads something he doesn't like and the line of his profile when he turns to the side, lost in thought. Sometimes I watch him outright, hoping he'll glance up and our eyes will meet so I can make a joke and he can shake his head ... and then what, I have no idea, but at least he'll be looking at me.

I want him to look at me.

But he doesn't. Except for a brief aside where he tells me my characters have glanced at each other eleven times in three pages, he practically ignores me, and I'm relieved when he takes a bathroom break and I'm able to tell myself in private to *get a freaking grip.*

It's the heat. The heat and the unplanned celibacy and the sad fact that, besides Maddie, I haven't spent this much time alone with another person in months.

I stand, staring out at the oak tree as I wipe the sweat from my forehead and then from under my boobs. There's barely a breeze today. Not so much as a leaf rustles, and the woods beyond don't move much either. I'm contemplating whether it would be worth moving to a shadier part of the house for the rest of the afternoon when a flash of colour in the distance catches my attention.

A second later it happens again, and I cup my hands against the glass, peering at the treeline as someone emerges from the woods and starts hanging things from the branches.

You've got to be kidding me.

'Stop that!'

I rap on the window so hard I'm surprised it doesn't break, but I'm too far away for them to hear it. Anger lashes through me, the familiar sting of it overriding everything else.

'Are you o— *whoa*.' Sam enters the room as I'm hurtling out of it, and he sidesteps me just in time. 'What's wrong?'

'Everything,' I mutter, and head down the stairs so fast it's a miracle I don't trip. A second later I'm out of the door, striding through the long grass in my bare feet. Sam catches up with me easily but doesn't ask what's happening as he catches sight of the intruder.

He can't be more than sixty, with curling white hair and sensible glasses. He looks harmless. Like a tourist who got lost and wandered down the wrong path.

But I know better.

'What do you think you're doing?' I ask. Sam tenses at my clipped tone, but, even though it's obvious to him, the stranger doesn't seem to notice, greeting me with a wave.

'I've got tokens from five different countries here,' he says proudly, not even pausing as he continues to tie bag after bag to the branches. There's a green ribbon brooch on his T-shirt, a sign of one of Dad's fan clubs. Either he or someone else has done the same to another tree behind him, and my stomach clenches at the sight. How many of them have been coming?

'This is private property,' I tell him, but as soon as I do, a younger woman comes marching into view, wearing a *I wish I was in Ravian* T-shirt.

'Dad, I couldn't find the postcards you— oh, my *God*.' She stops a few feet away, gawking at me. 'No way.'

I try again. 'You are trespassing on private—'

'That's Ciara Sheridan,' she says to the man as if I can't hear her. '*Dad*.'

'Is it?' he asks, looking at me with renewed interest. 'I thought she moved to France.'

'*She* is right here,' I say, practically seething. It's been months since I've had to deal with this and, unluckily for them, I no longer have the patience.

'Unfortunately, this isn't the best time,' Sam begins in an *incredibly* friendly tone. Still, neither of them pays him any attention as the woman scrambles to take out her phone. She angles it straight at me, with the house in the background, and I snap.

It's as though all those social rules, everything that's been drilled into me since I was a child, go flying out of the window as I bat the phone from her hand in a clean strike that sends it tumbling to the ground.

'Hey!' The woman glares at me as she stoops to pick it up, but I have run out of fucks to give.

'Private. Property.' I repeat. 'Didn't you see the sign? Get rid of all this stuff, and get out of here before I call the police.'

'You don't have to be so rude,' she says, astonished, but I don't wait to hear another word as I turn on my heel and march back to the house.

Sam stays behind to speak with them. I know he does because I'm already back in the office, seething in my chair when I hear him come through the front door. A glance out of the window shows me the people are still there, but at least it's because they're doing what I told them to do, and removing all the plastic they were about to leave behind.

I fold my arms, vindicated yet defensive as Sam appears in the doorway.

'Ciara—'

'Don't.'

'I know they're overstepping, but you really can't talk to your readers like that.'

'They're not mine! They're his.'

'They *will* be yours,' he says, his voice infuriatingly calm, and I'm so ticked off by it that all I can do is throw my hands in the air in a *whadda you want from me* gesture. It's a truly stunning comeback. One that probably turns my face bright pink, but hopefully he'll think that's from the sun.

I try again. 'They always think they can just do what they like,' I say. 'As if they have a right to this place.' A right to *me*. Familiar anxiety grips me. One that had started to fade these past few days but now comes roaring back with a vengeance as I remember what I've signed myself up to.

'I don't have the same relationship as he did with his fans,' I explain. Sam frowns at me, his hands shoved in the pockets of his jeans. 'There's a reason I published under a pen name.'

'I understand, but—'

'You don't,' I interrupt. 'You don't even believe me. Not really. I *told* you how some of them tore me apart when my name was leaked. There were whole forums dedicated to how I didn't compare to my dad or how I didn't deserve to get a publishing deal, and it's all going to start back up again as soon as we announce it and I know that and I'll be ready for it, but it's still a lot to deal with.' I take a much-needed breath, aware I'm starting to rant. 'I love these books,' I tell him. 'I do. And I want to write a good ending and I want to make people happy, I want to make Dad proud. But I'm not putting myself through that again. I need boundaries.'

Sam's quiet for a long moment. His face serious, his eyes narrowed in thought. 'Okay,' he says. 'I'm sorry. You're right. I don't get it.'

His words are sympathetic, and I don't know if he's disappointed in me or just realising what he's going to have to deal with, but a silence stretches between us that makes me want to fidget.

'I guess now's a bad time to tell you about my other surprise,' I add weakly.

Sam just looks at me.

'I thought we could take some time out tomorrow. There're some old castle ruins that Dad based the original fort on. I was going to take some pictures if you want to come with?'

It's something I've been planning for a few days. The church was step one, the statue step two. But this? This is boss-level, and I'm starting to get a real kick out of seeing Sam's inner fanboy come through. Something I never thought I'd want.

But Sam doesn't answer straight away. He's got this strained look on his face that I don't like one bit. 'I can't,' he says eventually. 'It's . . . I'm busy.'

'Oh.' My disappointment must be obvious because Sam grimaces, rubbing the back of his neck.

'Sorry, I should have said something.'

'That's okay.'

'Sorry,' he says again, and it's as though he can see right through me. My smile becomes strained.

'It's fine,' I say, just a *little* too curt. 'I'll go by myself. I'm used to it.'

I turn purposefully to my laptop and type randomly until Sam stops dawdling and returns to his spot on the couch. Which only makes me even more annoyed. I don't know when I started thinking of it as *his* spot, but I don't like that I do. I don't like anything right now, and Sam must realise this, because he takes the hint. Or maybe he just wants to get out before I have another meltdown. In any case, he doesn't stick around, barely lasting another five minutes before making up some excuse about emails and running out of the door.

Well, walking out of the door. But I could tell he wanted to run.

I wait until I hear him drive off before I stop typing, my frustration rising as I force myself to focus on the screen.

The faint smell of heather wSA THE FIRST SIGN THAT FINN WAS THROUGH THE WOODS. THHAT HE WAS HOME.. THe honey sweets cent tickled nos nose and he ;;ihed—

Christ.

I flick the laptop lid closed and stare unseeing at the wall.

It's not like the guy doesn't deserve a day off. God knows he's been working his ass off on this book ever since he came here. It's just that I wasn't thinking of the castle as a *book* thing. I was thinking of it as a . . . as . . . I don't know. Normal. Not work. Though I guess all things with me are work things to him.

Whatever. He's here to work. I'm here to work. We're all one big working family.

I reopen the laptop and get happy with the backspace, accidentally deleting a whole paragraph before I fix it and start again.

The faint smell of heather was the first sign that Finn was through the woods. That he was home. The honey-sweet scent tickled his nose and reminded him of when he was a child, collecting armfuls of the plant for the old apothecary. It was a scent that told him he would soon see his mentor. His family. His friends.

And yet.

I sip my now warm lemonade and slump down in the chair, settling in for the long haul.

And yet, despite how far he had travelled, despite the welcome he knew he was about to receive, as Finn began the final leg of his journey back to where he'd started from, he couldn't ignore the hollowness in his heart. The faint ache in his chest.

The slow, painful realisation that he'd never felt lonelier in his life.

CHAPTER FIFTEEN

Sam

'*Haaaaaappy birthday!*'

Amy's voice blasts through my headphones, and I quickly turn the volume down as she blows a streamer at the screen. The rest of my team, represented by their boxed-off heads, all do the same.

'Thank you for that,' I say when she's done. 'If anyone starts singing, I'm logging off.'

'What are you doing to celebrate?' she asks. 'Are you taking the day off?'

'She enquires on a work call.'

'I don't know what time it is over there!'

'Happy birthday, Sam,' Laura interjects. 'We'll get some cake when you're back in the office. Are you going out later?'

'Probably not.'

She frowns at me, ever the mother. 'But you'll do something to celebrate.'

'I don't like to make a big thing of it.'

At that, Amy scoffs. Loudly. I guess I understand why. Last year,

I booked out the bar in the building next door and invited the whole office. I may not seem like the type, but birthdays are kind of my thing. My parents always made a huge deal about them when we were kids and it's something neither Lizzie nor I ever fully managed to grow out of.

'It's fine,' I say as Laura's frown deepens.

'This is sad now,' Amy says. 'You're making me sad.'

'I'll probably go for a drink later,' I lie before she can continue. 'Did I tell you I'm staying above a pub?'

'You need to have a party, Sam.'

'He's thirty-six years old,' Deborah says. 'He doesn't need to have a birthday party.'

'I'm thirty-one!' I say, affronted.

Deborah just peers at me. 'Are you sure?'

'*Yes?*'

'You should wear a party hat,' Amy says. 'Or some kind of large button announcing your special day.'

'I won't be doing any of that. Can we work now, please?'

Deborah makes a *thank you* motion with her hands, and I'm relieved when the attention moves off me. But almost as soon as Laura starts reviewing the agenda for next month's acquisitions meeting, my mind starts to wander.

It's my birthday.

It was the first thing I thought of when I woke up this morning, and the knowledge was surprisingly anticlimactic.

My birthday.

I thought about taking a long weekend for it this year, but that plan obviously went out of the window. It didn't occur to me when Casey sent me over here, but now here I am. Over three thousand miles away from my family and friends and no one to celebrate with.

Well, I've got someone to celebrate with.

But for some reason, when Ciara gave me the perfect opportunity to do a casual little *Hey, I'd love to hang out on Friday. It's the anniversary of my dad breaking numerous traffic laws as he drove my mother to the hospital. No big deal, but it would be nice to have a beer.* Instead, I froze.

And I have no idea why.

'Sam.'

I snap back to attention to see the rest of the team staring at me.

'What do you think?' Laura presses.

'It's because he's old now,' Amy says, saving me from replying. 'His mind is starting to go. But as a young person with my whole future ahead of me, let me just say that I think that's a *great* idea.'

I do my best to refocus for the rest of the meeting, but it's useless, and, by the time we finish, even Deborah looks concerned. Laura pointedly suggests I log off a few hours early, but I have a whole other conversation to get through first.

Casey doesn't do video calls, so I have to get in touch the old-fashioned way, but at least that means I don't have to worry about my facial expressions this time.

'Sam!' he greets me when I dial his number. 'My computer tells me it's your birthday.'

'Your computer is correct.'

'I hope you have a good one,' he says, and thankfully leaves it at that. No streamers from Casey. 'How's our project coming along?'

'Great,' I say automatically. Except that the author completely freaked out at two readers yesterday and then started typing so hard I thought she was going to punch a keyboard-sized hole into her desk. 'Barring any major disasters, she should be on track for a first draft by late September.'

'I'm glad to hear it. How would you feel about letting the rest of the team know? I think it's about time I let Laura in on this at least.'

'Laura?'

'Unless you have a problem with that,' he says, clearly enjoying himself. He knows about our rivalry, just like everyone else in the office. Hell, he practically encourages it sometimes. But this isn't about that.

'Ciara doesn't want people to know yet. She's been pretty clear about it.'

'I think we can manage one more person. And we'll need to start thinking about publicity.'

'She doesn't want to do publicity.' I say the words without thinking and there's a moment of silence.

'You've discussed that?' Casey asks.

'Not exactly. But you've got to know she doesn't have the best relationship with his fans.'

'She'll have to do some appearances around the announcement. We can book her in for some media training, but we'll need to put a face to a name for something like this.'

'Can't she just write some articles or something?'

There's a long pause, and I'm grateful there's no video as I drop my forehead to the dresser.

'I understand the instinct to protect your authors,' Casey says eventually. 'But it's important that she's on board with this. And it's your job to make sure she is.'

'No, I know,' I say, backtracking. 'I'm sure she'll come around to it once she gets the draft finished.'

Except I don't think she will, but before I can dig myself into an even deeper hole there's a sharp knock on the door. I take the out, saying goodbye to Casey, only to find Mary waiting impatiently on the landing.

This place really needs a peephole.

'Hello again,' I say before noticing the plastic bag in her hands. 'What's—'

'Mangetout,' she announces. 'It's in season. Do you have any laundry?'

'I'm fine, thank you.' The nearest laundromat is by a gas station forty minutes away. It was still my first choice.

She doesn't seem put out, though, just peers behind me like last time.

'Is there anything I can help you with?' The question comes out more like a plea, but she just purses her lips.

'Just wanted to drop these by,' she says, handing me the bag. 'You should use them in a stir-fry.'

'I will.'

'And you'll need to be out by six p.m. Monday.'

'I— wait. What?'

'Five-thirty if possible.'

'What are you talking about?' I stop her as she turns to leave, almost dropping the vegetables.

'Room's booked up.'

'Yes,' I say, alarmed. 'By me.'

She just shakes her head. 'You paid for the month.'

'But on a rolling—'

'Got someone else coming. We've had a lot of interest.'

I glance back at the tiny space behind me. 'You have?'

'It's a very popular room,' Mary says, suddenly defensive. 'Competitively priced.'

'It is,' I agree quickly. 'I just thought—'

'Very popular,' she repeats.

'Right.' I look down at the mangetout. Shit. 'Okay. Well, do you know any other places nearby that I could—'

'No,' she says with a disapproving look. 'You should have planned ahead.'

I should have. And I tell her as much, trying to be as polite as possible as I close the door.

I spend the next hour Googling places nearby and coming up short. Unless I want to move to the nearest city, which is well over an hour away, my best shot is a campsite down the road. When I find myself seriously considering it for more than ten seconds, I know I've lost my mind and decide to make it tomorrow's problem.

But that, plus my conversation with Casey, only puts me in a worse mood than I already was, and by the time I'm finished for the day a strange kind of loneliness has settled in. The type I've never had before. The birthday messages that filter in from home over the afternoon just make it worse, and for the first time since I arrived I feel homesick, longing for New York, for my apartment and my things and my *people*.

When I can't take another minute of being alone, I have a quick shower and change my shirt before heading downstairs to the pub. It's still early, so I'm expecting to be the only one there as usual, but to my surprise I see someone already sitting at the bar.

The burger guy. Or at least that's what Ciara referred to him as. It isn't hard to remember the bulky, should-have-played-football man who now stares my way as the door shuts behind me.

We size each other up, but in the end he just sighs.

'I only wanted a drink.'

'Hey, no argument here,' I say. 'I'm just a tourist.'

'That makes two of us,' he says. 'Shane.'

'Sam.' I take a seat two stools away from him. 'You get your ketchup back?' I ask, and he grimaces.

'Found the delivery waiting for me by my truck a few days later. A real mystery,' he adds flatly. 'She a friend of yours?'

'Maddie? No. I'm with the other one.'

Shane just grunts.

'For what it's worth, I'm told she's not usually so ... passionate about her job,' I say. 'She thinks you're trying to close her business down.'

'I am,' he says bleakly, and on that cheery note he knocks back his Guinness. 'Is that what her friends call her? Maddie?'

I nod just as Ronan emerges from the back room.

'Sam!' He greets me like we're old friends. 'Haven't seen you about.'

'Yeah. Sorry. I've been busy.' I spent the past few nights working with Ciara. I've barely been back here.

'Ah, well, young love and all that. Another Guinness Zero?' he asks Shane.

'Please,' the burger guy says, and Ronan grabs him a fresh glass.

'Fancy a drink? Something independent?' His voice lowers. 'I've been tweaking the recipe. Or if you're up for it, a friend popped around with something a bit stronger.'

He gives me one of his scrunched-up-face non-winks, and it hits me that I like this guy. I like this guy, and I like this pub, and Shane I don't really know, but honestly, I can think of worse places to spend an evening in this world.

'All perfectly above board,' Ronan is saying to Shane. 'I just can't sell it to you. Monetarily.'

Shane looks a little green. 'I just don't think a bathtub is the best place to be brewing—'

'It's my birthday.'

Both men stop their conversation, turning to me.

'I mean ... today,' I finish. 'It's my birthday today.' And I have never felt less my age.

'Happy birthday,' Shane says, straightening on his stool. 'You should have said something.'

'You should have,' Ronan says, clearly unhappy at this development. 'Where's Ciara?'

'Oh, no,' I say quickly as he reaches for his phone. 'She's busy.'

'Busy?' He looks confused. 'On your birthday?' And then, before I can think of an excuse, his expression shutters. 'You didn't have a fight, did ye?'

'We ... yes.' That makes sense. Okay, it makes no sense at all, but ... 'We had an argument.'

He *tsks* as Shane whacks a heavy hand on my shoulder.

'Well, don't you worry about that,' Ronan says, rummaging beneath the bar. 'We know how to celebrate here.'

'It's not a big deal,' I begin, wishing I hadn't brought it up, but Ronan just shakes his head. A second later, he lines up five shot glasses before me.

Shane examines them warily, and, when he meets my gaze, gives me a look as if to say *you're on your own, pal*.

I jump as Ronan thumps an unmarked bottle of clear liquid on to the bar. A second later, another joins it.

'Now, then, birthday boy,' he says, deadly serious. 'Where would you like to start?'

CHAPTER SIXTEEN

Ciara

'Did you know I have never fallen for a scam?' I put the phone to my ear, relishing the excuse for a break. 'Not via email, not via text. Not by a salesperson coming to my door. I don't even play the lottery. I am scam-proof, my friend. Scam. Proof. So go ahead. Do your worst.'

There's nothing but silence on the other end of the line. And then: 'What the hell are you talking about?'

I frown at the vaguely familiar voice and double-check the unknown number that had flashed up on my screen. 'Are you not calling to tell me about fraudulent activity on my account?'

'I am not,' the voice says. 'I'm calling to tell you I have your friend.' A pause. 'But not in a kidnapping way.'

'Who's this?'

'Shane McCauley,' he continues. 'We met at the scene of the crime a few weeks ago?'

'I *gave* it back to you,' Maddie calls in the background.

'So you admit that you took it,' Shane replies.

'*No.*'

'Your friend's drunk,' Shane says to me, and yeah, I got that.

'How drunk?'

'She was singing Aerosmith at Delaney's.'

'Delaney's doesn't have a karaoke machine.'

'I didn't say anything about karaoke.'

Oh, my God.

'I'll be right there.'

'We're outside,' he says. 'I'd take her home myself, but I don't think she'd be comfortable with that. Yours was the only number she'd give me.'

'No, it's fine. I can be there in fifteen. Can you stay with her?'

'Not like I've got anywhere else to be,' he says, and I hear a mangled Maddie version of a Sinéad O'Connor song in the background.

I hang up and stretch my back until something cracks. I've been working all day and had only just taken my phone off Do Not Disturb when Shane called. I'd planned on making a giant bowl of pasta and collapsing in front of the television, but I guess I'll be doing that now with a drunk Maddie snoring on the couch beside me.

Not like it's the first time.

Luckily, it's a nice night for a drive. A warm breeze, a starry sky. I'm feeling pretty zen by the time I pull up to Delaney's, where it looks as though Ireland has won some sort of World Cup, judging by the number of parked vehicles and noise coming from inside.

It's weird, but I focus on Maddie, who's decided to wait for me in the middle of the road.

'That is not a safe place to stand,' I call.

'I'm keeping an eye on her,' a voice says from the shadows, and Shane steps out from behind the cars. 'Thanks for coming.'

'Thanks for calling,' I say as Maddie teeters over in high-heeled boots. She's all dolled up in a purple dress and her curls are pulled back in a matching claw grip. She looks beautiful.

And wasted.

'What happened?' I ask as she throws her arms around me.

'I got stood up,' she mumbles into my ear. 'So I thought I'd come here for a drink.'

'And what exactly did you drink?'

'Ronan started making whiskey in his bathtub.'

'I see.'

'It's not that bad.'

'I bet.' I squeeze her hand as I pull back, smiling encouragingly. 'Want to go mine? Watch a movie?'

'Do you have bathtub whiskey?'

'I do. I have so much of it, and I will give it all to you if you get into my car.'

She squints at me, swaying slightly. 'I think you're lying to me.'

But, before I can protest my innocence, a pair of headlights come speeding down the road, and Natalie pulls right up to us with her window down. She takes one look at Maddie and sighs.

'You're paying me overtime for this,' she warns.

'What are you doing here?' I ask as she side-eyes Shane.

'Ronan rang me. Said she needed a ride.'

'Why didn't he call me?' I'm weirdly hurt, but Natalie just shrugs as she hops out.

'You can take her if you want?'

Maddie puts her hand to her mouth. 'I think I'm going to vomit.'

Yeah. No. 'She's all yours.'

Natalie mutters something under her breath and takes hold of Maddie's wrist as she steers her towards the car. 'Come on, boss. Only because you'd do the same for me.'

'You're just going to hold this over my head.'

'Yes,' Natalie says seriously, and helps her inside, shutting the door firmly behind her. Not that that helps, as Maddie almost falls out of the window waving to me.

'I love you!'

'I love you too,' I call back. 'Talk to you in three days when you're not regretting your choices!'

Shane she ignores, which he doesn't seem to mind, waiting placidly by my side as Natalie drives off.

'Thanks again for staying,' I say, feeling the need to defend her. 'She doesn't date a lot because of the business, so she—'

'We don't need to talk.'

Oh. Good.

'I've got to get home,' he continues, already walking away. 'The birthday boy's in there, by the way.'

'Who?'

'Your friend? The American.' He unlocks a pristine silver van with his company's logo on the side. 'You're missing quite the party.'

I'm too confused to say anything back, but he's driving off anyway, his headlights sweeping over me as I turn back to the pub. As I do, a cheer rises inside, and with a sudden case of FOMO I push open the door.

For a moment, it's as if I've walked into another dimension.

The place is as packed as I've ever seen it, so much so that I'm not able to move another step without bumping into someone. I wasn't aware Delaney's even had a stereo system, which means somebody brought theirs from home, because what sounds like ABBA's greatest hits blares from wall to wall. A poker game is under way on my left, while there are so many people waiting at the bar to my right, I can't even see it.

I'm aiming towards it anyway, trying to spot Ronan, when there's a tap on my shoulder. I turn to find Sam grinning down at me.

At least, I think he's Sam. He certainly *looks* like Sam. Dressed like him, too. But his smile is a little too wide, his eyes a little too bright. There's a faint flush to his skin, and the top two buttons of his shirt are undone.

Drunk Sam.

'You're here!'

Happy drunk Sam.

'I am,' I say. 'What's going on?'

'Did you know Marcus can play "Waterloo" on the fiddle?'

'I didn't. And who's Marcus?'

'The guy with the fiddle.' Sam glances about as though looking for him. 'Do you want to hear it?'

'Not particularly. How much have you had to— *Whoa*.' I brace as he tilts towards me, and somehow manage to hold him upright. Looks as if Ronan's bathtub whiskey has been doing the rounds. 'All right, big guy. I hate to ruin a good time, but I think you're done for the night.'

'I'm fine.'

'You are. But you won't be in the morning. Trust me.'

'I've been thinking about the ending,' he says. 'When Finn's at the keep and he—'

'Okay, okay, shush.' I slap a hand over his mouth. 'Ixnay on the ookbay.'

He just smiles beneath my palm as I panic.

Crap.

'I'm taking you out of here before you start spilling state secrets. Let's go for a walk, hmm?'

'I'll get my stuff.'

'Do you have any stuff?'

'No.'

Okay. I latch on to his elbow in case he wanders off and pull him towards the bar, where I catch Ronan's eye in the crowd.

'Do I need to close a tab?' I yell over to him.

'Don't worry about it.'

'He's three sheets to the wind. I know he's good for it.'

But Ronan just shrugs. 'It's the lad's birthday. He had one drink on the house, and then everyone else chipped in. He's good.'

Birthday? Shane mentioned this too. 'Sorry, what do you mean it's his—'

A sharp tug on my arm cuts me off and I glance over my shoulder to see Sam gently petting Bernard's dog. 'You are very soft,' he tells it.

'Here,' Ronan says, dragging my attention back to him. 'Take the rest before it's gone.'

'Before what's—'

My free hand shoots out automatically as he thrusts what looks like a plate of half-eaten birthday cake into my hands. '*Best before* was a month ago, but it should be all right. Only thing I could find in the back.'

'Ronan—'

'Can't have a birthday party without any cake. We're not savages.' He leans over the bar, and I have to strain to hear his lowered voice over the noise. 'He said you had an argument.'

'He ... what?' I glance back, tugging at Sam as he tries to follow the dog.

'I like the lad a lot,' Ronan says. 'But to be clear, I'm on your side. No matter what you did.'

'I didn't do anything!'

'Exactly,' he says. 'But maybe be mad at him tomorrow, yeah?'

But before I can explain that I didn't even know it *was* his birthday, I'm jostled back by people trying to order.

I turn back to Sam, beyond confused, just knowing that I need to get him out of here. 'Okay,' I say, ushering him out the door. 'Let's roll.'

'Where are we going?'

'*You're* going back to your room. Where you will sleep.'

'Do you have a tent?'

I blink at the change in conversation. 'What?'

'Can't stay in the room,' he explains absently. 'Don't want to sleep in the car.'

'Why would you sleep in your— *Nope*.' I tighten my hold as he tries to go back inside. Sam just laughs, and I keep him there, considering my options.

Unless I lock the guy in, there is a high chance that as soon I leave he'll just make his way downstairs again, and while I know it's none of my business and that he can do what he likes . . .

'Sam? *Sam*.' I wait until he focuses on me. 'You want to go back to mine? Do some work?'

'Work?'

'Yes. You love work.'

'Now?'

'Uh-huh. Night owl, remember?'

'I remember,' he murmurs, and then glances down to where I'm still holding on to him. He makes no move to free himself. 'Are we walking?'

'No. I drove.'

'I think we need to look at the dungeon scene again,' he says as I take him to the car. 'I think you can go darker.'

'Noted.'

I open the passenger door for him, expecting a struggle, but he seems happy to go now that I'm not forcing him upstairs. In fact, he turns downright chatty, telling me all about Ronan's side-hustle as a brewer and how Shane isn't that bad a guy once you get to know him.

He's happy. Almost giddy, and at any other time I might enjoy this side of him. But instead, I'm just mad.

Mad that he didn't tell me it was his birthday when he told everybody else. That he might as well have lied to me about it.

That he didn't want me there.

It hurts me a lot more than it should, and doubt rears its ugly head as I drive, sinking my mood further and further, but Sam doesn't notice. He keeps up a running commentary all the way home and then hops out before I even turn off the engine, gazing at the house as though he's never been here.

'Have you ever tried writing horror?' he asks. 'I think you can lean into the horror in the dungeons. Make it dark.'

'You already said that,' I remind him, but it's as though he's talking to himself, speaking every thought that comes into his mind.

'You shied away from it in your books, but it didn't feel like your decision. It was like you were restraining yourself. Especially in your second one. With the poison.'

He climbs the porch steps, only seeming to realise I'm not with him when he gets to the door. 'Do you have the ...' He makes a twisty motion with his hand as he turns back to face me. 'Thing?'

'You read my books?'

'I read all your books,' he says, not seeming to register my surprise. 'May I have some water?' he adds politely, and I realise I'm staring at him.

I fumble with my key, my thoughts a confusing tangle as I let him inside.

He waits patiently as I turn off the alarm and then trails after me into the kitchen, humming something under his breath. He seems to have lost any understanding of personal space. He's so close that I can feel the heat radiating from his body. The man is like a furnace, but for some reason it only makes me shiver as I put the cake on the table and pour him some water. He chugs it back in three gulps.

'It was a commercial decision,' I say awkwardly.

'What?'

'With the books. They thought it would turn readers off if I made them too dark.'

He scoffs at that, switching back into Mr Editor mode so quickly I blink. 'They were wrong.'

'They said it was too risky.'

'You could pull it off.'

The compliment makes me flush, which is weird. It's not as if he hasn't said good things about my writing before, but this feels more personal somehow.

'I would have edited you better,' he adds stubbornly.

'Yeah,' I say. 'Probably.'

'Do you have a TV?'

'In the living room.'

'There's a movie I want to show you.'

'But you— Okay.'

I follow as he about-turns and heads across the hall, only to seemingly forget what he came in for. He stops by the couch, frowning as he places his hand on his stomach.

Uh-oh.

'Are you going to throw up?'

He takes a while to answer. 'No,' he says finally, but he sounds as unsure as he looks.

'Do you want to sit?'

'Yes.'

He does so gently, and I set the water on the table beside him.

'I'll get you something to eat,' I say, but he reaches out before I can, clasping warm fingers around my wrist. I freeze, my heart doing a little stuttering thing as I stare down at him. He's got that earnest look again. The one that makes any walls within me crumble into dust.

'I think you're a wonderful writer and I'm glad I came here.' He says each word slowly and clearly, as if he wants to imprint them on to me. 'And I really like your hair.'

'Thank you,' I say when he doesn't continue.

'You're welcome.' He lets me go and rubs his face hard, looking exhausted.

'You can lie down,' I tell him.

'My shoes.'

'You can take them off.'

He does, fumbling with them briefly before dropping them to the floor with a thump. Once that task is completed, he slumps back against the cushions with so much force that a dark wave of hair falls across his forehead. By my side my hand twitches with the sudden urge to fix it.

'Sam?'

'Yeah?'

'You're cute when you're drunk.'

A smile stretches across his face even as he closes his eyes. 'I'm going to remember you said that.'

'No, you won't.'

'Yes, I will.'

'Sam?'

'Yeah?' He drops his voice to a whisper, matching mine, and I lean in so he can hear me.

'I'm glad you came here too.'

'That's good.' He sighs, and his entire body seems to sink into the couch, the picture of relaxation.

'I'm going to get you some food, okay?'

'Okay.'

I leave him be and come back a minute later with some buttered toast, but he doesn't answer when I call his name, and when I set the plate on the table I find him fast asleep.

CHAPTER SEVENTEEN

Sam

I wake to darkness. The kind I'm beginning to get used to. The time on my watch says it's after two a.m., and the bed I'm on is actually a couch. A comfortable couch, but a couch all the same. One not above Delaney's but in Ciara's living room. And as soon as that little piece of information slots into my brain, I sit up so fast my head spins.

I thought after you drank like that you were supposed to forget everything that came afterwards. But, unfortunately, the night clicks back with crystalline clarity. The beer. The whiskey. More beer.

At least I integrated with the locals.

Someone – Ciara, most likely – left a glass of water on the coffee table, and I drain the whole thing as I stand. When I'm done, I use the bathroom before following the trail of lit rooms to the kitchen, where I find the woman of the house sitting at the table, fully dressed and eating a slice of cake.

'You really do sleep when you want, don't you?' I pull out a chair and take a seat, only for my stomach to roil dangerously.

Ciara gives me a knowing look. 'How are you feeling?'

'I think I'm in that space where I'm sobering up but not yet hungover, and I'm going to try to cling to that for as long as possible.'

'You hungry?'

'Oh, no. I can never eat anything ever again.'

Her smile is forced. 'Ronan said it was your birthday.'

Right. That. 'Yeah.' I sit up straighter, clearing my throat. 'Look, I wasn't planning on making a big deal of it. That's why I didn't tell you. It wasn't because—'

'I'm not mad you didn't tell me, Sam.'

'No, I know.' I pause. 'It's just that you *seem* mad.'

Her lips purse. 'Okay, I'm a bit mad. But I'm madder that you're thinking about sleeping in your car,' she says pointedly. 'What's wrong with your room?'

'Mary says it's booked out,' I explain. 'There's nowhere else nearby.'

She looks exasperated. 'Why didn't you ask if you could stay here? There's a ton of space.'

The same reason I didn't tell her it was my birthday.

Because her skin is soft and her hair smells like strawberries and sometimes when I'm with her, I only speak so she'll look at me.

But it's not like I'm going to tell her any of that.

'Casey used to stay here whenever he visited Dad,' she continues. 'So you can too. You can stay as long as you need to.'

'I'll ask him.'

She huffs, her jaw clenching before she abruptly plants her hands on the table and stands. 'Come with me.'

'But ... Yeah, all right.' My chair almost topples over as I get up, and I follow her as she leaves the kitchen and heads up the stairs. She takes them two at a time, as usual. But when she strides down the hallway she doesn't stop at her office. She goes one door past it and turns to face me.

'Dad always made a big deal about birthdays,' she says. 'I don't know if you do, but it's a thing in this house. And you're away from home and your family and your friends, and that's hard. My first birthday when I left Ireland was embarrassingly sad, and I don't want this to be a bad memory for you.'

'It's not,' I assure her, but she just shakes her head and twists the knob, swinging the door wide.

The smell hits me first. Paper. Leather. Woody with a hint of vanilla. I peer into the darkness, willing my eyes to adjust. And then she turns on the light.

'*This*,' she says, 'was my dad's office.'

It's as though someone's stolen the breath from my lungs. I don't move for a second, and, when I do, it's as if my limbs are not my own. They're stiff and foreign and glued to the floor.

'Sam?'

I don't answer as I join her inside, stepping over the threshold the way one would into a treasure trove. Because that's what it feels like. At first glance the room seems small, but the more I look, the more I realise that it's just filled with so much *stuff*.

Books, of course. Hundreds of them, crammed into shelves and piled high on the floor. Some have familiar paper slips sticking out of them, copies of novels sent to him in the hopes of receiving a glowing review back. I used to get such a thrill mailing them to him when I started working for Casey, but, before I can even wonder if any of the notes I wrote are there, I'm distracted by the next thing. A LEGO set of Ravian's keep. An illustrated map protected by a dusty glass frame.

A large cork board hangs on the wall opposite, and every inch of it is filled with handwritten pages. Some have so much writing you can barely see the paper underneath, and some only have a few lines. A word or two written in large capital letters that would make sense to no one but him and his mind.

There are drawings as well. A lot sent by fans, but others look shabbier and more exploratory. The ones done by him. By someone figuring out a world step by step.

There is no desk in the room, but there is the purple armchair with a flat white cushion and a small table where a tea tray rests.

This is where he worked. This is where he wrote.

This is . . .

'You said he didn't have an office.'

'I just didn't feel like showing it to you,' Ciara says, watching me take it in. 'And if you'd known it was here, I'd have had to.'

'What made you change your mind?'

She shrugs, looking uncomfortable. I don't push it.

'I'm glad you did.'

'Yeah, well . . .' She shifts her weight from one foot to the other, looking unsure, before she steps forward, plucking something from the tray and hiding it behind her back.

'Happy birthday, Sam,' she says and holds out her hand.

At first, I have no idea what she's giving me. It looks like an old envelope, opened and worn, like a bill you dump in a drawer and forget about.

Only when I go to take it, when I look at the address on the front, do I realise what it is.

My body goes numb, and for a moment I can only stand there, shell-shocked.

'This is mine,' I manage to croak out. 'This is . . . I sent this to him when I was a kid.'

'I didn't open it,' she says, scratching her arm in a nervous gesture. 'I just looked at the return address.'

I flip it over and there it is. My name and my parents' street name, written in my teenage handwriting. I read each word carefully to make sure it's not an illusion before running my finger over the opening in the envelope. It's a neat slash, probably made by a proper letter-opener. The jagged edges are softened by time, and the folded page inside looks creased, as if it's been taken out and …

'He read it?'

'Of course he did,' she says as I take it out.

Dear Mr Sheridan …

'Frank Sheridan read my letter.'

And he kept it. Frank Sheridan *kept* my letter.

What the fuck?

'I found it a few days ago,' she admits as I turn it over in my hands. 'I remembered what you said about writing to him, and I went looking for it when I couldn't sleep. I was going to give it to you when you left.'

'I can't believe he held on to it all these years.'

'There was no way he could have written back to everyone, but he made a point of reading everything he got.' She nods at the boxes lining the wall. 'There are more in the attic.'

'There must be hundreds.' If not thousands. And she went through them all, looking for mine.

Something in my chest starts to hurt.

'They're sorted by year,' she says, as if he didn't get a hundred of them a month or something. 'I'm sorry he didn't reply,' she adds.

'Don't be. I never expected him to. I mean, I hoped, but it was like hoping to win the lottery.' I look back down at it again, still in disbelief. 'This is everything, Ciara, thank you.'

'You're welcome.' She rubs her hands against her hips. 'Feel free to look around. Sorry for the mess. No one's been in here but me since he died.'

I pause, noticing the tension in her body for the first time. I can't imagine how big a deal it is for her to let me in here. For her to *be* in here. 'We don't have to—'

'No,' she says quickly. 'It's okay. It's nice seeing it appreciated.'

I take her at her word as I scan the bookshelves that take up the opposite wall. My eyes land on one near the window. 'Is that the secret passage?' I ask, remembering what I'd read about this place.

'Only one way to find out.' She tries to sound grumpy and fails miserably. 'I'll give you three chances,' she continues. 'But I promise I won't revoke your fan club membership.'

'Don't even joke about something like that.'

I try a dictionary first, pulling it out. Nothing happens. I pick a Tolkien novel. Same thing.

I stand back, considering before I make my final choice. *Alice in Wonderland*. I tilt it towards me and hear something click.

'This is so fucking cool,' I say, and Ciara laughs softly as I push on the shelves. The case swings open easily under my touch, revealing . . . 'Your office.'

'I used to do my homework here,' she says as I wander inside. 'There's one in my bedroom as well.' She grins at the look on my face. 'I know.'

I look down at the letter in my hand, marvelling at it all over again.

'This is the best day of my life,' I say, and she snorts. 'I'm serious. I can't remember the last time anyone has done anything so nice for me.'

'All right, that's enough,' she mutters, clearly embarrassed. But happy, too. Pleased.

'Ciara . . .' But I don't know what else I can say. Don't know how to put into words just how much this means to me.

I join her in the doorway, and, when she gazes up at me, it's as if my brain shuts down.

I don't know what I'm thinking. It's an instinct. An impulse. And as I dip down, I tell myself that this is what you do when you're thanking someone. You offer a hug. A peck on the cheek.

Only this isn't exactly a peck.

My lips linger against her skin, and she goes still beneath me, motionless except for the hitch in her breathing. A soft inhale of surprise.

I don't move away when it's done. My body doesn't let me, making me stay right where I am, pulling away only enough to let a hair's breadth of space between us. She stares back at me, her cheeks pink and her pupils blown, and I don't know what I'm doing.

No. That's not right. I know exactly what I'm doing.

And that's the problem.

'Thank you,' I say finally, and she smiles this little smile that has me staring at her mouth.

Shit.

Shit shit shit.

'You're welcome,' she says, her voice barely a whisper. And then, 'Please don't sleep in your car. Just stay here. There's like a million bedrooms.'

'There are five bedrooms,' I correct.

'Stay here.'

'Okay.'

Okay.

Another beat passes, another moment where my body doesn't listen to my brain, and then she presses a hand to my stomach. Her fingers spread and my muscles clench, the thin cotton of my T-shirt doing nothing to keep out the feel of her. She pushes gently and I step back, putting space between us again.

I've definitely had too much to drink.

'Now,' she says, peering up at me. 'Are you going to pretend this is all about your big promotion, or do you want to look at my father's custom LEGO set?'

'Do you have any original artwork?'

She pretends to roll her eyes and I want to touch her again so badly, I have to shove my hands in my pockets.

'There are definitely some maps,' she says, leading me back through the bookcase. And if she notices how awkward I am for the rest of the night, she doesn't say a word.

CHAPTER EIGHTEEN

Ciara

I don't see Sam for the rest of the weekend, and when I rock up to the beach on Monday things feel almost back to normal. Whatever normal looks like to me right now.

I offered to make him up a bed, but he insisted he was fine with the couch, and when I woke the next day it was to find him gone, with a note left in his place.

He has very adult handwriting. Adult like my parents' generation. The ones who didn't all stop using a pen and paper when they were ten and start typing instead. It's neat and elegant, and I found myself admiring it for a good five seconds before reading the words.

Thank you for the birthday present. Get to the end of chapter ten by Monday.

He might as well have written *or else*, but I still smiled like an idiot. I didn't realise how miserable I was at the thought of him shutting me out before he let me back in. And now that that door's open again, I intend to keep it that way. After all, communication between an author and their editor is good. Healthy and normal and important.

Especially if he's going to be moving in with me.

If that's still happening.

He hadn't said it wasn't.

Last night, we'd casually agreed that he'd bring over his stuff this evening, but he hasn't double-confirmed since, and I haven't brought it up because I'm a coward, so what's a girl to do? Overthink it?

Me?

My laptop screen goes black due to my not typing anything or doing any work whatsoever, and I try to do what I've been doing for the past few hours and push Sam to the back of my mind as I focus on my book. Or at least I do for five seconds, before Maddie sticks her head out of the door again.

'How's it going?'

'Fine,' I say. 'Just like it was fine ten minutes ago when you asked me then.'

'Sorry for caring,' she says, not even looking at me as she peers over the cars.

I didn't want my laptop to melt in the sun, so I'm sitting in the shade behind Maddie's truck, hunched in a fold-up chair with my laptop balanced on my knees and a fan directed at my face. There's more space now Shane's truck isn't parked directly beside hers. He's moved, as requested, to the other end of the car park, which is far enough away that I can't even see him any more unless I squint hard.

The way Maddie's doing right now.

Beyond a few *choice* words about the guy who bailed on her, she didn't have much to say about Friday night. About being stood up or the drinking or any of it. But I didn't push her. She's been working even harder since the schools got out, and I know she's hanging on by a thread. I offered to help out, but she promptly shut me down and told me I had enough to be getting on with.

She isn't wrong.

I drain the last of my smoothie as I stare down at my laptop. I've been working on the same scene for over an hour, and at the rate I'm going it will be another five before I'm finished.

I've tried to shake it up by alternating between the screen and some pages I printed this morning, but my brain doesn't fall for the trick. All words are bad to it right now.

Maddie disappears back inside as I minimise the document, weighing up my need to pee with the effort of getting up and using the public toilets, when a notification appears in the corner of my screen.

An instant message from Sam.

Why do you hate love?

I stare at the question. At the little words that I have no idea how to respond to. Hate love?

I don't hate love, I type back. Then I throw in a few *????* for good measure.

His reply is instant.

Then why aren't they kissing in the library?

Finn and Maeve?

He's talking about the pages I sent him last night. The ones that definitely had kissing in them. I check the email I sent him, worried

I might have attached the wrong file. It only takes me a few seconds to find the scene. *Finn holds her close as he—*

> *They are kissing!!*
>
> *That's not a kiss scene. That's barely anything. They need to have sex in this book.*
>
> *I know they do, and I'm describing it here.*
>
> *You're not. You've written a prolonged hug. They have SEX in this book. Please tell me you've planned a sex scene.*
>
> *Stop saying sex.*
>
> *Start writing sex.*

'You okay?'

My head snaps up as Maddie swaps my empty cup for a fresh one, using it as a paperweight on top of the printouts beside me.

'I'm working. This is my working face.'

'Whatever.' She sighs and leaves me alone again.

I glance back at the screen to find another message from Sam.

> *?*
>
> *I haven't thought about it. Besides, they're busy. I don't know if you noticed that they are LITERALLY AT WAR.*

Something that never leads to heightened emotions.

You're distracting me.

I'm editing you. And then his words come rapid-fire, the messages popping up before I can even begin to think of a response. *Readers read for different reasons. And a lot of his readers are reading for this moment. The one that Frank was building up to for two books and that you are now glossing over. You've got to give them this.*

I type three variations of *I will* before I stop. I'm lying to him. Lying to him because I won't. I haven't considered a sex scene. I haven't even considered the kissing scene. Finn is about to get stabbed by his supposed friend in the council meeting three pages later, so forgive me if my mind is more focused on that.

But even as I rage artistically, I know he's right.

My dad never shied away from the romantic side of things. It was why his readership base was so big. The way he balanced emotions with the politics and war of his world was what made the books so different. He always had something for everyone.

I re-read the scene, trying to view it from different eyes. And okay, I guess we could go a *little* steamier. His hand on her waist or something. And hers on his ... arm?

I sit back, trying to picture it as I hold an imaginary mini-Finn on my lap. Where do I put my hands when I'm kissing someone? Where do I even—

Well? Sam asks. I tell the truth.

I've never written anything romantic before.

So practice.

With you?

I type the words without thinking, trying to infuse as much snark as possible into them before realising what I just sent.

'Oh... shit.'

'You okay?' Maddie calls.

'I'm fine!'

What do I do? What do I do what do I do what do I do? Throw in a classic *lol*? It's never let me down before, but I don't think even that could save me now.

My fingers hover above the keyboard, frozen as I stare at the screen. Maybe if I look hard enough, the words will simply disappear.

There's no point in deleting it because he's already seen it. It says it right there under the message. *Seen.*

He just hasn't responded. He's not even typing. None of those dancing dots that would tell me he's taking my message in the tone I intended and is about to come back with an equally snarky response.

There is nothing but silence from his end, which would make me think he's not even there if it weren't for that little green circle by his name indicating that he is.

The one that promptly flicks red as soon as I look at it.

Offline.

Right. Great. *Superb.*

'Maddie?' I yell, and a second later, she sticks her head out the door. 'I need to change my name and move to Switzerland.'

'Drink your juice,' is all she says, and disappears inside again.

Maybe I should add in a *haha*.

Everyone loves a *haha*.

I reach for my drink, feeling sick as the fan whirs back my way, and as if this moment couldn't get any more embarrassing I realise too late just how good a paperweight the smoothie was as my first few chapters go flying, pages scattering around me.

Maybe Australia would be better.

Much further away.

I lurch to my feet, putting the laptop on the remaining pile as I aim for the closest ones first.

'Let me help you with those!' a woman calls on my left, but I barely look up as I grab at a page before it can drift under the truck.

'I'm okay! Thank you.'

I snatch up another few as the stranger does the same.

'Honestly,' I say. 'It's fine.'

She nabs the last one near her and straightens with a friendly smile. She looks in her early forties and is dressed in a bathing suit and flip-flops, her soaking blonde hair pulled back into a short ponytail.

A dog-eared copy of the fifth Ravian book is in her hands.

Panic courses through me so fast that my body goes into shock, every part of me shutting down as she approaches.

'Think we got them all,' she says cheerfully. 'What are you working on?'

'It's . . . it's nothing.'

I hold out my hand for the paper, but she doesn't even notice me asking. She's staring at me, her gaze assessing as her smile fades.

'You look just like . . . ' She trails off, her mouth falling open. 'Are you Frank Sheridan's daughter?'

'That's me,' I say, going for extra-casual. It doesn't work.

'Oh, my gosh!' Her free hand flies to her chest, and she laughs as if she can't believe her luck. 'I'm such a big fan of his,' she gushes. 'It's why we came here. We've been talking about a trip to Ireland for so long and when I found out he died I knew I had to come and pay my respects. I wanted to be over for the convention, but the kids have camp, and it just wouldn't have worked out and I'm babbling. I'm sorry. I'm just ... could I get a picture with you?'

She reaches for her phone at the same time she seems to remember the pages in her hands, and she laughs again, holding them out to me. 'Sorry!'

It takes everything within me to take them from her like a normal person. As soon as I do, I shove them under the laptop with the rest, feeling doubly sick now. If she were to see them ...

'Is everything okay here?'

I look over my shoulder to see Mary rounding the truck, eyeing the woman suspiciously.

'Everything's fine!' I say with enough cheer to make her stop in her tracks. I suppose I'm not usually the merriest of people, but the last thing I need her to do is blow that damn whistle again. 'This is ... uh ...'

'Linda,' the woman supplies.

'Linda. She's a fan of my dad's.'

But something in my tone must clue Mary in that I am on *edge* right now, because she doesn't leave as Linda pulls me in for a photo.

'Thank you *so* much,' she says again, and I tell myself to smile as she holds up the phone. It's been a while since this happened. Years, in fact. Only his biggest fans recognised me once I stopped going to events, and even then it was only in places like bookshops or if they were literally peering through my window. I'm out of practice.

'You don't still live at the house, do you? Only my husband and I were hoping to get a picture of it, seeing as how we've come all this way. It's impossible to find, and everyone keeps giving us different directions!'

Mary doesn't like that. 'That house is private property,' she says, as though she doesn't show up uninvited every week. 'And you shouldn't be back here. There are generators. It's dangerous.'

'Oh, of course,' Linda says, not bothered by her tone. 'I'm sorry. I'm just so excited to meet you.' She squeezes my hand. 'You must miss him so much.'

My smile is so fixed on my face it feels frozen. 'Every day.'

Another squeeze, another smile. This one filled with pity. It's clearly what she wanted to hear, and despite her friendliness my stomach sours as she gives her final goodbye and disappears in the direction of the beach.

'Thanks,' I say to Mary. 'I wasn't expecting ... That's mine.' I straighten as I see the piece of paper clutched in her hand, but she just *tsks*.

'You spelled apothecary wrong.'

I hold out my hand, fighting the urge to snatch it from her.

'You're finishing his final book?' Mary asks, ignoring me. 'Is this why you disappeared?'

'I didn't disappear.'

'You didn't leave that house for months. You stopped coming to the pub. Ronan thought you were smoking drugs.'

'You do drugs, you don't— he thought *what*?'

'I knew you weren't,' she says, examining the page. 'You had terrible asthma as a child. I did think maybe a nose job.'

'Mary.'

'But I see you've still got that little bump—'

'*Mary.*'

Her eyes dart to mine, and she finally hands it back to me. 'Is it a secret?'

'*Yes.* So you can't say anything.'

'Why not?'

'Because that's what a secret is,' I say, reaching for the very last of my patience. 'I'm only just getting into the swing of things and I don't want people to start harassing me before I at least get something down. I'm barely halfway through yet.'

'But—'

'Please,' I interrupt, starting to get nervous. 'Swear to me you won't say a word.'

'Of course I won't,' she says, affronted. 'But I think ... '

'What?' I ask, glancing behind her to make sure Linda is definitely gone.

'Your father would have loved this,' Mary says. 'It's nice that you're doing it.'

I stare at her, surprised. So surprised I can't think of a response. Not that she seems to expect one.

'You look better now,' she says finally. 'Not as ... ' She gestures half-heartedly at my face. 'Sickly.'

And any fuzzy feeling I had for her vanishes. 'All right, thank you.'

'It's a compliment,' she says, and gives me one final look before heading back to the beach.

CHAPTER NINETEEN

Sam

There's no response from Ciara as I once again find myself standing on her porch in the blistering heat, wondering if she's even in. Wondering though I already know the answer.

There's no car in the driveway. No windows open nor signs of life.

I've been here for ten minutes, and no one's answered the door.

She's not here.

So, of course, my brain conjures up the worst reason why.

With you?

I put my bag down and sit on the porch steps, easing my legs out as I stare at the garden.

I'd been thrilled when she said I could stay here. Professionally, I wanted to do anything to get this book done. Personally, the opportunity to stay in Frank's house is not one I could turn down. And then the other part of me, the quiet, selfish part, just wanted to spend more time with her.

I just don't let myself think about what I want that time to look like.

I drop my head into my hands, rubbing my face harshly as if that might erase any thoughts of her.

I'd love to say it was the hangover that kept me away this weekend, but no, it was just plain cowardice. Just me putting space between us so that I could have a clear head. Except it doesn't feel clear. It still feels as hazy and addled as ever. It still feels full of her.

And it's because of that that I'm probably able to hear her car long before I see it. I'm like a pet dog waiting for its owner to come home, and I only fuel that comparison when I jump to my feet, watching her car approach. By the time she pulls up, I'm ready to be my most professional self, and even throw in a wave when our eyes meet through the windshield.

She doesn't look happy. I'd go so far as to say that she looks distinctly *un*happy, which makes my stomach sink, but thankfully, she seems to snap out of it as she gets out, and by the time she climbs the porch steps she's smiling.

'Sorry I'm late.'

'Is everything all right?'

'It's fine.' But the words come out like a grumble as she slots the key in the door. 'This morning was just a solid reminder of why I don't write in public.'

'Because of the faces?'

'What?'

I grab my bags and follow her inside. 'A lot of my writers make faces when they work. They're usually worried about that.'

'*Now* I'm worried about that,' she says, turning off the alarm. I close the door behind me and for a moment the two of us just stand there, looking at each other.

'So,' she says. 'Welcome.'

'Thanks again for letting me stay.'

'Yeah, well. It's not like I don't have the space. I made up a bed for you and everything.'

'Such luxury.' I follow her up the stairs. We turn right this time, going opposite to where the offices are as we head to another wing of the house.

The room she leads me to is nice. Much nicer than the one in Delaney's. There's a bigger bed for one, and a mirror and a desk. She's wheeled in a rack that I presume is to serve as my closet and has even set a small vase of daisies by the bed.

'Shut up,' she says when I pick it up. 'It's a nice thing. I'm being nice.'

'The nicest,' I say, setting it back down. 'Do I get a full tour now?'

'You've already had a full tour. Do you want to see the attic? There's nothing but spiders in there. And probably a ghost, I haven't checked.'

'Is there a basement?'

'Irish houses don't have basements. Please don't bring your American ways into my home.'

'You had a basement in your last book,' I say, and roll my eyes at the look on her face. 'I told you I read them.'

'Yeah, but don't quote them back to me. That was lazy writing. I was untrue to my setting, and for that, I apologise.'

'Uh-huh.'

She lingers in the doorway, her hands shoved in the pockets of her shorts. 'Bathroom's across the hall. Help yourself to whatever you want in the kitchen. And I guess that's it.' She takes a step back. 'Try not to disturb the ghost,' she adds and disappears down the hall.

I unpack.

It takes about as much time as it did in Delaney's, which is to say, no time at all. A quick test of the bed proves it to be *much* comfier, and yeah, awkwardness or not, this will do just fine.

I put my suitcase away, plug my laptop in to charge and open a window before grabbing my washbag. There are two doors on the other side of the hallway, and I reach for the one opposite mine, expecting to find a tiled, plain bathroom like the one by her office.

I don't.

But I know what I've found instead.

It's the smell that hits me at first. A clean, floral scent that stops me in my tracks. That I didn't even know she smelled like until it's like she's standing right in front of me. Close enough to touch.

Ciara's room.

It doesn't look like the rest of the house – a clean, orderly world that feels like no one lives in it at all. This space is very much lived in. Very much hers.

An unmade double bed is pushed against the wall with plain white sheets rumpled at the bottom. There's a vanity table and an overflowing laundry basket. A yoga mat and a fern that looks like it has two to three days left to live. An enormous, tasselled lamp dominates her bedside table, barely leaving any room for the stack of crime novels balanced on the edge, and above it she's hung a painting, a large canvas of green and gold swirls that catch the setting sun perfectly.

This must have been her childhood bedroom, because the bookcase door she mentioned before is to my left. It looks as if it leads to her closet, though most of her clothes are strewn about the room.

I take a cautious step inside, unable to help myself even as the floorboard creaks beneath me. But as soon as it does, Ciara calls from downstairs as though waiting for that exact moment.

'Get some beer!'

I take one final glance around and close the door before dumping my stuff in the bathroom. Downstairs, I find the beers in the fridge and Ciara on the porch, sitting along a bench with her legs propped up on an upside-down basket.

'Gimme,' is all she says when she sees me, and she makes a grabby motion with her hands as I step over her legs and pass her a bottle.

'This is nice,' I say, stating the obvious. It's more than nice. It's blissful. You can't hear any traffic out here. Can't hear anything but the low buzz of crickets and the faint calls from farm animals in the distance. 'You must come out here a lot.'

'Yes, because it's always like this,' she says. 'It is never windy or cold or wet or—'

'Okay.'

'I feel like I need to hammer home that this is not a normal summer for us.' She takes a sip, staring out at the garden. 'At all. Plus, we're due some storms soon. Big ones.'

'Never work for the tourist board.'

She readjusts her legs, crossing one over the other, and I watch from the corner of my eye as she brushes a blade of grass off her thigh.

Golden hour. I get why they call it that now. The soft warmth of the light highlights every strand of hair, every inch of skin. As though the universe is pointing a spotlight right at her, guiding me her way, telling me to look.

I force my gaze to the trees. 'How did your writing go?'

'You mean, how did my sex scene go?' she asks with a sly look that I don't know what to do with. 'I got interrupted. But I've taken your feedback on board even if I don't agree with it.'

'You don't agree with it?'

'I think I'm already going over the word count with a fifth of the book still to go, and after you made me cut a whole council scene for *pacing*, I don't understand why we need to add a bedroom scene.'

I can't tell if she's joking or not.

'We'll need at least two bedroom scenes,' I tell her. 'And probably a bit more in between.'

'Where the hell are we going to put them?'

'We'll figure it out.'

'But there's no room for—'

'We'll find room.'

She gapes at me, looking so confused that I can tell she truly doesn't get it.

'You know *The Last Mountain* is a love story, right?'

'*The Last Mountain* is an epic saga about the ravages of war and the greed of men.'

'It's a love story,' I repeat. 'It's Finn and it's Maeve. That's the whole point of the book.'

'That's a large part of it, sure, but—'

'It's the whole point,' I interrupt. 'And it's the ending. You think we can give them their happy-ever-after with no build-up?'

'There is build-up,' she says, but I can hear the doubt in her voice. 'There's just other stuff as well.'

'But nothing as important. Think about it. Why else are they still going? Every other character has either died or given up. What do you think they're both fighting for?'

'Territory expansion.'

'Ciara.'

She smirks, but I know she's listening. 'A love story,' she says, and I nod. 'Okay, well now I feel dumb.'

'Don't.'

'Hmm. No, I do. Feels extremely obvious now that you say it.'

'Makes it simpler, though, doesn't it? With a big series like this, authors tend to lose their story four or five books in, but your dad knew what he was doing. We saw in his notes that Finn and Maeve were always his ending. And you need to remember that in every word you write or else you'll—'

I break off when she smiles at me. A wide, happy smile that makes me forget what I was saying.

'What?'

'I like it when you go into editor mode,' she says. 'You get all passionate. Use your hands.'

'My hands?'

She gestures her own in the air, exaggerating the motion until I scoff. 'All right, I'll stop.'

'No, it's cute,' she protests.

'Cute when I talk, cute when I'm drunk.' I sit back against the bench, and she cringes.

'You remember that, huh?'

'Told you I would.'

'Lesson learned.'

I feel her eyes on me as I take my first mouthful of beer, and, when I look over again, I find her contemplative.

'I've never written a love story before.'

'You're writing one right now,' I point out.

'I guess so.'

'Just don't be afraid to give them their moments.'

'And lose their clothing,' she adds, but there's no mockery behind the words. She still sounds as if she's thinking. As if she's taking it seriously.

'We can discuss it if you're not convinced.'

'I'm convinced,' she says, relaxing back. 'I put my faith in you, Sam. You're the only one here who knows what they're doing.'

And to that I have no answer. Because when it comes to the woman beside me, more and more, I realise I have no idea what I'm doing at all.

CHAPTER TWENTY

Ciara

There is a man in my house.

It's the only thing I can think of that night as I stand in the dark hall, gazing at Sam's sneakers lined neatly by the door. That upstairs, across the landing from my room, there is a man, and he is asleep. And I put a vase of flowers by his bed. I don't know why I did that. Probably because I panicked. It's been a long time since I've hosted anyone.

We had another beer over dinner and chatted about the book and then he got some work done and I got some work done and it's so domestic it's downright confusing. It's nice, though. Easy.

There was only one awkward moment when he fell asleep in front of the television and I stressed out, wondering if I should wake him, but he solved that dilemma by rousing a minute later. And then he gave an apologetic smile and took himself off to bed.

That was an hour ago. And now here I am. Staring at his shoes.

I'm not used to it. Sharing the house with someone other than Dad. I mean, sure, Maddie's crashed here a few times, but that's about it. Not that Sam's a bad guest. He washed up after dinner. He got rid of a spider. He has not, as far as I can tell, stolen anything.

But it's more than that.

Ever since Dad died, this house has never felt like home to me. But now it feels different. More comforting knowing that Sam's upstairs in bed, sleeping soundly.

I wish I could sleep. I wish my brain could swallow the hours. That I could close my eyes and when I open them again it'd be morning.

I slept fine when I lived in London. I shared a small house with an opera singer and a quiet, tidy man who told us he worked for the civil service but who I was convinced was some sort of James Bond spy. I'd moved there after the whole pen-name debacle, wanting a fresh start. The plan was to eventually get back into writing. Maybe travel a bit.

And then everything went tits-up.

Dad got sicker, and I moved back to look after him. He'd been doing okay before then, but he needed full-time care, and I wanted to be the one to do it.

The insomnia began a few weeks later. Stress about the move. About him. I thought it would stop, but it didn't. If anything, it got worse.

I didn't want to sleep in case he needed me during the night. In case something happened and I missed it. So, instead of resting, I would spend hours lying in my bed and thinking about all the bad things that could happen to him, snatching a few hours of sleep only when someone else was in the house with him.

That was when Maddie started coming around. It was as though she sensed it. And then Ronan would pop in before opening the pub and someone else would drop by with food or flowers and another just to sit with him and chat. Whatever we needed to get through.

I don't know when I stopped that. When I started hiding from the doorbell instead of answering it. No one was trying to pry. They were just doing what they'd always done.

I leave Sam's sneakers where they are and move into the kitchen, where I work in fits and starts for the next few hours, taking only short breaks. I nap on the couch. I eat some cheese and crackers I didn't know I had. I move chairs and wipe down the counters. I write and write and write.

Sam wakes just after seven.

It terrifies me at first. The sudden noise. I have a real *guess I'm about to be murdered* moment before I remember his existence, and then I'm just nervous. Expectant.

I track the unfamiliar footsteps across the floor, the snip of the bathroom door followed by the rush of pipes followed by more footsteps getting closer and closer until he appears in the doorway, his eyes scrunched in sleep and his hair sticking up in such a way that I realise Sam Avery is someone who must style his hair every morning. I file that away as if I'm keeping a catalogue of him, right under *early riser* and *likes maps*.

He shuffles into the kitchen, scratching his stomach through a grey cotton T-shirt, and I stare at him. I know I stare at him. I just can't look away. I try to. I command myself to. But I can't.

He just looks so darn sleepy.

So sleepy that he doesn't realise I'm here until I say good morning, at which point he definitely wakes up.

'Jesus!' His back hits the fridge door hard enough that its contents rattle, and I wince.

'Sorry.'

Now it's Sam's turn to stare. 'I'd ask if you normally get up at this time, but let me guess.'

'I couldn't sleep,' I say with a shrug. 'It's no big deal. Are you usually up this early?'

'No. Well, sometimes.' He glances at the fridge. 'Do you mind?'

'Go for it.'

'I'll go into town and get some food today.'

'You don't have to,' I say as he grabs some orange juice. 'Maddie keeps me well stocked. Besides, you're a guest.'

'You want some?' he asks, pointing to the carton.

I shake my head, watching him grab a glass from the shelf. Remembering him doing that another time when he had his hand on my hip and his chest against my back and—

His phone buzzes in his pocket, and he checks it briefly before placing it on the counter.

'Who the hell is emailing you at this hour?' I ask.

'Film agent on the West Coast. It's late over there.'

'And my question still stands.'

He just smiles at me, as if I'm being funny. 'Did you get much done?' he asks.

'Too much. My brain is dead. I think I've re-read the last page twelve times now.'

'You should go to bed.'

I nod, because I should, but I am not sleepy. I am the opposite of sleepy.

I am wide fucking awake.

'Can I ask you a question?' I say as he takes a seat at the table. 'When did you get Finn's mark?'

Sam pauses, glancing down at the tattoo on his underarm as if he forgot it was there. 'My eighteenth birthday,' he says. 'My parents were furious.'

'Really?'

'Mostly because they felt they had to be. And that I didn't tell them. And that I didn't "think about it",' he adds in air quotes. 'As if I hadn't been thinking about it since I read the book. But they gave me money towards the next one, so I think they forgave me.'

'You've got more than one?' I don't know why this shocks me so much. My gaze drops down his body as if I've got X-ray vision, and it suddenly becomes incredibly important that I know exactly where else the man has ink. His chest? His legs? His d—

'I guess you wouldn't have seen it,' he says, thankfully interrupting my imagination. He puts the glass down, deliberating for a moment before he stands.

Putting me at eye level with his hips.

I fidget as he reaches a hand behind his head and tugs his T-shirt off. He turns as he does, and I get a glimpse of the flat length of his stomach and a light dusting of dark hair before he shows me his back. And then all I see is ink.

This is not a small symbol on his arm. This is art. An intricate weave of spirals that represent the arrival of the ancient kings and queens. The heroes of old.

Sam shifts self-consciously in front of me. 'This one took a little more time.'

'I bet,' I murmur, reaching for the smallest circle in the centre. He flinches as soon as I touch it, and I draw back immediately. 'Sorry.'

'It's okay. Just wasn't expecting it.'

'Cold hands,' I say, and he nods in agreement even though they're not. 'Can I . . . ' I trail off, watching as his whole back tenses, making the design move.

'Go ahead.' This time, he relaxes when I press a finger to his skin, tracing a Celtic knot that must have taken hours. Heaviness settles between my thighs, and I press my legs together, following each line until there's no part I haven't explored.

I don't stop. I don't think anything could make me.

Instinct overwhelms reason, and I keep going, trailing a straight path down his back. My touch is so light I wonder how he even feels it, but he reacts as though he does, his muscles bunching and releasing beneath me as I reach the elastic waistband of his sweatpants.

I pause, but he doesn't move away, and after a beat my eyes drift back up as he turns his head over his shoulder.

The look he gives me is like a dare.

A moment passes, thick and heavy. My heart is beating so hard I can hear it, and my imagination runs wild, warm, needy thoughts of him flooding my mind, giddy and heady and—

A sharp, ugly buzz ruins the moment, and another a second later kills it altogether.

Reality crashes in, embarrassment swift on its heels as his phone lights up, and I let my hand drop away as I stand. Sam just stares at me as if he didn't even hear it.

'West Coast,' I whisper, clearing my throat, and I avoid his gaze as I snatch up my laptop and flee back upstairs.

Our new routine continues as June becomes July. I sleep most of the day and work during the night, and in the hours that Sam and I overlap we tease out plot points and smooth over writing and, bit by bit, connect the dots until an actual book takes shape.

One day, we work so hard that I fall asleep on the couch in my office and wake up in my bed some time after eleven, completely disorientated and absolutely starving. Sam must have carried or corralled me, which is all sorts of embarrassing, but I'm mainly relieved because the last time I slept on that thing, I had a crick in my neck for days.

Judging by the soft light streaming from under the crack in his bedroom door, he's still awake, but I still creep by, trying not to disturb him.

I'm not inclined to make a proper dinner, and my stomach can't decide what time of day it is anyway, so I make do with a bowl of cereal and an apple while I watch a YouTube video on medieval plagues and then a make-up tutorial by a woman with skin so clear it looks airbrushed. When I'm finished, I clean the kitchen and do twelve minutes of a thirty-minute yoga video before finally heading back upstairs.

Sam's light is turned off now, so I'm extra-quiet as I shut myself in my office. And then I get to work.

I write until my brain gives up.

I know when it does because I'm not able to type a single sentence without hitting the backspace twelve times. Experience has taught me that this is not something I can just 'push through', and so I give in, pleased with the word count as I tidy up the room, gathering the empty mugs and glasses and sorting all the notes and papers into neat little piles. Sam had been using some of my Ravian books for reference and I pick those up too, slotting them back on to the bookcase that still lies open from when I showed him Dad's office.

I didn't leave it that way to make a point. It was mostly because I forgot about it and then because I told myself that I should start using it. Maybe look around for more inspiration on the off chance he wrote a detailed three-act structure and hid it in one of his boxes.

But I didn't. Until now, anyway, when I linger on my side, peering in. If I did believe in ghosts, this is where I would see him, sitting in his chair, writing away. But I don't, so it's just a room filled with memories. Though I guess that's what all ghosts are, anyway.

I wrap a hand around the side, pulling it open fully as I step inside.

This is the fifth time I've been in here since he died.

The first time was during the house clearance, when I put everything of his I didn't want to throw away inside. The second time was when I looked for information on *The Last Mountain*. The third was searching for Sam's letter. The fourth time was with Sam.

And now here I am.

The moon is so bright tonight that I don't need to switch on the lamp. I open a window, though, letting in some air along with the faint rustle of the oak tree outside.

This is the one room I've yet to tackle, and I'm not so obtuse that I don't know why. I threw myself into sorting the house because I didn't want to think of him as *not* being there. And I don't go into this room because here he still is. In the smell and the books and the pages. In the mess and the dust and the indent of the chair.

My father lives on in this room. And I'm going to have to deal with that eventually.

But for now, I sit cross-legged in the centre, alternating between enjoying the silence and hating it.

I always liked sitting on the floor. I did it all the time when I was a kid. Now, if I do it too long my lower back is like, *why*, but a little while longer won't hurt. You can see things differently down here. Things you wouldn't usually. Like the books along the bottom shelf. The dropped coin underneath the armchair.

The name *Ciara* written in marker along the side of one of the boxes.

Well. If ever there was a sign . . .

I crawl over and try to pull it out, but it's heavier than I expect and the cardboard is flimsy, tearing in my hands. I get closer and try again, grasping it by its sides to pull it out more carefully.

It is a box that is, shockingly, all to do with me.

My school yearbooks. My report cards. My projects and paintings and various things I brought home to him over the years.

God, I couldn't draw for shit. Even as a kid. But he kept a lot. Maybe even all of them. Every glittery crayon monstrosity that I proudly presented to him. At least that was better than my baking phase. At least he never had to *eat* my paintings. He'd just put them on the fridge or tape them to the front door when he knew someone was coming over. So everyone would see it.

I don't know what it says about me that when a drop of water hits the drawing I look up to see if there's a leak in the ceiling. Why it takes me a second to put a hand on my cheek and find it wet.

As though someone's flicked a switch, I've had enough. My hands are shaking when I put everything back in the box. Shaking when I push the box back in its place. As I do, I disturb the dust and sneeze twice in violent succession. The kind of sneeze that makes you feel like you're blowing out your lungs.

I return to my office, grabbing my laptop and sitting on the floor with my back to the couch.

From this angle, I can see into his room, silent and still, as if I weren't just in there.

I didn't know he kept all that stuff.

And do you know what would have been great? If maybe he told me he had.

Despite how young I was, most memories of my father are from before the books. Because, once the series took off, I barely saw him. I didn't give him the drawings after school. I slid them under his door because he'd be working. I baked because that meant he'd come downstairs. That I'd get to see him for a few minutes as he marvelled over a distinctly average brownie.

I'm old enough now to know how hard it must have been. A single parent. A career like that. I can't imagine how he managed it all.

But it still *hurts*. That he was barely around. That, whenever he was, I always had to share him. With these books. With his readers.

When I left home, I did it to forge a new life for myself. Something that was just for me.

And yet here I am.

I upended my whole world to come back here. To look after him and then to . . . what? Stay in his house, writing his books and doing it half as well? I can't even figure out the central relationship, so how the hell am I going to—

I look back at the screen, stopping my thoughts in their tracks. I'm running behind, back to where I was at the start, where the words are coming but they're all the wrong ones. But Sam's expecting something tomorrow and I don't want him to make his disappointed face at me.

So I force all memories from my mind, thinking of only Finn and Maeve as I draw my laptop on to my lap and write.

CHAPTER TWENTY-ONE

Sam

Three a.m. and Ciara still hasn't gone to sleep.

About an hour ago, I woke when she came up the stairs, but she didn't go to her bedroom. She went to her office instead and she's been there ever since.

Maybe she fell asleep on the couch again.

Maybe it's none of my business.

But whenever I close my eyes, it *feels* like my business. As if I can't rest unless I know she is too.

I stare up at the ceiling, running through my options. I could get up and pretend to get a glass of water while I check on her. Or I could be normal and go to sleep.

Or I could get a glass of water.

I kick the sheet off before I can stop myself and slip down the hallway. I'll just stick my head in. I'll stick my head in and check that she's . . .

I pause outside her office, rocking back on my heels as a muffled shriek breaks through the silence. A second later, something thuds against the wall, as if she's thrown something at it, and, concerned now, I push open the door.

The first thing I notice is how bright it is. The windows are open and the lights are off, but it's a clear night, and the moon is out, illuminating the space. It's changed a lot since she first showed it to me, a natural consequence of the two of us spending most of our days there. The couch is now full of cushions she brought up from downstairs and two large corkboards hang on the wall, filled with flashcards from when I tried to help her visualise the chapter breakdown.

Ciara kneels in the middle of the room, surrounded by scattered pieces of paper and scrawled-upon legal pads. Her laptop lies open beside her, the screen glowing with dim light.

'Are you . . .'

Her head snaps up at my voice, and I'm relieved to see that she's not crying.

'. . . okay?' I finish hopefully.

She scowls at me. 'It's shit.'

'It's not shit,' I say automatically.

'You haven't read it.' She climbs to her feet, her movements stiff, as though she's been down there for a while. 'And I don't want you to read it because it's *shit*. It's the worst fucking thing in the world and as soon as you finish it you're going to hate me and Casey's going to hate me and readers are going to hate me because it's *shit*.'

Oh, boy.

First proper author breakdown. Honestly, I'm surprised it's taken her this long. But I usually only ever deal with them over the phone, or respond to carefully worded emails that never fully manage to hide the panicked *I CAN'T DO THIS* scream between each line.

'You're doing a great job,' I say. 'I need you to trust me to tell you if you aren't.'

But Ciara's not listening, back in her own head as she snatches her laptop off the floor and puts it on the desk.

'I don't think about sex.'

'You . . . excuse me?'

'When I'm having sex,' she continues, sounding *extremely* annoyed that I'm not following her thought process, 'I don't think about it. I don't think about what I'm doing. I'm just doing it. I'm not analysing every moment because *I'm* not a pervert. Is this what romance writers do? Because that's weird. Someone should tell them that.'

Wait.

My brain, which had wiped clean in some sort of weird self-preservation move, snaps back to life as I realise what she's saying.

'You're freaking out over the bedroom scene?'

'I don't *do* romance.'

'You're overthinking it,' I tell her. 'It's just a kiss.'

'It's more than a kiss!' she exclaims. 'It's the whole point of the book. That's what you said.'

That is what I said. I just never expected that *this* would be the thing that breaks her.

And she must see it on my face. 'Don't you dare laugh at me,' she warns, almost slipping on some loose paper as she moves closer.

'Does it look like I'm laughing at you?' I gesture to the laptop. 'Where have you got to?'

'Absolutely nowhere because I don't know where his hands go! And I don't want to use the word *tongue*. And you keep telling me to add more tension instead of just saying they're horny for each other, but they are! They're horny! Sometimes you don't need a chapter of build-up. Sometimes people just—'

She cuts off abruptly as I tense, her eyes going wide as she looks down to where she's planted her hands on my chest. She looks confused. As though she's not exactly sure how they got there. But she doesn't move away. She doesn't stop touching me. And maybe it's the late hour or the topic of conversation or the way her tank top is riding up her stomach, but I don't want her to.

'Act?'

Her gaze shoots up to mine. 'Huh?'

'Sometimes people just act,' I finish for her, and she blinks rapidly as though she's trying to focus.

'Exactly,' she says, though the word sounds unsure.

'And you don't know where his hands go?'

'I just mean . . .' She trails off, her brow furrowing as I wrap my fingers around her biceps. 'Sam . . .'

'His hands go here.' My voice comes out unfamiliarly low, unrecognisable to my ears.

Still, she doesn't move away. She doesn't move at all. And I wait for her to tell me to fuck off or to be serious, but she doesn't.

I suddenly become hyper-aware of her. Of all of her. The piercings in her ears. The freckles on her shoulder. The faint line on her forehead and the low arch of her brows and the small birthmark on the side of her neck. The more I notice, the more I see. And the harder it is to look away.

Ciara's lips part, and I watch the movement of her throat as she swallows. 'Then what does he do?' she asks.

'You tell me. Talk me through it. Where are they?'

'Her bedroom. It's before the execution. All her guards are outside.'

'They can be heard.'

'Exactly.' She's staring at my left shoulder now. 'So they have to be quiet.'

I pause, trying to visualise it. 'That's good.'

'I know,' she mutters, and I fight back a smile.

'How did he get past the guards?'

'He snuck into the castle earlier. They're looking for a man with long hair, so no one recognises him.'

'How did he know where her room—'

'It's a plot hole and I don't care,' she says, finally bringing her eyes to mine. 'There's a big tourist map. He paid five euros for it.'

'Ciara.'

'He guesses. All castles are the same. He grew up tending one. He knows how they work. And he's willing to risk it all because he has to see her. That's all he wants.' But she pauses, doubt creeping into her voice. 'Unless that's too much,' she says. 'They've already slept together.'

'It doesn't matter. They haven't seen each other in months. And if you've been following the—'

'Of course I've been following the timeline,' she interrupts, sounding exasperated. Another smile pulls at my lips. But it disappears as she shifts on her feet, reminding me I'm still holding her.

Somewhere in the back of my mind, a little voice asks, what the *fuck* am I doing? But I barely hear it. I definitely don't pay attention to it.

I don't know what I'm doing. But I know I can't stop.

My fingers trail down her arms, stopping just above her wrists.

'Keep going,' I say, squeezing gently when she starts to fidget. She looks distracted, but I need her back on track. 'She's surrounded by enemies. Is she scared they might be found?'

'Her guards are in the corridor outside. She's supposed to be asleep.'

'What about Finn?'

'He's not scared. He just wants to see her. He wants to know that she's safe. And he . . . he's forgotten what she looks like too,' she says, and her eyes drift to my collarbone, where, in the book, Finn has a long, jagged scar. 'She'd been younger, in his head. Softer. But living in the castle has changed her. She's not a princess any more. She's a queen.'

'Go on.'

'He's awed by her,' she continues. 'And he's nervous. He was always the one who knew what he was doing in their relationship. But now he's unsure. He's tongue-tied. For the first time in his life, Finn has no idea what to say to her.'

I know the feeling.

'So that's where they're at,' I say after a long second. 'Now we need to break it down. Where are my hands?'

'Really?'

'Where are my—'

'My wrists.'

'And where would Finn—'

'Her hips.' Ciara's cheeks go pink, but I say nothing, resting them carefully on her waist. She shuffles the tiniest step forward. And then nothing. We hover there for a minute, as though neither of us wants to take the next step.

I take a deep breath. 'Then what would he—'

She kisses me.

Every thought, every wall, every single line in my mind dissipates into nothing as her hands shoot up to cup my face. As her lips press to mine.

I tighten my hold on her, drawing her into my body until she lets out this little noise that makes my knees go weak. It's like my body breaks out in a fever, going warm all over as she plasters herself against me.

When she sweeps her tongue into my mouth I taste lemonade, and when she leans against my chest, I swear I feel her heartbeat.

I feel starved for her. Alive for her.

And maybe Ciara's right, because I'm not even aware of my hands moving. I'm too focused on her. Too lost in the sensations to think about how one second I'm holding her to me and the next my hands are under her tank top, fingers spanning her back. I move to the soft skin of her ribcage, aiming for her breasts, and only regain some sanity when she jerks away, breaking from me with a gasp.

'Wait, wait, wait,' she says rapidly, and I stop immediately, worried I've gone too far, but she's almost laughing as she squirms.

'Maeve isn't ticklish,' she says between heavy breaths. She stares at where she clutches fistfuls of my T-shirt, making an *oops* face before loosening her grip.

After a second, the roaring in my ears goes down, and I cover her hands with mine.

'Then what happens?' I ask thickly, and it takes her a moment to answer.

'He leaves,' she says finally. 'He needs to get to the prison. He doesn't have time for much more.'

'Through the door?'

'Out of the window.'

'I think you can use your imagination for that part,' I say, and she laughs quietly as her gaze flickers to mine.

'Yeah,' she says quietly, dropping her hands. 'Okay.'

Okay.

'Try to get some sleep,' I say, because I don't know what else to, and she gives me a little salute that makes me want to kiss her all over again. I don't, though. I let her go instead, even though every part of me is screaming *NO. WRONG*. And I—

'Sam?'

'Yeah?' I stop so abruptly I nearly walk into the door.

Ciara's mouth twitches and she looks so beautiful in that moment, it takes me a second to remember I'm not dreaming. 'This was very helpful. Thank you.'

'Sure,' I say, and have to clear my throat with how hoarse it sounds. 'Any time.'

CHAPTER TWENTY-TWO

Ciara

I would love to say that, with a bit of space and a couple of hours of sleep, I woke up without my editor on my mind. That I wasn't thinking about his hands on my waist and his eyes on my lips and everything that happened after.

Instead, after typing furiously for as long as I could, I went to bed thinking about him, and when I woke to bright, monotonous sunshine what felt like like a second later, it was as though he was in the corner of my mind, waiting for me.

Maybe I have a crush.

Or maybe I just haven't had sex in a really long time.

Whatever it is that's altered all the chemicals in my brain, I find myself staring at my bedroom door and imagining him walking through it.

My whole body perks up at the thought, and I grow impatient as I stare at the handle, willing for it to turn.

Like . . . *now*.

Except it doesn't. Obviously. Nothing happens. The house is

silent except for the usual birdsong outside, and after thirty more seconds of waiting because, you know, just in case, I fling the blanket off me, admitting defeat.

Of course, as soon as I stand up, I hear his door open.

I jump so hard that I lose my balance and whack my heel on the bedpost. Under the stream of curse words flooding from my mouth, I listen to him head to the bathroom. A second later, the shower turns on.

It does not help things.

Visions of a soaking wet, soaped-up Sam Avery fill my mind and that's the moment I know I need to be out of my house today.

I dress quickly, throwing on the first things I find, before slipping out of the room. The shower's still going, and I keep my gaze firmly ahead as I stride purposefully past it, down the stairs and out the door.

A walk is good. Will clear my head.

Or at least that's what I tell myself as I keep going, putting more and more distance between us until I find myself halfway to the village. By this point I'm already starting to regret my decision. It's still early but already getting warm, and I meet only one or two other people on the way before I get to the pub, where Ronan's outside, accepting a delivery.

'Is that Ciara Sheridan?' he asks, squinting exaggeratedly my way. 'In the daylight?'

I hold up my arm. 'I think I'm burning.'

'Better get inside, then,' he says, and I don't need to be told twice as I flee into the main room.

This pub was my happy place when I first moved back. It was the only place I could escape to when Dad was sick. Mainly because it was the only place in the village I could go to that wasn't my house.

'How's the boyfriend?' Ronan asks, striding in after me.

'He's not— Fine. He's fine.' I hop on to the stool. 'Can I have a drink?'

'No.'

'Seriously?' I check the time. 'Not even a mimosa?'

'Not according to the Habitual Drunkards Act of 1879. So blame that and not me.'

'I will,' I say. 'I will write it a strong letter.' And I slump as he pours me a glass of orange juice.

'Use your imagination,' he says at the look on my face.

'Hmm.' I take a sip, eyeing him over the rim. 'Did you get a haircut?'

'Flirting won't get me to break the law.'

'Says the guy with an unlicensed microbrewery in his back room.'

'I am a man with hobbies,' he says, unruffled. 'And that's a thing to be praised. Maybe you should think about getting some yourself.'

'I have lots of hobbies,' I tell him. 'Number one: drinking before noon.'

'You should get out. Do a class.'

I stare at him. 'What class? And *where*?'

'In the city,' he says, as if it's obvious. 'You can't stay cooped up in that house all the time.'

'I'm sitting here now, aren't I?'

'And what happens if I'm not around?'

'You mean if you keep drinking that whiskey?' I ask before realising what he's saying. 'You're not thinking of closing down, are you?'

Ronan just shrugs. 'I'm getting on. And so are the costs. A good summer season isn't enough to keep me going through the winter.'

'Yeah, but . . .' I shift on my stool, not knowing what else to say. This place has been the same ever since I was born. No matter how long I stayed away, Ronan was behind the bar and my dad's picture was on the wall and the only wines available were 'white' and 'red'. It isn't supposed to change.

'Stop that.'

'Stop what?' I ask, taking another sip.

'Whatever it is you're thinking about. It will do you no good.'

'I'm thinking about how sad I'm going to be when you retire.'

At that, he snorts. 'You will not. You'll be long gone.'

'Gone where?'

'Anywhere!' he exclaims. 'Back to Dublin, at least. Or London. You're doing no good here. You're barely around enough as it is.'

'That's not true,' I protest. 'I'm an active member of the community.'

'What community?' he scoffs. 'Sure, there's barely any of us left. School's closed down. Church closed down. Half the houses around here are holiday lets, and there aren't even that many of those any more.'

'What are you talking about?' I frown. 'The room upstairs is booked out for the summer.'

'It is not,' he huffs. 'I've got one backpacker down for a few days next month, but that's about it.'

'But Mary told Sam ...' Oh, for fuck's sake. 'She is ... meddlesome,' I say, unable to think of another word.

Ronan nods gravely. 'That she is.'

'She told Sam he had to move out.'

'Did she now?' he says, not looking surprised at all.

My mouth drops open. 'You *knew*?'

'I don't know anything,' he says. 'Except that it sounds like he needed a push to begin with. Ten-thirty,' he adds, looking at the clock, but the moment has passed.

'Just a coffee,' I sigh, and he busies himself with the machine. As he does, my phone vibrates in my pocket, and I take it out to see a text.

Did you leave?

Sam.

The little burst of giddiness I feel is alarming. *He's thinking of me!!* inner teenage Ciara squeals, which is odd, because real teenage Ciara had been a self-conscious introvert and would have run a mile in the other direction.

I don't want to tell him I'm in the pub this early lest I perpetuate a national stereotype, so I tell him a half-lie instead.

Decided to help Maddie at the beach.

Because I'm a good friend, and definitely not because I keep thinking about you in the shower.
Feel free to come down, I add because I am so brave, but his reply pings barely a second later. I'll never get over how fast that man can type.

I have meetings this afternoon.

I can't tell if I'm relieved or disappointed by this, but a new message appears before I have time for my soul-searching.

I'll take a look at chapter eleven for you.

Eh?

What's wrong with chapter eleven?

Nothing. Once I edit it.

The middle finger emoji seems appropriate here, but I'm smiling as I send it, and then I realise I am and stop because Ronan is watching me with a knowing smirk.

I spend another hour with him before Maddie swings by to pick me up. I won't lie; when I texted her, I mostly expected to spend the day detailing every confusing thing happening in my life while she nodded in all the right places and told me exactly what to do. But of course the reason she agreed to let me help her was because the beach is completely rammed. I barely have time to catch my breath, let alone chat, as the customers line up by the dozen for the next few hours.

But even with the constant activity my thoughts have a habit of returning to the man in my house. At every single moment, I'm either wondering what he's doing or what he's thinking or remembering how big his hands felt around my waist. How soft his lips and how hot his mouth.

It could have been awkward afterwards, but it wasn't. Even when I sat back down in the room when he left and waited for it to be.

It felt natural.

And fuck me, but it *worked*.

If that's how you get over writer's block, then that's how you get over writer's block. It reminds me of the time I took a creative writing class when I first moved to Dublin, and the tutor spent the whole session talking about how he spent three months in Venice doing some *vital research*.

Maybe Sam is my Venice.

It would explain how I wrote three thousand words last night. Most of them will probably have to be cut, because reading it back it's just a lot of touching and clothes coming off, but who am I to not give the people what they want? And according to Sam, it's what they want.

Judging by the look on his face yesterday, it's what he wants, too.

And, while that thought alone make me want to go straight back to the house, it's Maddie who drove me here and so it's Maddie I'm chained to, unless I want to walk for two hours in this heat.

I'm exhausted by the time I finish, my feet aching from standing all day and my face tired from smiling. We don't end up closing until after five, and then I help clean up before we grab a pizza from one of the seasonal restaurants along the strip because she wants to check out the café again. We eat our slices sitting on the kerb outside and I listen patiently as she describes exactly what awning she wants.

It's dark by the time we finally head back. Late, too.

I don't exactly *expect* Sam to be awake, but I'm still disappointed he's not as I grab a glass of water and sneak up to the office. I'm weirdly eager to get to work after a full day away from the book, and when I open my email I find that he has indeed gone over chapter eleven, and his suggestions make sense. Enough sense that I work my way through them first, just so he won't be smug about it in the morning, before spending another hour polishing the words I wrote last night.

Maeve wasn't alone in the room. She sensed this instantly, something deep within her making her pause just inside the door. But it wasn't alarm she felt. There was no danger here.

At least not the kind she feared.

His mouth on mine. His taste on my tongue.

My skin prickles as if he's standing right here, and I swear I can feel the pulse of my blood in the places where he touched me. Burning flashes of memory sear across my mind, mixing with my imagination as I think about what would have happened if I hadn't stopped it. How he would have kept going. How I'd lift my arms and he'd lift my top and he'd—

WRITE YOUR BOOK, CIARA. WRITE YOUR DAMN BOOK.

I get to my feet, annoyed with myself as I stare out of the window, at the sky and the moon and the stars.

I should be *channelling* these feelings, not writing fan fiction for my own life.

And yet all I can think about is that it's a beautiful moon. A beautiful night. And it's been so, so long since I've shared it with someone.

CHAPTER TWENTY-THREE

Sam

'Sam.'

My eyes snap open, my heart racing as I twist my head to see Ciara standing in my open doorway.

'Hi,' she whispers, stepping inside. 'Did I wake you?'

'Yes?' I reach for the light. 'You're literally in my room calling my name.'

'I know. I was being rhetorical.'

'My mistake.' I sit up, squinting her way as my eyes adjust. 'What time is it? Are you okay?'

'I'm fine. There's a full moon tonight. Did you see it?'

'Can't say that I did,' I say. 'Because I was asleep.'

'Well, it's pretty spectacular, and I wondered if . . . ' She trails off, looking unsure, and I try very hard not to look at her bare legs in those tiny shorts.

'Are you asking me to look at the moon with you, or are you asking me to join some sort of ritual sacrifice.'

'No one ever wants to look at the moon with me,' she says, just short of pouting. 'I used to have this tradition where I'd go and stargaze, but I haven't done it in years and I don't want to do it alone. Plus, it's massive tonight. It must be a special one.'

'It's the same one as yesterday. It's just our perception that—'

'*Sam.*'

'I would love to look at the moon with you.'

'Yeah?'

'Yeah,' I say, swinging my legs out of bed.

'And you won't make fun of me?'

'Not to your face,' I say, and the smile she gives me makes me want to pluck the thing from the sky and give it to her on a silver platter.

'I'll get my keys.'

Keys? 'We can't look at it in the garden?'

She shakes her head. 'I know a much better spot.'

Which is how ten minutes later, I find myself sitting next to her as she drives down the empty roads. It's not like I would have said no to her, anyway. I've been on edge all day waiting to see her. Needing to know that she doesn't regret what happened. She doesn't act like she does, smiling as she sings along with the radio, and I'm so absorbed by her that I don't even ask where we're going. Don't even realise where we are until we get there.

The beach is deserted. Devoid of the cars that usually fill every space. Ciara passes Maddie's shuttered smoothie truck and parks right by the sand, the world going silent as soon as she turns the engine off.

It's the kind of silence that freaked me out the first few nights I was here. I'm used to noise, to a constant hum. A taxi in the distance. Music from a house party. But in Carrigwest there's nothing. Or at least nothing but the ocean lapping at the shore.

'Where is everybody?' I ask as we get out. It's late, but I thought there'd be a few campers around. Or some college kids having a bonfire.

'There's a smaller beach about fifteen minutes away,' Ciara says, catching what I mean. 'It's more secluded. Plenty of dunes to sneak into.'

'Speaking from experience, are we?'

She winks, stretching her arms overhead as I admire the view of the ocean.

'I could definitely be a country person,' I say, but Ciara just gives me a look.

'You'd miss New York. I bet you do already.'

I do, but I'm not letting her ruin my little fantasy. 'I think I can even see it,' I say, peering exaggeratedly at the ocean.

'New York?'

'Yeah. That tiny dot in the distance? Brooklyn.'

'Try Newfoundland. And then try looking at a map.'

'I'm a fantasy editor, Ciara. I love looking at maps. In fact, I have a whole book of—'

I shut up as she grabs my chin, tilting my face upward.

The moon is just as big as she promised. Just as brilliant. But all I can focus on are the points where she's touching me.

'It's a supermoon,' she says, her voice hushed. She drops her hand and eases her neck from side to side. 'The water looks nice.'

It does.

'Are midnight swims another tradition?' I joke, but she just nods.

'Yes.' And then she peels her shirt off.

Just like that.

No warning. No sly glance or teasing movement. She just grabs the hem and pulls it over her head before throwing it on top of the car. Her shorts go next: a quick flick of a button before they're pushed down to her ankles, and then she's standing in her bikini before me.

Thin black straps, red polka dots. I catch only a glimpse before she turns and strides across the sand. She doesn't even pause at the water's edge; just goes straight in as if she's never going to stop.

She does, of course. She lets the water get as high as her waist before turning and slowing down, moving languidly backwards until it reaches her chest. I'm too far away to see her expression, but I'm going to guess it's a real *you scared?* one.

I'm not scared. I'm terrified.

But what's a guy supposed to do when a girl invites him for a midnight swim?

I dump my T-shirt next to hers and kick off my sneakers and jeans before striding after her.

It's only when I reach the water that I realise how hardcore Ciara Sheridan is.

'What the *fuck*,' I curse as she throws back her head and laughs, delighted by my misery. Determined not to be undone, I keep going, not stopping until I'm right next to her. 'It's freezing.'

'It's the Atlantic Ocean.'

'I'm getting hypothermia.'

'You'll warm up to it,' she says, and takes an exaggerated breath before disappearing beneath the water. She pops up instantly, wheezing from the cold.

'Do it,' she gasps.

'No.'

'It will make you warmer.'

'I don't believe a word out of that mouth,' I say, and she plants her glacial hands on my shoulders. 'I am, like, ten times stronger than you,' I remind her as she tries to push me in.

She just clicks her tongue before stilling. The wicked glint in her eye is the only warning I get before she jumps, wrapping her equally icy legs around my body. My hands automatically go to her waist to keep her steady, but I lose my balance in the process, and she shrieks as I fall backwards, and we hit the liquid darkness with a loud splash.

I was right. I do not feel warmer.

I get back to my feet, shaking the water from my hair, only to find Ciara's grip on me hasn't lessened, and, when I rise, she does too, her body pressed tight against mine. Hip to hip. Chest to chest.

She's still smiling at me, her eyes as bold and bright as the moon, and I can't help but feel like she's something out of a storybook, or one of those legends from her father's books. Something not of this world. Because how can someone human feel this good, feel this right in my arms?

We watch each other for a long moment, and eventually, although I'll never admit it, I start to feel warmer, the initial shock giving way to something comfortable as my body gets used to the temperature. Maybe helped too by the woman in my arms.

'Do you know anything about astronomy?' she asks, looking at the sky.

'No.'

'Me neither.' Her chin dips back down and we're eye to eye once more. And I think she's going to let go. I think she's going to slip back into the water like something from a dream and she'll make a joke and I'll make another and on and on and on.

But she doesn't. She doesn't do any of that.

She just gets this very serious look before her hands move to cup my face, holding me there.

'I'm going to kiss you,' she says, and she waits for me to nod before closing the final gap between us. There's no build-up, no hitched breath or moment of anticipation. One second she's looking at me and the next, my eyes are closed and her lips are on mine and all I can think is thank *God*.

I haven't been able to get her out of my mind all day. If I'm being honest with myself, I haven't been able to get her out of my mind since I got here.

We're both hesitant at first, but we don't stay that way for long. Her mouth is hot and open against mine and a ball of heat barrels through me, spreading its way through every inch of my body until it feels as if my blood is boiling from within.

We move with the ocean, and I hold her tighter, my hands snaking down to her ass as I get a steadier grip. As soon as I do, her hips push against mine, small unconscious movements that make the water ripple gently around us, but there's nothing gentle about us now. The kiss deepens, and I want her so much it's as though a match someone struck has turned into a blaze, one that's made all the hotter because I know she feels it too. She's practically writhing against me, her breath growing ragged as she runs out of it, but still, she kisses me. Still, she presses her body to mine like she can't get enough.

I spread fingers up her back until they hit the small knot of her bikini top and I thank God for my scouting days because I know that one quick tug and it will come loose. One quick tug and she'll be bare in the moonlight, and however much she's willing to give tonight, I'll take it. I'll take it and I'll—

She breaks away a second before I hear it, the car engine impossibly loud in the quiet of the night. Ciara grips my shoulders as we look towards the beach, just as a pair of headlights sweep around the corner.

It's a campervan. Old and noisy, with surfboards attached to the roof. Just a couple of tourists bunking down for the night.

Neither of us moves, staying as still as statues as they continue driving until they reach the bend and disappear.

Once they're gone, I turn back to her, my nose skimming along her cheek, but her attention remains firmly fixed on the beach.

'Do you think they're hiding a body?' she whispers.

'Do I think they're *what*?'

Her eyes swing back to me. 'Too crimey?'

'Too crimey.'

'Sorry.' She licks the salt water from her lips, but her expression softens even as I feel the faint tremor of her body under my hands. She's cold.

'We should probably get back,' I say reluctantly.

'Yeah.' A line appears between her brows. And then, 'Thank you.'

'For what?'

'For looking at the moon with me.'

Something happens then between one breath and the next. Something sweet and piercing that makes me want to hold her closer and never let her go.

But she's already moving away, extracting herself from my grip and catching my hand in hers as we wade back to the beach.

CHAPTER TWENTY-FOUR

Ciara

Sam is very quiet. Very, very quiet. To the point where I wonder if I took things too far. Except I don't think I did. He matched my every move in the water, and though he doesn't say a word I can feel his attention as I drive, his gaze a searing heat on my cheek.

Still he says nothing. All the way home. All the way to the door.

Even when I let us in and turn to face him in the dark hallway to find his eyes fixed on me.

'Okay, then,' I say when he doesn't move, '... goodnight.'

It's as though I've said the magic word. I barely take a step before his hand grasps mine. And in the next breath he pulls me back, catching me in his arms and holding me to him.

The restraint he'd been holding himself under for the whole journey snaps. Our lips clash together as his hands delve under my shirt and mine go to his zipper, tugging it down as I slip a hand into his boxers and delight in his groan. He's hot and hard in my grasp, and he presses into my touch as I stroke until he tugs me away.

I push his trousers to his ankles, and he kicks them off before tugging my shorts down to join them. There's a frantic energy to both of us and I stumble back, trying to move this to anywhere but the hallway, only to almost trip over the stairs.

'Mother of—'

He kisses me again, cutting me off, and wraps his arms under my butt, gripping me tight as he lifts me into the air and starts to climb and, okay, this works too.

I trail kisses down his neck as I spear my fingers into his hair, trusting him not to drop me as he carries me up and up and up.

He sets me back down when we reach the landing, his mouth returning to mine, and the breaths I manage to gasp in aren't enough, but I don't care.

I pull him closer, clutching handfuls of his T-shirt as I chant his name in my head, my only thought. My only need.

Sam. Sam. Sam.

Only maybe I'm not thinking at all. Maybe I'm saying it out loud because his whole body shudders as he pushes me back, moving me until I fall with a bounce on to the bed.

The carefully tucked sheets under me tip me off that we're in his room, not mine, and I squirm against the unfamiliar mattress, getting more comfortable as he follows me down. My heart hammers against my chest as he licks a path up my throat, his fingers playing with the thin strap of my bikini bottom until I feel like I might combust.

'Wait,' I gasp, and he stops immediately, pulling back to check on me. 'Do you have a condom?'

'I have two.'

The snort I let out is so loud that he lets go of me altogether.

'I do,' he protests.

'Okay,' I say, fighting a smile. 'You just sounded so proud of yourself.'

'We're lucky I have them at all.'

'We need to work on your dirty talk,' I tease, only to fall silent when he reaches back to pull his T-shirt off.

'Get the damn condoms,' I mutter. He doesn't need to be told twice, taking two strides across the room to grab them from his wallet. He moves back to the bed so fast he almost trips on the clothing he just discarded.

The weight of what's happening hits me then, powerful enough that something threatens to burn behind my eyes, and I can only watch as he glides his hand across my cheek and down my neck, through the valley of my breasts and the soft curves of my stomach. My stomach, which moves up and down with each panting breath, is starting to glisten with sweat from the heat of the room and our bodies and this thing between us that makes me burn all over. I beg him silently to go all the way, to move down to where I need him most, but instead he lingers on the hem of my tank top, a question in his eyes.

I raise my arms in answer, and he pulls it off me and tosses it to the floor, where it's joined immediately by my bikini top because I'm getting too hot and bothered with all this foreplay and take that off myself. His lips twitch, the only sign that my impatience amuses him, as he leans in.

It's baffling how addicted I've become to kissing Sam Avery. It helps that he's good at it. Very, very good at it. But still, I know it's strange that after only a handful of times we already have a rhythm. As though I've learned him over a lifetime.

Because that's what it feels like. I know this man. I've known him since the moment I laid eyes on him. And it makes sense, doesn't it? The way just being around him calmed my soul more than anything else. The way, after a few weeks, the mere thought of him leaving made me feel as though the ground was splintering beneath me.

After a few minutes, he pulls away, pushing sweaty strands of hair from my face as he meets my gaze. His eyes glint in the dark, his pupils dilated. But the hungry, naked need in them softens as he stares down at me, gentling into a tenderness that steals the breath from my lungs.

'How do you like it?' he murmurs.

'Like this,' I tell him, watching as he loses the last of his clothes and rolls the condom on.

I sit up, pressing against his chest until he takes my place, sitting against the pillows as I swing my leg over his hips.

His head tips back; his eyes squeeze shut. A shift of our bodies and then I lower myself on to him, guiding him into me with small rocking motions that make him grunt.

'You good?' he asks hoarsely, and now I'm the one amused.

'Yeah. You sure you are?'

'Just thinking really hard about typefaces.'

'Maybe recite an ISBN or two?'

'That's actually a massive turn-on for me.'

I ease down another inch more until I'm fully seated on his lap, and we pause, our bodies tensed, and all I can think of is him crouched in the grass with me. Of his knee pressed against mine in Delaney's. Of the look on his face when I gave him the letter and the way he holds a pen and the smile he gets right before he laughs and how I think I could fall for him.

I really truly do.

And I don't know how I didn't realise it before.

'What?' he murmurs, and I shake my head.

'Nothing,' I whisper, even though it's everything, and I push those thoughts to the side, focusing only on the here and now and the sensations rippling through me.

When I feel ready, I start to move, exploring what feels good. Sam seems content for me to do so, letting me set the pace as his hands wander, caressing my body like a thing to be worshipped.

I plant my hands on his shoulders, moving faster and faster until my muscles start to protest, and even then I keep going, even when the sweat slicks our bodies and our movements grow clumsy with heated desperation.

Sam watches me all the while with a look of pure concentration, as if he's trying to commit every second of this to memory; and it's only when his fingers find where our bodies are joined that I realise he's studying me, learning what touches I like, what feelings I chase.

And what will send me over the edge.

My hips stutter as he takes over, and I gasp into his mouth as he kisses me with an intensity that sends sparks through my blood. His tongue moves hot and demanding against mine and I'm so close. So *close*.

'Ciara – *fuck*.' He breaks the kiss, swallowing hard as I grind down against him, shouting my release. He barely lets me take a breath as his arms band around me, holding me tight as his hips move fast, powering into me until suddenly he stills. His groan is the sexiest thing I've ever heard in my life.

Eventually, his hands move up and down to stroke my back, my hair. Eventually, I pull back and lean in for one more kiss, soft and sweet, before he releases me.

I flop to the side, boneless as a rag doll beside him.

Sam seems to feel the same way.

He collapses on to the bed, one hand on his stomach as he stares at the ceiling. I stare at his profile, basking in the afterglow, in just being next to him, and when I reach out a finger to trail a pattern down his arm, his head tilts towards mine.

'I think we're both really good at that,' I tell him.

'Ciara.'

'What? We are. We—'

I shriek before dissolving into laughter as he rolls over until he's on top of me.

'Two condoms?' I tease, and he just dips his head to mine and kisses me all over again.

Sleep is for the weak.

I turn away from the morning sun, nestling into the pillow as Sam shifts beside me. He doesn't like it when I try to move away from him, that much I've learned, and his grip around my hip tightens, drawing me back into him until I settle down again.

'Sam?'

He doesn't move. Though his breathing changed a few minutes ago so I know the man is definitely awake. Or halfway there, at least.

I run my finger down his nose, watching his brow furrow.

'*Sam.*'

'What?' he mumbles into the pillow.

'I proved my point.'

'Which one?'

'I didn't think once about where my hands were,' I tell him, and he cracks an eye open to peer at me. I smile. 'Not even when you—'

He's on me so fast I don't have time to react. I just let myself go, sinking into the mattress as he covers my body with his.

'I think you're right about the bedroom scenes,' I say between kisses. 'I think there should be more. And I think you should help me to practise. I think we needs lots and lots and lots of—'

'Ciara?'

I freeze as a voice yells from outside. Maddie.

'It's okay,' I tell Sam as he pulls back, propping himself above me. The doorbell rings. 'She can't get in.'

Sam just winces. 'She still has a key.'

'She has a *what*?'

A second later, I hear the front door open, and I shove him off me, scrambling from the bed.

'Ciara!' she calls, and I spin in a circle, looking for my clothes.

'Go!' I tell him, pulling on my bikini bottoms.

'What?'

'*Go.*'

'This is *my* bedroom.'

I throw the sheet over him as footsteps sound on the stairs and just manage to find my top on the floor as the door swings open.

'Boobs much?' I snap, holding it up to my chest.

Maddie stands in the doorway, her curls wild and her eyes narrowed as she takes me in. 'I heard voices.'

'I'm getting dressed.'

'And Sam's staying naked?' She rolls her eyes at the look on my face. 'I wasn't born yesterday. There are clothes all over the hallway, and I don't care.'

'That doesn't mean you can just barge—'

'You didn't answer your phone!' She holds up her hand. 'Whatever. It's fine. Congratulations on whatever this is. And look, I know you're working hard and I promise you that, as always, I am one hundred per cent here for you, but right now I need you to come with me and be my back-up because I need someone on my side here.'

'Side where?' I ask as Sam cautiously brings the sheet down to reveal his face. 'What's going on?'

And, in the most serious voice I have ever heard, Maddie utters one word.

'War.'

CHAPTER TWENTY-FIVE

Sam

I'll give her one thing: the girl knows how to make an entrance.

'How did you even find out about this?' Ciara asks as Maddie speeds towards the coast.

'Mary told me. She was watering the plants under Bobby Brennan's front window and heard him on the phone to his son. *His* wife works at the newsagent's by the beach.'

'Why was she watering—'

'She thinks he's in an open marriage.'

Ciara looks intrigued. 'Is he?'

'Unconfirmed. Anyway, that's not the *point*.' Maddie slaps the steering wheel, and I close my eyes as we make a particularly vicious turn at a speed that, again, should not be legal on roads this narrow. 'The point is his son's wife works at the newsagent's and *she* said this morning that the boards came down off the window and that someone was in there making noise. So she went to investigate and said she met an estate agent who was in there cleaning up because he was showing it to a prospective buyer this morning.'

'And you think that's Shane?'

'"Shane"?' Maddie blinks. 'Since when have you been on a first-name basis?'

'He's not that bad,' Ciara insists. 'He looked after you when you were drunk at Delaney's.'

'What are you talking about? Natalie said she picked me up from you.'

'And I was only there because Shane called me. He must have been minding you for at least forty minutes by the time I got there. You were wasted.'

'That's . . . ' Maddie scoffs. 'I'd remember that,' she says. 'I'd remember if he . . . ' She trails off. 'At Delaney's?'

'All coming back to you, huh?'

'Oh, whatever,' she mutters and presses down on the accelerator.

We're at the beach in no time. It's still early and only a few cars are around, some young families and a couple of walkers getting their steps in.

Maddie keeps going, though, driving up the coast until we come to a street of cheerful-looking shops. A corner store. A clothes boutique. A chemist. A gas station. And there, in the centre, is an empty slot.

The building is obviously vacant. The old newspapers covering the door and the FOR SALE sign overhead would tell you that. There's also the fact that it looks like it's about to fall down.

'*This* is the building she's been saving for?' I ask Ciara as we get out of the car.

'It's the only one available,' she whispers back.

'And has she asked herself why?'

Maddie doesn't pay attention to either of us, striding up to the window and cupping her hands around her eyes. It barely takes a second before she whirls around, victorious.

'I *knew* it,' she hisses as we join her.

I peer through the gaps in the newspapers and spy two men with their backs to us. One stands by the wall with a black clipboard in his hands, while Shane looks as if he's dressed for a construction site and is already rolling out a measuring tape as Maddie pushes the door open.

Ciara rushes after her. 'Maybe just wait until they're— Okay, we're going in. Yep. Sorry,' she adds to me, but I just shrug as she tugs me in after her.

The two men look up when we enter, their identical expressions of surprise turning to annoyance.

'Oh, for fuck's *sake*.' Shane's head falls back, and he stares hard at the ceiling as if he's looking for some divine presence to intervene.

The agent just smiles at her. 'Is there something I can—'

'*Yes*,' Maddie snaps. 'You can answer my calls for once. Or my emails. You've been avoiding me.'

'I understand you were interested in this location,' he begins patiently.

'More than interested! This place is mine.'

'Actually, this unit belongs to the owner, who has entrusted me to sell it on his behalf.' The mask of professionalism slips just a fraction. 'Ideally, to someone who can pay for it.'

'*I* will pay for it.'

'And I'll need to see proof of funds before I can—'

'I'm getting them! That's what I've been trying to tell you.'

'—proceed. Then, if you'd like to arrange a visitor with a surveyor, you can make an appointment, as Mr McCauley did.'

'A *private* appointment,' Shane adds, looking tired.

'Why do you even want it?' she exclaims. 'Why? Because I think it's because of me. I think it's because *I* want it. This place has been vacant for two years and do you know the reason for that? Do you? It's because it's *shite*. So shite that anyone with an ounce of sense would take one look and turn the other way. But not you.'

'And not you either.'

'Because I don't have another choice,' she says, spreading her arms wide. 'This is me scraping the bottom of the barrel. I know it and everyone else does, too, but I don't care because it's the same reason I have been working every day this summer. The same reason I have lost friendships and relationships and any hope of not developing premature wrinkles. I found my dream, and this is it. This shitty, stressful, financially ruinous dream is mine, and I'm not going to let you take it just because you think it might be a fun little challenge. There's a toilet in the kitchen. Did you know that?' She whirls on the estate agent. 'Did you tell him that?' she demands.

The man clears his throat. 'I think—'

'A *toilet* in the *kitchen*.'

Shane rubs a hand over his mouth as though he's fighting back a smile, but he just shakes his head.

'This is my second viewing,' he says. 'I've seen the toilet.' He takes a step towards her, and her shoulders stiffen, but she tilts her chin, meeting him head-on. 'I have more money than you,' he says.

'I have more history.'

'Let's see which the bank prefers, shall we?'

'Maddie, we should go.' Ciara tries to grab her hand, but Maddie shrugs her off.

'You think you'll survive more than the summer here?' she asks him. 'Tourists are all well and good, but if you don't have the locals, then you don't have anything.'

'Is that right?'

'It is,' she says, jabbing a finger at him. 'I grew up here. I've lived here my whole life. I know everyone, and they all like me because *I* am extremely likeable. People want me to succeed. They'll come out on the rainy days, and they'll come out on the cold ones, and they'll come out for *me*. You can go anywhere else in the county. Anywhere else in the *country*! I can't. This is my home. This is my community, so I need you to *find somewhere else*.' She speaks the last few words slowly and clearly, as though begging him to understand, and Shane falls quiet for a long, weighted moment. There's an assessing glint in his eyes as he examines her, and I'm guessing Maddie knows better than to make her case again, because she doesn't say another word.

None of us do.

And then Shane smiles. 'No.'

Ciara mumbles something that sounds a lot like *oh boy*.

'You'll be out of business within a year,' Maddie says. 'Less.'

'Not if you're my partner.'

'And if you think for a *second* that I'll— What?' She stares at him. 'What did you say?'

'I said, not if you're my partner. In the business sense, that is.'

'Could you be serious for one—'

'I am,' he says, crossing his arms. 'You just spent the last minute outlining all the reasons I won't be able to do this without a local. You're a local and you want to do this. Go into business with me.'

She scoffs, though the noise is a little high-pitched. 'No.'

'Why not? It's been made perfectly clear that this town isn't big enough for both of us. This is a solution.'

'What, like fifty-fifty?'

He shrugs, as calm as if he was offering her a cup of coffee. 'Maybe. We can discuss terms depending on how much you have to put in.'

'I ... you ...' She stumbles over her words, glancing around the room as though we're all in on some big prank. 'Why?' she finally asks.

'Because I like it here,' he says simply. 'And, magnificent though you are when you're mad, I'm not leaving just because you asked me to.'

The back of Maddie's neck goes bright pink, but Shane seems to take her silence as agreement and turns expectantly to the baffled agent.

'You said I could see the space out back?'

'I did?' He tears his gaze away from Maddie, blinking back into professionalism. 'I mean, I did. You can. There's more than enough room if you want to expand. You could build a separate storage area or knock it through for a private parking space like next door have ... ' The man's voice trails off as he leads Shane through the doorway at the back of the building.

Maddie jerks as though she's going to follow, but Ciara grabs her hand before she can move. 'What are you doing?' she whispers, although it sounds more like a hiss. 'You're not considering this, are you?'

'No!' A pause. 'Maybe.'

'You can't go into business with him. You don't know him.'

'I don't *not* know him.'

'Oh, my God.' Ciara turns to me, seeking support, but there's no way I'm wading into this one.

'I'm just a tourist,' I say, holding up my hands, and she shoots me a look before refocusing on Maddie.

'You have other options.'

'No, I don't. There's nowhere else around unless we build from scratch. And besides,' she adds, her back straightening, 'I can handle him.'

'Absolutely,' Ciara says. 'You totally can. But also, maybe you can't. What if this is a trap?'

'You're the one who was saying in the car how great he was.'

'I didn't say he was great. I said he was not bad, and that's because I thought you were coming here to *murder* him.'

'You want to look at this toilet or not?' Shane yells, and Maddie's eyes spark as she tosses her curls over her shoulders.

'Keep your pants on,' she shouts back. 'Give me ten minutes,' she adds to us, and then strides off after them, her flip-flops slapping against the bare concrete.

It's another forty minutes of Maddie passive-aggressively following Shane around before she finally drives us back to the house. She and Ciara argue the whole way there, but even I can see that Maddie isn't going to be swayed on this one. At least not yet. And I get it. To be so close to your dream. Who wouldn't barrel through the first door that's cracked open for them?

'What about up in Kilashan?' Ciara suggests hopefully. 'There are loads of vacant buildings there.'

'Yeah, because it's a shithole,' Maddie says. 'The pilgrims stopped going there years ago.'

'Pilgrims?' I ask.

Ciara twists in her seat to face me. 'Some guy in the eighties claimed he saw the Virgin Mary outside a pub.'

'And he didn't?'

'We'll never know for sure. But we do know that he'd had at least eight pints and fell asleep in some bushes.'

'He saw her when he got up to pee,' Maddie adds. 'Very sus. But a bishop came to check it out and everything.'

'I thought it was a cardinal,' Ciara says absently.

'The Pope said no, but it didn't stop them from making a shrine, did it? Gift shop, too. They sold these little bars of soap that smelt amazing. I think my aunt bought five of them when— What are you *doing*?'

Maddie breaks off in alarm as Ciara ducks down, cursing when she hits her head on the dashboard.

'Don't stop,' she hisses. 'Just drive.'

'Why are— Oh.'

I lean forward, peering through the windshield. We're almost at Ciara's house, but on the usually empty road several cars are now parked, and a handful of people mill about, taking pictures.

'Red alert,' Maddie calls and drives even faster. Ciara stays hidden, and I twist in my seat, watching them as they zoom past. They pay us little attention, but they're all clustered around her driveway, obviously looking for the house.

'Are there usually so many fans like that?' I ask.

'Never,' Maddie says. 'Is it a Ravian anniversary?'

'I don't think so.' Ciara gets back up, pushing the hair out of her eyes. She doesn't look happy. 'Let's just go to Delaney's.'

'You don't want to call the guards?'

'They'll go away soon.'

Maddie makes the turn for the village as my phone chimes in my pocket, and I take it out to see Casey's number.

'Hi, boss,' I say, and Ciara glances back at me. 'Now's not a great time. Can I call you back?'

'I'm afraid this can't wait.'

'What's happened?' I ask, and strain to hear over the rush of wind in my ears. Ciara frowns.

'Someone's leaked it,' Casey says. 'Someone's leaked the book.'

CHAPTER TWENTY-SIX

Ciara

The news is everywhere. Every social media platform. Every blog. Every entertainment site. My only consolation is that they've only got half the story. They know there's a book but don't know who's writing it. For now, I'm in the clear.

I can cling to that much, at least.

'No one's getting through that,' Ronan calls from the pub door. He slaps the wood with his palm and double-checks the lock. 'You're sure Maddie will be all right?'

'She said she's going to "disperse" them,' I say. 'I think it's best not to ask questions.'

'Certainly never failed me,' he agrees as Sam emerges from the back room, his phone in one hand and a glass of water for me in the other. He's been on and off with Casey for the last while and puts him back on speaker now as he sits in the booth beside me.

'Hey,' he chides when he sees my own phone in my hand. 'Don't look at that.'

I ignore him, continuing to scroll through a sea of comments.

'Ciara. Come on. Nothing good is going to come of reading that stuff.'

'They're not all mean.' Only the ones I'm paying attention to.

Sam and Ronan share a look before Ronan plucks the thing from my hand.

'You have no self-control,' Sam says as I sputter, and Ronan makes a show of putting it behind the bar.

Whatever.

I know he's right, even though I hate to admit it. It's just that at some point in the last hour, I've become a glutton for punishment.

There's a lot of excitement. A lot of exclamation marks. But not everyone is happy about the book. A lot of them are furious. They don't think the series should be touched. And the rest just want to know who's writing it. A gazillion forums and threads have appeared, all dedicated to discussing who it could be.

My name's come up a few times, which I guess should be expected, but it's still startling.

'I just don't understand how they found out,' I say for the millionth time.

'Who else knows about the book?' Casey asks over the phone.

'Just Maddie. But she's known from the start.' And no way would she leak it. No one here would. 'There was a woman at the beach who saw me writing it,' I say. 'She said she was a fan, but I don't think she realised what it was. She never said anything. But maybe?'

'It's unlikely, if she didn't ask you about it at the time. Anyone else?'

'No one.' I pause. 'Except . . . well, Mary did—'

Sam's eyes dart to me. 'Mary knows?'

I frown at his tone, feeling weirdly defensive of her since she helped me with that reader at the beach. She's a gossip, but she's *our* gossip. 'She wouldn't say anything.'

'You sure about that?'

'Yes.'

'But she's—'

'It wasn't her,' I say sharply, and Casey clears his throat.

'It doesn't matter how it happened,' he says. 'All we can deal with right now is what we're going to do going forward. I have Laura on the phone here, Ciara. She works with Sam in editorial.'

'It's nice to meet you,' a woman's voice chimes.

'You too,' I say, unable to help myself as I glance sideways at Sam. 'I've heard so much about you.'

He gives me a look.

'I'm going to get right to it,' she says. 'I'm sorry that this happened, but in these kinds of situations fan theories tend to run wild, and we want to put a stop to that. I think the best thing to do right now is to be truthful and explain exactly what's going on to our readers.'

'What?' I sit up, panicked, and Sam immediately jumps in.

'We're not releasing Ciara's name as the author.'

'Oh, no,' Laura says quickly. 'Don't worry. I'm talking purely about the book just existing at this stage. It's a good news story, and we should treat it as one. But we need to control it. I think we should make an appearance at Ravicon this Saturday.'

I suck in a breath as Sam goes still beside me. Neither of us answers.

'Are you still—'

'We're here,' Sam says, his eyes on me. 'I get where you're coming from, but I don't think that's an option. Even if she's just representing Frank's estate, if Ciara shows up, people might—'

'Sorry, Sam, I didn't mean Ciara,' Laura interrupts. 'I meant you.'

'Me?' His surprise would be funny if I weren't freaking out.

'Unless you want to break the news now, Ciara? Get ahead of the game?' I can hear the hopefulness in her voice, but the thought fills me with such anxiety that I don't even consider it.

'Can't we just put out a statement?' Sam asks when I don't respond.

'Yeah, if we want to be bad at our jobs,' Laura says bluntly, and despite everything I decide that I kind of like Sam's work nemesis. 'Look, obviously this isn't how we wanted the news to break, but it couldn't have come at a better time. Ravicon is the best place for us to speak directly to his readers and you're already in the country. It's all anyone is going to talk about anyway.'

Sam opens his mouth, but I put a hand on his knee before he can respond, and when he looks at me I nod.

You sure, he mouths, and no, I'm not sure, but Laura's right. We have to do something.

'If you think we should,' I whisper, and don't miss the flicker of relief on his face even as my chest tightens. It's the right choice. I just don't like it.

'Okay,' he says out loud. 'So long as I know what I'm saying, I can do it.'

'Great,' Laura says briskly. 'There's a flight that night we can book you on and then Casey has agreed we should have an all-hands-on-deck meeting on Monday to—'

'Flight?' Sam interrupts. 'What flight?'

'To New York,' Laura says.

Sam's eyes flash to mine, but it takes me a moment – one distracted, lost moment – before I realise what's she's saying.

'We need you back here,' Casey continues when Sam doesn't say anything. 'I know you wanted a few more weeks, but there's too much work to do now.'

He keeps talking, but it's like he's speaking in a different language, one I can't even hear owing to the sudden roaring in my ears. New York? He can't go back to New York. He can't—

'You're doing great work, Ciara,' Casey says, and I zone back in with a snap. 'I know you're worried about this, but you don't need to be. Your only job here is to focus on the book.'

'Okay,' I say weakly. Though I don't know how I can do that when right now all I can focus on is the man sitting beside me. The one who doesn't look any happier than I do.

'Could you give us one second?' Sam asks abruptly, and doesn't wait for a response before putting us on mute. 'I don't have to do it,' he says to me. 'Any of it.'

'Of course you do.'

'Ciara—'

'I'm okay,' I lie. 'I get it. This is your job.' And I'm just a part of it. The little-girl pity party in me is having a field day, but the adult me smiles, trying to be encouraging.

His dark eyes study me, but I don't know what he's looking for. What he wants.

'Would it be better if you went back?' I press, and his jaw clenches.

'Yes,' he says eventually. 'Casey put me on this book. That means that I'm in charge of it. That every decision should go through me. It would be easier for everyone if I were in the office.'

'Then that's where you should be.' The words sound forced even to my own ears, and I nudge his knee with mine. 'Especially since Laura seems to be in charge right now.'

He doesn't smile at my attempt at lightness. Doesn't even pretend to, and, when he doesn't respond, I lean forward and unmute the call. 'Okay,' I say. 'Keep going.'

'Sam?' Laura asks.

'Yeah.' He clears his throat, pulling his gaze from me. 'Okay. What are we putting out in the meantime?'

Laura launches into the details, saying things like *statement* and *sign off* and *Entertainment Weekly*. Sam jumps in every now and then, switching to editor mode before my eyes, but I say nothing. Do nothing.

I felt as though my world was just starting to make sense again, and now it's being ripped apart in real time. And when Ronan sets a small glass of clear liquid before me, a gentle expression on his face, I don't even ask what's in it before snatching it off the table and knocking it back in one.

We spend the rest of the day at Ronan's before returning to the house. Thankfully the people lurking on the road have gone by the time we get back, Maddie having done as she promised.

Once inside, I say something about needing a shower and take the stairs two at a time, letting the water wash the day away before I dress for bed. It's well before my usual time, but I'm so exhausted I can't even think.

'You've been staring at the wall for five minutes now.'

I look up to find Sam standing in the doorway. His hair is wet and he's changed his clothes and the thought of him leaving makes me want to throw something at him.

'The only way to know that is if you've been staring at me for that long, too,' I say instead.

'I don't deny it.'

'You can come in,' I tell him, and he hesitates only briefly before sitting beside me on the bed. He smells like my soap.

'You okay?' he asks.

'No.' And then, 'I want to go with you to Ravicon.'

He frowns at that. 'You don't have to.'

'I want to. I mean, not *attend*, but I could go with you to Dublin. Especially since you're leaving straight after.' My throat closes up as soon as I say the words and an awkward silence stretches between us.

Sam is the first to break. 'Ciara—'

'I don't want to talk about it,' I interrupt. 'I know we should, but I don't want to. Not tonight.'

He seems torn but relents, as if knowing one wrong move will break me. 'Of course you can come,' he says quietly. 'You can stay in the hotel if you don't want to go in. The convention's been booked out for a few weeks, but they set rooms aside for panellists.'

'And you're going to do a panel?'

'They're calling it "The Future of Ravian". It was supposed to be on fan fiction but slotting me in there made the most sense. I'll be as vague as possible about everything else, and that's it.'

'That's it,' I echo.

And then he'll get on a plane and go back to New York and I don't want him to go.

'I'm fine,' I say, even though he didn't ask. 'Honestly. I'm just tired. It's been a long day and I'm worried about Maddie and now, with the book, and I'm just . . . really, really tired.'

Sam stays silent, letting me babble even though I wish he wouldn't. I wish he'd order me back to the office, tell me to get to work. But he just sits there, his leg pressed against mine and his gaze on me, and when I try to take a breath it shudders, as though something's stopping it from coming in all the way.

'Shit,' I mutter because I don't cry. I *never* cry. I get moody and quiet and don't speak to people for days, but I don't *cry*. But now the tears are slipping down my cheeks and my throat feels tight and my head feels full and Sam's putting an arm around me, not drawing me into his side but on to his lap, and I wrap myself around him like a goddamn koala.

His hand creeps up into my hair, and I bury my head into the crook of his neck, inhaling deeply.

We stay like that for so long that I must fall asleep. I must, because one moment my eyes are closed and the next, they're open and we're lying on my bed above the sheet, as wrapped up in each other as two people can be with their clothes still on.

Sam is dead to the world, and I spend a few minutes just staring at him, trying to commit every inch of him to memory, because he's leaving. He's leaving and I'm too scared to ask him to stay because I don't know what I'll do if he says no. I don't think I could take it.

I watch him until my eyes grow heavy again, and, this time, I fall asleep to the sound of his heartbeat beneath me.

CHAPTER TWENTY-SEVEN

Sam

On Saturday, Ciara and I leave early to drive to Dublin.

Or to the outskirts of Dublin, at least.

Turns out Ravicon is being held in one of those big, anonymous hotels near the airport. It's not the most scenic of surroundings, but it's one of the few places in the city that can host the huge number of people visiting over the weekend.

We're driving in separate cars since I need to drop off the rental and she'll need to get home, but she solved the issue by keeping up a phone call the entire time. I think she meant it to be fun, but all it makes me think about is how I'll have to get used to that. How, from tomorrow, this is how I'll hear her voice. Through a speaker. On a screen. An ocean away.

The past few days have been strange, though neither of us admit it. We haven't spoken about what comes after today. As though if we don't then it doesn't happen. But it's not as if we've had much time to speak, anyway. I've been busy dealing with the leak, and Ciara's been writing. Or at least she keeps telling me she has. All I've seen her do is scowl at her computer screen for several hours a day and then refuse to show me anything. So I guess we're back to that again. The weather hasn't helped, either. The long-promised summer storms are on their way, and the thick cloud overhead gives the world a gloomy, desolate feel, as if everything's been stripped of colour.

Our hotel is across the road from the convention centre, and the room we're put in is a standard one. Basic and clean, if a little worn, with a stunning view over the dumpsters. Ciara barely gives it a second glance as we come in, just dumps her bag by the bed and locks herself in the bathroom.

My attention goes to the large gift bag left on the desk.

Dear panellist, reads a generic greeting card. *As a welcome to Ravicon, we enclose a small selection of what will be available for purchase over the weekend.*

List of suppliers, *be sure to tag us*, etc. etc. etc. Guest passes, water bottles. I grab a decent-looking pen from the top of the pile because you can never have too many pens and examine the fridge magnet.

'Does this hotel have a spa?' Ciara asks as she re-emerges.

'Nope.'

'Does it have a pool?'

'No.'

'Does it have *anything*?'

'It's a three-star budget airport hotel. You'll be lucky if they make you a cheese sandwich.'

'I want to at least get drunk later.'

'I'll see what I can do. Hey.' I draw out a packet of Ravian-themed cookies. 'Snacks.'

'We get presents?' She wanders over as my hand closes around something soft, and I draw out a cheap red wig.

'Cute,' she says. 'Suits you.'

'It's Maeve's.'

'Then we should give it back to her.'

'Funny.'

She slips the wig from my hand, draping it over my head. 'Please wear it.'

'No.'

She spins away from me, opening the snack as I unpack my notes. She's trying, I know she is, pretending not to care when she's hating all of this, and not for the first time I wonder if I should have asked her to stay at home. We could have said our goodbyes in Carrigwest. Dealt with it properly instead of stretching it out. But it's too late for that now.

She flicks through the television channels as I take a shower and change into fresh clothes. After that, it's time to go, but I linger, feeling the need to say something. Ciara acts like I'm not even there, pretending to be absorbed by a cooking show even as her shoulders visibly stiffen.

'I'll be a couple of hours and then I'll come straight back,' I say eventually.

'Sure.' She smiles at me. It's a fake one. 'I hope it goes well.'

'If you need me—'

'I'm fine, Sam. I'm going to work. I'll see you later.'

'We'll talk then.'

'We will.'

My phone vibrates in my pocket, and I take it out to see Lizzie calling me. I silence it, focusing on Ciara, who's now working her way through the snacks.

'I'll text you before I go on,' I say, and she calls *good luck* as I close the door.

For a moment, I just stand there looking at it, feeling in my gut that this is the wrong thing to do, before I force my feet to turn and head to the elevators.

It's a short, sweltering walk to the convention centre, but the hall has air-conditioning at least. Giant fans that keep the place blissfully cool. They'd probably have to cancel the whole event if they didn't. The centre is packed. I didn't look up the numbers, but it has to be a couple of thousand, judging by the crowd around me. People of all ages rove around in costumes and themed T-shirts, bags of merchandise clenched in their hands. There are babies in strollers and groups of laughing teenagers and grown men studiously examining replica figurines. I hear a dozen different accents. A dozen different languages. Frank Sheridan's reach was worldwide, and all the world is here.

I sign in at the desk, am given a booth map and sent on my merry way.

I barely take two steps before I see the first bookstore. There'll be more, but this looks like the biggest, with the books and board games and branded stationery. The more expensive stuff is up front, and I pause at a display of gift items, checking to see what they have.

'You seen this one?'

A middle-aged man approaches on my left, pointing to an illustrated edition of the first book. We published it a few years ago.

'The details are incredible,' he continues, peering at a battle drawing.

I feel a burst of pride. 'They are.'

He admires it for a few seconds before flipping it closed again. 'Pricey, though. They charge anything these days.'

'Colour printing is much more expensive than black and white,' I protest, and the guy blinks at me. 'And printing costs have increased by forty per cent in the past few years.'

'It's still sixty bucks.'

'But the shipping alone means— Okay. Yeah.'

He wanders off, and I straighten the stack he messed up a little more passive-aggressively than I should. I can practically hear Lizzie in my ear. *You're being you again.*

I sigh, and am doing a quick glance around to make sure all our other titles are front and centre when my eyes catch on a table towards the back.

A few years ago, for the fifteenth anniversary we re-released the first edition with the same cover as the one I used to read in the school library. The one I kept checking out until my parents bought me my own copy. It's the kind of cover that went wildly out of fashion before becoming painfully cool recently. The title in big, bold text, the cover a colourful illustration featuring a young Finn holding up his sword to the stars. And maybe it's because of where I am, or because I've been working on these books all summer, but just the sight of it pulls at something in me, and I buy it, even though there are shelves of them back in the office.

It feels different buying it in a bookshop. Purer. As though this is the way it's meant to be.

And all I can think about as I flip through it is that I wish Ciara were here with me. That she could see this. The goodwill. The excitement. It's almost like I want to say, *See? We're not all bad.*

'Mr Avery?'

At the entrance to the panel rooms, a blond-haired teenager in a bright orange vest bounds up to my side. He's got a lanyard and a headset and a grin as wide as his face as he introduces himself. 'Simon Ridley. I'm here to take you backstage. We're so excited you're joining us.'

'Great.'

'*So* excited,' he repeats with an enthusiasm bordering on hysterical, and okay, maybe it's best she's not here.

I follow him away from the chaos and into a long corridor. Other events are already under way judging by the murmur of voices from behind the closed doors, but Simon leads me to a small green room, which consists of a few chairs and a table of snacks. There's no one else inside.

'The others are out watching another panel,' Simon explains.

'Others?'

'Yep.' He checks the clipboard. 'Alison Smith moderating. And Austen Mitchell is joining you on stage for a reader's perspective.'

Austen's name rings a bell, but I can't figure out why. 'I thought it was just Alison and me.'

'The panel's on the future of Ravian,' he explains. 'We've brought storytellers from both sides.'

Fan fiction.

That's where I know the name. Austen Mitchell is one of the biggest names in the fandom. He'd been writing short stories and sometimes full-length novels for years online, which was completely fine until he tried to sell them as an official continuation of the series. It's as though the guy woke up one day and decided his work was too important for such trivial things like US copyright law. I was only in my second year at Richardson Books when we sued for infringement. He dropped it pretty quickly, but the guy had an attitude about it that he's yet to shake.

I go to shoot off an email to Casey, annoyed that we weren't told this in advance, only to see another missed call from Lizzie. Crap.

'Did you ever meet him?'

I look up to find Simon still here, watching me. 'Who?' I ask, before I realise he means Frank. 'No. I've met his daughter.'

Simon's eyes go wide. 'I thought she died.'

'She – what?'

'My sister said she died.'

'She's extremely alive,' I say, alarmed. 'She's just private.'

'Right.' His neck goes bright pink. 'Sorry. My mistake.' He takes a step back, embarrassed. 'I'll come to get you when it's time to start.'

'And maybe tell your sister not to go around spreading rumours in the meantime,' I begin, but my annoyance snuffs out as soon as I say the words, something tugging at the back of my mind.

'Please help yourself to some fruit,' Simon continues, but I'm barely listening as he beats a hasty retreat out of the door.

Frowning, I unbutton the top of my shirt, and look at my phone. The missed call notification from Lizzie stares up at me, and my stomach sinks.

I've been so sure the leak came from someone in the village.

But what if it didn't?

CHAPTER TWENTY-EIGHT

Ciara

Less than a minute after Sam leaves, I stand at the window, watching the crowds outside. I'd been trying to play it cool beforehand. I don't know why. It's not as though I needed to impress Sam with how blasé I am. I just didn't want him to worry about me. Something which I obviously failed at, seeing as how he looked as if he expected me to have a breakdown as soon as he closed the door.

I mean, he's not far off.

I shouldn't have come here.

I should have stayed at home and said my goodbyes. I should be finishing my book. I should at least close the hotel curtains.

Any one of those options would be better than what I'm doing now. Standing eating dry Ravian cookies while I watch some of my father's most ardent readers funnel across the road to the hotel. All to celebrate him. All while I stay away.

My phone buzzes in the pocket of my shorts, and I take it out, hoping for some distraction, only to see my second official text alert of the day.

Status: Orange Wind Warning.

Storm Bessie is well and truly on her way, and the Irish meteorological service is taking no chances despite the innocent-sounding name. Probably as bored as we are by reporting nothing but sunshine for the past three months. I'm not too worried, though. It's not supposed to hit Dublin until the early hours of the morning, and Sam's flight will already have left by then.

So, you know. That's great.

Laughter draws my attention back outside, and I watch a group of teenage girls grab at each other before dashing between stationary traffic.

'I used to have fun once,' are words I actually say out loud, and then I make myself step back from the window, brushing cookie crumbs from my chest as I stare at the wig on the bed.

I don't know what it is that's chipped away at my usual wariness when it comes to his fans. Maybe I've been subconsciously readying myself for events like this, or maybe all these weeks working on the book have started to rub off on me. Perhaps it's because freaking Sam out just by showing him a pencil belonging to my dad has become my new favourite hobby.

Or maybe I'm just tired of hiding myself away.

Before I can second-guess myself, I stride over to the bed and upturn the gift bag. More snacks and stationery tumble out, joining the long mass of plastic hair.

It would have been better if they'd given us a soldier's costume. At least that would just be a mask. But no.

I get the wig.

Ten minutes later, I'm in the convention centre. No one gives me a second glance, and I just show one of the passes that was included in the gift bag and then I'm through.

It's more than a little overwhelming. It's the largest one I've ever been to, but it's not my first. Dad took me to one or two when I was younger, but I grew bored of them. The large, deafening spaces, the standing on your feet for hours. I would sit in the back room and play video games on my phone. It's been years since then, so I'd forgotten how intense they could be. How loud.

Everywhere I look, I see my dad. T-shirts with his face on them, with quotes from him. There are even a few people *dressed* like him, and, while I guess some might find it flattering, it borders on weird for me, and so I try instead to focus on the booths where they're selling everything under the sun. Posters and figurines. Umbrellas and sweaters. Shoes. Stickers. Pyjamas. Anything that could be branded is branded. I even see the discontinued Maeve make-up line they launched when the film came out.

There are smaller stalls too, where people sell homemade artwork and everything from recipes to pottery based on my father's world.

It's times like this when the whole thing still boggles me. How vast his reach was. How many people he inspired.

Not bad for an English teacher scribbling at his kitchen table at five a.m.

I feel a wash of pride as I take it all in, one so strong that it overpowers any nerves, and I smile when I catch the eye of a young woman behind one of the booths and purchase a woven bracelet of the kind described in the books. I make a mental note to include one in mine, and head towards the back, where there's a sign for the panels. I find the nearly full room where Sam's one is supposed to start, but there's no one on stage yet. On a whim, I keep going, heading down a side corridor where there are far fewer people. There's no one to stop me, and I pause by a door with a handwritten sign taped to it saying *Guests*.

I prise it open, peering inside.

I don't see anyone at first. Just an ambitious snack table and some boxes of books. And then Sam appears, slumped over in a chair. He doesn't notice me, too busy staring at his phone as it rings out in his hands.

I'm about to step into the room when the call connects.

The phone is on speaker. 'Hey,' a female voice says. One that doesn't sound like Laura. 'Sorry, the boys were at soccer practice, so I thought I'd—'

'Was it you?' Sam interrupts.

'What was me?'

'Did you tell someone about the book?'

I freeze where I am, the glow I'd been feeling vanishing in an instant.

'Lizzie,' he prompts, and I grow only more confused. His sister?

His sister, who doesn't respond.

Sam's entire body tenses. 'Liz—'

'I swear I didn't mean to!'

'Are you fucking kidding me?'

I startle, as shocked by his angry tone as she must be, because all of a sudden it's as though a dam has burst, and the words come pouring out of her.

'I swear, Sam. I promise. I was at book club and Joanne was there and you *know* how she is and she was going on and on about her new house and all her travelling and I'd had a few wines and I just wanted to get a word in edgeways and mentioned you were in Ireland working on it. It just slipped out, but she wasn't even that interested. She told me she hasn't even read them! But her husband works at *Variety* and she must have said something, and I'm sorry. I'm so sorry.'

'Do you have *any idea* what kind of shitstorm you've caused?'

'I know,' she says, sounding miserable. 'I know how big this is for you. And I know Casey is probably furious.'

'He will be when he finds out it's because of me.'

'I'll talk to him. He likes me. I made him potato salad once.'

Sam drags a hand through his hair as Lizzie's voice turns hesitant.

'Are you going to tell Ciara?'

'No,' he huffs, and I feel sick at the way the word whips through me. 'I'm doing enough damage control with her as it is. The last thing I need is for her to—'

Applause from the main hall thunders behind me, cutting him off, and Sam looks my way, hanging up as soon as he sees me.

I've never seen him look so guilty.

For a moment, we just stare at each other, and then I step inside, pressing my back against the closed door. It takes me a second to speak.

'You weren't going to tell me?'

Sam's face pales. 'I don't . . . She didn't mean—'

'I heard,' I say, my voice bitter even to my ears. 'And thank God I did, or I never would have known.'

Standing here, I realise how much I'd come to trust him. How I'd completely given myself over to him. My father. My writing. Myself. And he was going to keep this from me? Hurt blooms like a bruise inside, along with something deeper and heavier. Something like betrayal.

'She didn't mean to say anything,' Sam continues.

'You shouldn't have told her in the first place.'

'That happened before I met you. Before I knew what it meant. I told you we're close. I tell her everything.'

Of course he does. He tells her everything and he's leaping to her defence because he's her brother and she's family. Family that he'll go back to because he's not going to stay forever. He's going to leave, and I'll be here and we'll go to talking only through emails and edits and a phone call every few weeks.

'Please don't be mad at her,' Sam says, and I see red.

'Why wouldn't I be mad at her? She spilled my secret for *bragging rights*. And you were going to pretend you never knew! You were going to lie to me.'

Damage control. I want to yell at him some more when I remember his words, but I can't. I'm frozen. My thoughts spiralling and my stomach twisting until I feel as if I'm going to throw up.

My feelings come second – the book comes first. Why am I *always* second place to these books?

'Mr Avery?'

We both whirl towards the door as a teenager steps inside. He doesn't seem to notice the tension in the room, barely taking me in as he sends a cheerful nod my way.

'Time to shine!'

Sam looks as though he's about to snap at the kid but stops himself at the last minute.

'I'll be there in one second,' he promises. 'Just give me a minute,' he adds as the boy is about to object.

There's a beat of silence as he goes. I feel I want to cry.

'Can you stay here?' Sam asks. 'Please? I have to go do the panel.'

I shouldn't have come. It's all I can think. *I shouldn't have come I shouldn't have come I shouldn't have—*

'Ciara.' He's pleading with me now, but I can barely hear him over the rushing in my ears. 'I have to do this.'

'I know.'

'I'll be right back.'

I nod, and it must look convincing enough, because he finally edges away, his eyes on me the whole time as if he's afraid I might bolt. But I don't. I stand there watching him go until the door swings shut behind him, leaving me alone.

CHAPTER TWENTY-NINE

Sam

Okay, so I fucked up.

I massively, massively fucked up.

My mind spins uselessly as I follow Simon out of the room, trying to ignore everything in me that's screaming to go back to her. To wipe that look of betrayal off her face and fix this. I needed just a bit more time.

As it is, the panel is directly across the corridor, and I blink at the unexpected flash of cameras as Simon opens the door. The room is packed with hundreds of people, and it takes me a dazed second before I can take it all in.

'Sam?'

A woman approaches. Black dress. Dark hair. Chunky turquoise hoops in her ears.

'Alison Smith,' she whispers, holding out her hand. 'We talked via email?'

We did.

Alison Smith, owner of Ravian's largest fan site. I shake her hand

and force myself to smile as she leads me to the side of the low stage, where I'm handed a microphone.

A man who must be Austen is already waiting. He's tall and bearded, with glasses that look too small for his face. He also doesn't acknowledge me, too busy smiling at the people in the front row, who seem thrilled just to be near him.

The room hushes as Alison gets on stage. I'm introduced first and climb the two steps to polite applause before taking the furthest chair.

I don't get stage fright, but I feel instantly better when everyone's attention moves from me. I'm not a personality here. They're more interested in what I have to say than in who I am, a fact further proved when Austen gets a more rapturous welcome. Fan fiction writers are big in this world.

Alison is just taking her seat when the door I'd come through cracks open again. No one notices but me as Ciara slips through. The wig was a good idea. Half the room is wearing something similar and so no one gives her a second glance when she settles against the wall, watching me.

'Sam?'

My gaze snaps to Alison.

'We're going to have to address the elephant in the room. A few days ago, several outlets broke the news that Richardson Books was working on the tenth novel in the Ravian series. You didn't deny it. In fact, you confirmed it.'

'We did,' I say, and can't help my smile at the excited murmuring in the crowd.

A camera flashes and Alison leans forward. 'So why keep it a secret until now?'

'Because it's not finished yet,' I say honestly. 'We weren't trying to trick anyone. We just wanted the manuscript completed before we went out to the wider world.'

'Which dispels the rumour that Frank finished it before he died.'

'Yeah, that would have made things a lot easier.' Laughter sounds. I relax a little. 'He'd started researching it,' I explain. 'He'd made some rough notes, knew the overall story. But there's a lot of work still to do.'

'But you're sticking to his plan.'

'We are. And we're confident about where we're going. I think readers both old and new are going to be very happy.'

'So long as you haven't fed it into an AI machine,' Austen says.

I smile his way. 'We haven't.'

'And you keep saying *we*,' Alison says. 'Obviously you've already chosen a writer to continue his legacy. I presume you can't say anything on that just yet.'

'I can't.'

'And it's not me,' Austen quips with a look at the crowd. There's more laughter alongside some disconcerted whispers. I try very hard not to look at Ciara.

'Austen brings up a point, though,' Alison says. 'How did you pick the writer? Was there an audition process?'

'I'm afraid I can't get into any of that,' I say as Austen huffs.

'More secrets,' he says.

'We're just asking for patience while we get the book done – that's our focus at the moment,' I say, ignoring him. 'We didn't intend for the news to come out so soon. That's why I'm unable to share anything else right now.'

'But that brings up another point,' Alison says. 'Some people might rally *against* publishing *The Last Mountain* if Frank Sheridan wasn't the one to write it. Did it ever occur to you to simply leave this be?'

'No. Frank wanted this series to be finished. He told us he did. And it's my promise to you that we're going to do everything we can to honour these characters and his storytelling. We also have the full approval of the Frank Sheridan estate and—'

'His daughter,' Austen interrupts, and I tense. 'You mean his daughter.'

'His daughter is the executor of his literary estate,' I confirm after too long a pause. 'Anything to do with him must go through her for approval. Again, as per his wishes.'

But Austen isn't done. 'Frank was always easygoing with that kind of stuff,' he continues, and I'm starting to understand why this gets under Ciara's skin so much. He says Frank's name like they were best friends, when I'm pretty sure Casey said Frank couldn't stand the guy. 'He gave back to his community,' Austen continues. 'He encouraged creativity. Can we expect more of the same going forward, or is there going to be a shutdown now we have to go through *her*?'

A sting of anger races through me at the derision thrown into that last word. At Ciara.

'We don't have any problem with inspiring other writers,' I say. 'Copyright infringement aside.'

Austen says nothing, that insipid smile still on his face. But I swear the man's jaw ticks.

Alison glances at her notes. 'Why don't we—'

'See, as a reader, my main worry is that they approach this as something purely for the masses,' Austen continues, speaking over her. 'I bet you all the money in my wallet right now that they'll have brought someone in who does exactly what they're told. Sticks to a beat sheet and plays it safe, instead of giving the fans what they really want.'

'Which is?' Alison prompts.

'I mean, if it was me...' He trails off with a laugh as some people in the audience shout encouragement for him to continue. Not everyone is on his side, though; I clock a few people giving him the stink eye. 'It was Finn's other life that always interested me most,' he says. 'Before I realised I could write my own versions, I used to stay up for hours imagining a separate story where he travels to the fifth mountain and rescues Lord Guerin. And the dark dawns never happen.'

'But if he travels to the fifth mountain, then no one meets Maeve at the cliff,' Alison says.

'Well, that's the point. I believe that Maeve was meant to die. I do,' he adds when murmurs start. 'I think that's what Frank intended. Her death would have given Finn a more hardened outlook that would have served him better. That's the journey he started on, even if it wasn't how he ended up.'

'What do you think made Frank change it?'

'Editors, maybe,' Austen says with a goading look at me that I pretend not to see. 'Commercial pressure. The fourth book came out at the same time the movie was announced, and, not to be sexist, but these things are gendered. Maybe it was Hollywood. All I know is that his hand was forced in order to bring in that female audience.'

A smattering of applause, mainly from the men in the crowd, echoes around the room. My gaze flicks to Ciara to find her scowling.

'Frank Sheridan wrote those books,' I say before Alison can move on. 'Him and only him, for almost twenty years. It's only natural for a writer to change as they grow. But I can tell you right now that he wasn't swayed by anybody but his own characters.'

'That's not true, though, is it?' Austen asks. 'He spoke all the time about outside influences. Other authors, his readers. His daughter. In fact, he said he initially wrote the character of Maeve for her. That the whole story changed *because* of her.'

'And that's your issue with it?' I ask, all patience lost. 'That Maeve took on a central role in the books?'

'At the *expense* of Finn. He betrayed his original story for her. And when readers ask why, we get ignored. Even now, we're not listened to. When Frank died, we had over five thousand signatures asking his daughter to hand the rights over to the fans so that we could end Finn's story properly. We never even got an acknowledgement.'

I can hardly believe what I'm hearing. 'So you're pissed because Ciara Sheridan didn't respond to a half-assed petition complaining about her recently deceased father?'

'Well, it wasn't exactly a surprise that she didn't bother to respond,' Austen says. 'This is the woman who rode on his coattails for three mediocre books and then disappeared off the face of the planet. And I'd hoped,' he adds, raising his voice when I go to argue, 'that when she took on the estate she'd finally understand, but she's shown over and over again that she doesn't care about the fans. So no, I don't trust her to know what's best. And I don't think she should have control of these books.'

'Well, Frank did,' I snap. 'And she understands more about them than you ever will.'

'It takes a storyteller to truly—'

'She *is* a storyteller. She's a hard worker and a phenomenal writer and she's going to do an incredible job.'

There's a collective intake of breath before the room goes quiet, and I'm confused for an instant before I realise what I just said.

The panel is silent. Alison's mouth is agape and even Austen is staring at me, shock finally making him shut up.

I feel as if I just stepped off a cliff.

'An incredible job at what?' Austen asks after a beat, and this time I can't help it as my eyes go to Ciara. Ciara, who's gone as white as a sheet, who's standing rigid against the wall.

Whose biggest fear has just come true.

CHAPTER THIRTY

Ciara

My body grows cold as Sam stares at the fan fiction writer, looking like a deer caught in the headlights.

The question hangs in the air, and I want to move, want to flee, my fight-or-flight response very much alive as my heart starts to race, but I'm too horrified to move. Sam's eyes flash to me, and I shrink back against the wall, terrified that they'll put two and two together. As if realising the same thing, he turns to Alison, who thankfully takes the hint.

'*Okay,*' she says with a nervous laugh. 'Why don't we just—'

'Now hang on,' Austen interrupts. He's frowning, looking as confused as everyone else. 'An incredible job at what?'

Alison smiles wide. 'Sam's come all this way to give us an update so let's not—'

'Is Ciara Sheridan writing *The Last Mountain*?'

The room is deathly quiet, and this time Alison says nothing.

Sam brings the microphone to his mouth. 'She's . . .'

I wait. Wait for a miracle. For him to deny it even though I know he can't. Even though I know we'll have to admit it eventually and it will be so much worse if we lie now. I know it and Sam knows it.

He stays silent, and then Austen starts to laugh, and then the room erupts into chaos.

I have a brief daydream then. One where I stride up the aisle between the chairs like a protesting suitor on a wedding day. Where I announce who I am to the room and give some wonderful speech that will turn the whole thing around.

But I don't. I just stand there. Listening to them talk. To these people who don't know me and didn't know my father and yet still make me feel like the smallest person alive.

Alison finally starts to speak, trying to regain control of the crowd, but it's too late. There's movement all around as people get up, recording on their phones, taping the whole thing. Sam gets up too, but I don't wait to see what he does next, whirling back through the door and escaping into the main hall.

I swear it's even busier than before. Waves of heat wash through me; the wig scratches and pulls at my scalp, and I whip it off, throwing it in the nearest bin. I need to get out of here, I've never needed anything more in my entire life, but Sam catches up with me, grasping my elbow.

'I'm sorry,' he says, breathless from chasing me. 'I'm so sorry, I didn't mean for that to happen.'

The room empties out behind him, the audience chatting excitedly, and my panic only rises.

'I need to go.'

'Just let me talk to—'

'*No*, Sam, I want to—'

I break off, blinking as he vanishes. Or maybe not so much vanishes as is blocked by a tall woman in another Maeve wig, clutching a plastic goblet that smells as though it's filled with coffee.

'Oh, my God,' she says, her voice far too loud for comfort. 'You're Ciara Sheridan.'

It's not like the movies. The hall doesn't fall silent. Whispers don't scatter through the crowd. But a lot of people do turn my way. And when they do, even more look, until Sam is pushed further from view.

A phone is shoved in my face, and I see an Instagram post of me and the reader from the beach, smiling nervously at the camera. *Guess who I just met!!* reads the caption, but I barely have time to take it in before it's pulled away again.

'Are you doing a talk?' the woman asks, and another man stops, his gaze snagging on mine as he does a double-glance back. Another woman does the same. And another and another until a small circle forms. One that feels as though it's pressing into me on all sides.

'Excuse me,' I mutter, trying to push through. 'Sorry.'

They don't hear me. Or maybe they do, but they don't care, because no one budges an inch.

'*Move*,' I snap, and then I do it for them, shoving my way through the bodies as I make my escape.

I know Sam's following me – I can feel him as surely as if I could see him – but I don't slow down. I'm barely keeping it together as it is, so I just keep going, not caring who I bump into or who curses me out as I follow the signs to a propped-open fire exit.

For a moment I forget where I am and expect to be back in Carrigwest when I emerge out into the heavy air. The roar of traffic startles me, the smell of tarmac and petrol and the busy road beyond. My pause gives enough time for Sam to catch up with me again and he bursts through the doors a second later, stumbling to a halt when he sees me.

Before he can say anything, my phone starts to ring, and I silence it blindly, not bothering to check who it is. I can only guess the news is out there. All over the internet.

God, what did I think was going to happen? I've done nothing but dig my head into the sand and hole myself up in that house pretending the world outside didn't exist. But it does. And now I have to face it.

And I'm not ready.

I'm not ready at all.

'I couldn't lie to them,' Sam says, and I know this. I know he didn't mean to. Know he felt that he had to defend me. But it still doesn't change what just happened.

I wonder if this is what people mean when they say their heart is breaking. Because that's what it feels like. This ragged pain inside.

Curious faces peer through the doorway, and I turn and stumble further around the building, away from prying eyes.

'Ciara—'

'I'm just freaking out,' I tell him as he follows. 'I'm allowed to freak out.'

He nods, as if to say *of course you are*, but it doesn't make me feel any better. I don't know who he is right now. I don't know if he's my editor or if he's just Sam, and, what's worse, I don't know which one I need.

'Tell me what you want to do,' Sam continues, a desperate edge to his voice. 'Tell me and I'll make it happen. Whatever you want.'

What I *want*? I want to cry. I want to ugly-cry right here in this car park. I want today to never have happened. I want to never have started this book. I want to go home and I want my dad.

I want my dad so badly it hurts.

The familiar urge to hide overwhelms me, blanketing me until it's all I know.

'I want to leave,' I begin, and he's already nodding.

'Okay,' he says instantly, looking relieved. 'We can do that. I just need to drop off the car and then we can—'

'Without you, Sam.'

His mouth slams shut. He stares at me as though he can't compute what I'm saying.

'I'm going to get my stuff,' I say carefully. 'And then I'm going back to *my* house. And you're going to go and get your flight back to New York.'

'Forget the flight. I can get another one.'

'That's the point, though,' I say wearily. 'You will get another one. Why delay the inevitable? You belong there, and I need to be here.'

He's shaking his head before I'm even finished. 'Look, I know what just happened is a lot but we need to talk about this.'

'We *need* to do our jobs. You're my editor. Go and do your ...' *Damage control.* I lick my suddenly dry lips, trying to make him understand. 'This is what I want to do. And you've got to do what you have to do. That's what we agreed.'

We've both got to go home.

He doesn't say anything at first. He looks wounded. Every muscle in his body is tense, as if he's holding himself back. From what, I don't know, but in that instant I wish he would just let me go. I don't want to fight any more.

I am so, *so* tired.

'Will you text me when you get there?' he asks finally, and there's an odd detachment in his voice I've never heard before. One that hurts more than anything.

I feel sick. Physically sick. As if I might throw up here and now, but I don't. I nod, and, before he can say anything more, I weave my way back through the cars, leaving him behind.

CHAPTER THIRTY-ONE

Sam

I hate airports.

Always have and always will. Trapped and waiting and paying the equivalent of sixteen dollars for a sandwich.

But that might just be because I'm several hours early and I'm not allowed through security for another two.

I'd built in that extra time to spend with Ciara, but now she's gone and I'm here and news that Frank Sheridan's daughter is writing *The Last Mountain* is all over the internet.

And it's all my fault.

I check my phone again, swiping away weather warnings, only to see Ciara still hasn't messaged me. Which means she's not home yet. Or she never wants to speak to me again. I'm not sure, because she didn't answer my text checking in. Or my call. And a guy can take a hint, but Jesus.

I've never felt like this before. This lost. I've always known what to do, I've always known what steps to take, and I thought I was doing the right thing in leaving her. In doing what she asked. But I'm miserable. I'm miserable and Ciara's miserable and Lizzie's miserable, judging by the flurry of texts she keeps sending me.

'Ridiculous, isn't it?'

I glance to my left to find a man looking at me, and I'm confused for an instant before I realise I've been glaring at the departure board.

'The delays,' he adds. 'A bit of wind and everything goes up the wall. You'd think they'd build a stronger plane.'

'I think it's more complicated than ...' I stop myself. 'Yeah. Ridiculous.'

He nods and returns to his phone just as mine starts to ring.

Casey.

I strongly consider not answering it, but then remember I'm probably close to being fired.

'So,' he begins when I accept. 'That didn't go to plan.'

'I'm sorry.'

'Don't be. Someone was bound to piece it together at some point. How did Ciara take it?'

'Badly.'

'She's with you now?'

'She's gone home,' I say, straightening in my chair. 'I didn't mean to—'

'I know, Sam,' he cuts me off. 'Laura sent me a clip of the panel. He was goading you and you were protecting her. It was a slip of the tongue. I understand.'

It doesn't feel as though I was protecting her, but I don't voice that little insecurity.

'I think you should take me off this book,' I say, feeling a headache form behind my eyes. 'Laura would be a better fit from—'

'No.'

'—here on ... what?'

Casey sounds amused. 'I'm not taking you off the book, Sam. I meant it when I said that you were the best person for the job.'

'Maybe you were wrong,' I say. 'And besides, we have Ciara to think about. After today, she's probably going to ask to move to another editor anyway.'

'She hasn't yet.'

'She doesn't trust me any more.'

And trust between an editor and author is paramount. The whole partnership breaks down without it.

Casey is silent on the other end of the phone. So silent, I check to see he hasn't hung up. And then he asks out of the blue, 'Do you know why I hired you?'

'Are you implying it wasn't because of my middling English literature degree and two weeks' unpaid internship?'

'It's because you wouldn't leave me alone about those books,' he says. 'I was used to it, of course, but the difference between you and every starry-eyed graduate who came in for an interview was that you also told me what was wrong with them.'

'I did?' I have no recollection of that. Probably because I erased it from my mind out of embarrassment.

'Oh, yes,' Casey says. 'You seemed very critical about the ending to the second book in particular. Not to mention High Lord Aengus, who you said was, and I quote, *a waste of space*.'

'You're making this up.'

'I'm doing no such thing. I gave you the job not because you were passionate about the books, but because you weren't afraid to tell me what could have been done better. Even back then, you were thinking with an editorial brain. You have never been afraid to tell the truth. Not to me and not to your authors, and I bet not to Ciara either. You're a fantastic editor, Sam. You understand what makes a story great and you have a knack for knowing the market before it even knows itself. I've considered every manuscript you've brought to us seriously because I trust your judgement. I trust you.'

'*But?*' I say, hearing one coming.

'But,' he echoes, 'over the years, I've watched that passion leave you. Yes, this is a business and you need to treat it as one. But it's one about art. About stories. And I think that you forgot about that somewhere along the way. You can manage as many budgets as you like, you can negotiate like hell and win every auction, but you can't reach your full potential if you lose sight of what we're doing in the first place.'

I frown, watching another flight get called to the gate. 'Please tell me you didn't send me all the way to Ireland so I would regain my love for the written word.'

'No,' he says. 'I sent you to Ireland because I needed to get this book written and Ciara was ignoring my calls. And I hate any flight over three hours.' His voice softens, inviting me to listen. 'It's about balance, Sam.'

I stare at the tiled ceiling as I take in what he's saying. As I realise what I've been thinking myself for a long time.

'I also have an email from your sister,' he adds cheerfully, and I bang the back of my head against the wall. 'Begging me not to fire you.'

'She told you she was the leak?'

'She did. And promised me a four-course home-cooked dinner of my choice to make up for it.'

'I'd take her up on that,' I tell him. 'Or you'll never get rid of her.' My fingers tighten around the phone. It's not like I can get into any *more* trouble. 'I need to tell you something. And it's not just about what happened. Ciara and I—'

'I don't want to hear it,' he interrupts. 'I've known that girl since she was seven. Anyway, what's that saying? What you don't know can't hurt you?'

'*She's* hurting though,' I say. 'And I don't want to leave her like this. Not yet. I need to take a few days off.'

'Oh, sure. It's not like Laura's drinking twelve coffees a day trying to keep up with everything.' He sighs. 'Sam, this book was always going to be—'

'This isn't about the book,' I say. 'It's about her.' About us. 'It's personal,' I add, and there are a few beats of silence on the other end of the line.

'And if I say we can't spare you?' he asks finally.

'It would do wonders for my ego but that's about it.'

'I'm starting to think you're not actually asking me here,' he says wryly, and I smile.

'Not this time, boss. I'm sorry. I'll be back next week.'

We say our goodbyes, his more resigned than mine, and I look up at the departures board, watching them flicker in unison before I jump to my feet.

'You're in some rush,' the same man says beside me. 'Forget your passport?'

'More like my priorities.'

'Eh?'

'Nothing,' I say, shouldering my bag. 'Have a good flight.'

He just nods, watching me with a baffled expression as I turn and all but sprint towards the entrance.

'Wrong way,' someone calls with a laugh, but I ignore them, smiling as I weave between travellers.

For the first time in weeks, I know exactly what I'm doing.

CHAPTER THIRTY-TWO

Ciara

The panel goes viral. I know this because I look it up at a service station halfway home, not able to wait until I get back.

> **Frank Sheridan's daughter to write final Ravian book.**

I suppose it's kind of funny. I was so worried about my name getting out there and in half the posts they don't even use it.

I thought she died, someone wrote under an article. *Didn't she die?*

I think that's another chick.

Christ.

I sit in a McDonald's just off the motorway, listening to the rain fall against the window as I read take after take and watch reel after reel. It's as though every image ever taken of me with my father is now plastered around the internet. And some teenage years just shouldn't be unearthed, you know?

They shouldn't even be touching it.

She can't write for shit.

In it for the money.

I replay one of the clips from the panel, getting angry all over again as I watch Austen smirk at the audience. '... his hand was forced in order to bring in that female audience.'

That's not what happened. That's not what happened at all. And I would know. I was in the room next to Dad as he moved in and out of his office, muttering storylines out loud while checking I was doing my homework. He wasn't forced to do anything. He ignored the naysayers and tore apart drafts and had long conversations on the phone with Casey at a time when international calls were *not* cheap, and he did it because Sam was right. My father loved Finn and Maeve. And as soon as he realised they loved each other, that was all he needed.

The video finishes, flicking automatically to the next, and I'm unable to look away as Austen appears again, speaking to someone off-camera. 'Nepotism. That's all it is. Nepotism, pure and simple. Both his daughter and his publisher clearly just want to make some money and think that all it takes is slapping the Sheridan name on the cover to say their job is done. I don't even believe what they said about the outline. If it exists, then let us see it. Let us know what Frank wanted these books to be before we—'

I pause the video, unable to watch any more.

It's not as though I can say they're wrong. It's why I said yes in the first place. Because I wanted the money. I *needed* the money. I wouldn't be able to keep the house otherwise. It was the only reason I replied to Casey. That's what I told Maddie. That's what I told myself.

But it wasn't the truth.

It was never the truth. It was a defence mechanism. A way to protect myself from people just like Austen Mitchell. If I was doing it for the money, then I wouldn't care. And if I didn't care, then I couldn't be hurt.

I love these books. I love these characters. And I wanted to write their ending more than anything. Not just for my father or his fans, but for me too.

I wanted to prove that I could do it.

I wanted to say goodbye.

And that's what this is, isn't it? A way to move on.

Because as I sit here on this hard plastic stool, running away once again, I know that I haven't. Hell, everyone knows that. That's why everyone treats me with kid gloves. Why Maddie drives out of her way to see me every day. Why Ronan lets me run up a bar tab. Why Casey sends an editor across an ocean just to give me the help I need.

Because I refuse to admit it.

I tuck my phone into my pocket, staring out at the gathering storm. Pathetic fallacy. That creative writing teacher would eat this shit up.

Still, it's apt.

I start to wonder if Sam's flight got out okay, only to stop myself before I can feel even worse. Now that I've had some time to calm down and get some food to eat, my anger has just left me feeling hollow. But there's no point in even trying to talk to him until he's landed. And even then, I don't know what I would say.

I crumple my food wrappers and toss them in the bin, knowing

I should get home before the storm gets worse. There have been no more weather warnings other than to stay away from the coast (i.e. *don't be an idiot*), but there are already reports of fallen power lines and electricity cuts. I usually love the rain. But this is almost tropical in its chaos, and uneasiness fills me as I get back on the road.

It's late afternoon, but the clouds are so dark it feels like night, and I drive extra-slowly as the rain shows no let-up. Despite there being no traffic, the final hour's drive takes me two, and I'm about ten minutes from the house when I come across a Garda van parked in the middle of the road.

The poor lad on duty waves me down, but whatever he says is lost on the wind and I have to roll down my window so I can hear him.

'You'll have to turn back!' he yells. 'It's not safe. Storm's making the branches fall.'

'But I live up—'

He just backs away, motioning for me to turn around, and, not wanting to make his job any worse than it is, I follow his instructions.

Still my anxiety churns, an unsettling sense of dread leading me to cut across the bridge by the village, aiming for the coast road. The wipers work overtime as I circle back, coming at the house from the other side. There's no patrol this way, no one to stop me but nature itself.

I've never been much of a daredevil. Never not played it safe when it comes to the important things in life. And, right now, I know the safest thing to do would be to drive back and take refuge at Ronan's until the storm passes. But be it intuition or what, I can't.

Something's wrong.

I'm halfway up my drive when I find out what.

My headlights sweep across the grass, and I brake immediately, slamming to a halt as I stare up at my home.

Or what's left of it.

The large oak tree in the middle of the garden, the one my father bought this house for, has been uprooted by the wind and crashed directly into the house, ripping through the east wing. Through his office and mine.

I can't speak. Because, while I may be alive, I'm not well. I'm not well at all, and as I stare at that place where the oak once stood, there's a pain in my chest that's worse than anything I've ever experienced. That's almost unbearable. And before I know what I'm doing I'm out of the car and then I'm running. I'm running and the alarm is blaring as I throw open the front door and go up the stairs, nearly tripping in my haste.

I'm down the hall in the time that it takes me to draw a breath.

Someone shouts my name, but I barely pay attention to it as I shove open the door.

The rain hits me first. A blast of it on the wind, striking my whole body and making me stumble back before I push forward into what is left of my father's favourite room in his favourite place.

It looks even worse than it does from the outside.

The hole that's ripped through the wall is so large that it's taken out half the roof. His armchair has disappeared, his lamp too, and I can't see the garden beyond; my view is blocked by the top of the oak tree, which now takes up half the room. Everything that's left is in chaos. Books lie scattered among notebooks and broken picture frames, all destroyed, torn apart by the elements.

I take two steps inside before the walls groan ominously. The tree hasn't fully collapsed, its fall broken by the house, and I have no idea if I have minutes or seconds before it might keep going, crashing through the floor. Another horrific creaking sound shudders around me, and my legs give out, the shock making them collapse from under me, and then I'm crawling, grabbing whatever's within reach. Saving what I can.

I'm horrified at the thought of losing anything. But to lose it all?

My name is called again. Closer now. But I keep moving, scrambling further inside as I try not to look at the gaping hole where the wall should be. Splinters dig into my bare knees and something stings sharply against my cheek, but I ignore it all, barely feeling the pain. I'm frantic. Desperate. And when I catch sight of a lined yellow page filled with my father's writing, it's as if my whole world centres on it. It's snagged on the tree, fluttering violently, but, once upon a time, he sat down and wrote it. The paper is his, the ink is his, and I clamber towards the gap, dropping whatever is in my arms as I stretch out my hand as far as it can go.

The floor beneath me seems to tilt as my fingers graze the page's edges, but before I can shuffle another inch I'm yanked backwards, strong arms encircling my waist, pulling me from my prize.

'What are you doing?' Sam yells in my ear. Because Sam is here. He's here, and he's holding me so tight I can't move. 'You almost went over!'

I struggle against him, not listening as he tugs me back further, and I watch in horror as the paper disappears, snatched by the wind as if it were never there at all. Another one follows. And another and another as the storm whips around us, screaming into my face and stealing the breath from my lungs.

'We've got to go,' he says, his voice barely audible even though he's shouting at me. 'It's not safe up here.'

'But his work!' He, of all people, has to understand what's in this room. What we're about to lose. 'It's important! We can't just—'

'*You* are important.' He cups the side of my face, forcing me to look at him. 'It doesn't matter. None of this matters. *You* matter. Come with me. Come on.'

He keeps talking at me, not taking his eyes off mine as he drags me out into the hallway, kicking the door shut behind him.

The alarm is still blaring as he brings me down the stairs, but I can barely hear it over the howl of the wind. A rental car sits just outside, the engine running and the driver's side thrown open. Sam doesn't stop until he pushes me in and slides into the passenger seat.

He whirls on me as soon as he slams the door.

'What the hell were you thinking?' he explodes.

He's furious. More than furious. Incensed. There's a panicked, frenzied air about him that I've never seen before, and my own hysteria fades at the sight of it, leaving me strangely numb.

'It looks as though it's about to collapse,' he continues when I don't say anything. He grasps my shoulders, turning me to face him as he scans my body, looking for injuries. 'You could have—' His hand goes to my cheek. 'You're bleeding,' he says, horrified.

I move willingly as he tilts my head, his touch turning impossibly gentle as he examines the scratch.

'I'm okay,' I tell him.

'You're not.'

'I am.'

He finally starts to calm, some of that manic energy leaving him when he sees that the scratch is the worst of it.

'Never do that to me again,' he croaks.

'I won't.'

'You could have fallen.'

'I'm sorry,' I say. 'I wasn't thinking. I was—'

I break off as he pulls me into a rough embrace, and I instantly wrap my arms around him, clinging to his soaked-to-the-skin shirt.

The rain hammers the roof of the car, as hard and fast as his heartbeat, and when I turn my head to press a kiss to his neck he feels unusually cold. Guilt lances through me when I realise just how much I scared him, and I pull back a fraction so I can see his face.

'What are you even doing here?' I ask. 'Your flight—'

'I couldn't leave you like that.' He runs two hands through his hair, straightening as best he can in the cramped space. 'Everything got so messed up, and I'm sorry. About all of it. You have to believe I never wanted to—'

'I know,' I say, hushing him. I'm the one comforting him now, which is all sorts of ridiculous, but I'm a sucker for when he gets all sincere like that. A sucker for him.

He reaches up to cradle my jaw, fingers delving into my hair as his thumbs sweep my cheeks.

'I don't know what's going to happen,' he says. 'But I promise I'll be there for you when it does. No matter what you need, I'll be there. For as long as you want me to.'

The tears come then, and I don't think he'd believe me if I said it was the rain, so I just let them fall. Let them fall, and let him kiss them away until there are none left.

Something flashes in the corner of my eye, and I flinch, thinking it's lightning. But lightning isn't blue and red. And it doesn't make a noise like that either. A wailing siren that grows louder and louder as the first emergency vehicle screams up the driveway.

'The house,' I whisper, because that's all I can say. All I need to. And as more lights flash, and a fire engine pulls up beside us, Sam wraps me back in his arms, holding me so close I feel as if he's never going to let me go.

CHAPTER THIRTY-THREE

Sam

It could have been so much worse. That's what the paramedic tells her. A tall, plain-speaking man who arrives along with two fire engines, answering the call of her alarm. He sits us in the back of an ambulance, where he produces a cup of tea out of nowhere and presses it into Ciara's hands.

Ciara, who won't stop shivering.

Ciara, who doesn't say a word.

A team sweeps through the house to ensure no one else is inside, and then the building is cordoned off. But the worst of the damage is done as the storm passes over us, continuing east. Almost as soon as it does, more cars appear in the driveway, and then, suddenly, everyone is there. Every face I've come to recognise, whether I know their names or not. They all come for Ciara, carrying food and blankets and offers of accommodation.

Mary's the first to arrive. Mary, who always seems to know what's going on. She brings two cartons of milk just as she did the first time I saw her, and it's used for the tea that's passed around, followed by a tray of sandwiches that Ronan made.

A pale-faced Maddie is one of the last to arrive. She brings an overnight bag for Ciara and tries to insist we stay with her, but Ciara doesn't want to be so far from the house and so she drives us to the room above Delaney's instead.

Then we're left alone.

I make Ciara take the first shower, and I'm touched when I find Maddie brought new clothes for me as well. I use the T-shirt and sweats as pyjamas once I've washed the rain from my skin and try not to think about what would have happened if Ciara had been in the room. Try and fail, seeing as how I haven't stopped thinking about it from the moment I saw the damage.

The horror that gripped me was like nothing I've ever experienced and I never, ever want to feel it again. It's the memory of that feeling that makes me irrational. And I'm barely in the bathroom three minutes before I'm back out again, needing to see her with my own eyes.

The bed feels even tinier than it used to, but Ciara doesn't say a word as she climbs into it and drags me down with her. Any lack of space is made up for by the way she drapes her body over mine, and for the first time since I've met her, when the world grows dark, she sleeps.

I know I should try to as well, but I don't. I can't. All I can do is lie there and watch her dream, ready for the moment she might wake. For when she might need me.

Eventually, though, I must lose the battle, because the next time I open my eyes, pale sunlight filters through the thin curtains, telling me a new day has begun.

A glance at my phone tells me it's just after dawn.

Ciara hasn't moved an inch.

Her body is warm and so very real beside me, and when I draw the fallen sheet over her shoulder her eyes open, finding me immediately.

'Sorry,' I say. 'Did I wake you?'

She shakes her head. 'I've been awake for a while.'

'You hungry?'

'No.'

'Thirsty?'

'I'm okay. Has anyone called? Or . . .'

'It's early,' I say.

A strand of hair falls over her face, catching on her eyelashes, and I hesitate for only a moment before I tuck it back. She shifts closer, her nose brushing mine. 'Does my breath smell?'

'Yes.'

She groans, rolling away. 'You're supposed to lie,' she mutters, but she doesn't protest when I pull her back into me. 'I feel like I've been hit by a bus.'

'Just rest. You don't need to do anything today.'

'I need to get my stuff.'

'We'll go by later and get what we can. But they might not let us inside yet.'

She makes a non-committal noise, and I don't hide my relief when she relaxes against me. There was a moment at the convention where I didn't think we'd get past this. That I'd fucked it up completely.

'I'm sorry I said I wasn't going to tell you about Lizzie,' I say quietly. 'It's just that you were finally starting to enjoy writing again, and realising I might be the reason that that stopped was . . . I didn't want to hurt you.'

'It hasn't stopped.' She sighs. 'And I'm not mad at you. Or at Lizzie. Not really. I was just frustrated about everything, and it felt like . . .'

'What?'

'Nothing,' she mumbles, but I'm already urging her around to face me, surprised when she doesn't meet my gaze.

'Felt like what?' I insist.

'I've lived my whole life in the shadow of those books,' she says. 'And I love them. I do. I owe so much to those characters. But it's still hard. I share everything with them. The house, my dad . . . you.' She says the last word softly, almost sadly, and my hand tightens around her hip.

'You think, if it came down to it, I would pick the books over you?'

'No,' she says, clearly lying. 'I just—'

I sit up, turning so I'm braced above her. 'I think I need to be clear,' I say, forcing her to meet my eye, 'that, given the choice, I will choose you every time.'

She looks up at me. 'You're using your editor voice.'

'Because your mind needs editing. You come first. Always.'

'So you're saying, if I asked, you would *burn* Richardson Books to the—'

'I'm serious.'

She falls silent, looking faintly embarrassed. But I know she hears me. 'You'll still tell me when my story's shite, though, right?'

'Of course,' I say, lying back down beside her. 'I've got a reputation to uphold.'

She burrows into me immediately. 'Is it bad that I don't feel bad any more?' she whispers. 'I'm lying here, and I don't feel bad. I'm exhausted and bruised, but that's physical stuff. The emotional side of me . . . ' She trails off, her gaze searching mine. 'I think I'm relieved.'

'Then you're relieved,' I say. 'You should never feel guilty for how you feel.'

'I know, it's just . . . ' She licks her lips, her jaw working as though she's searching for the words. 'It's, like, now I don't have to decide any more, right? I've put off thinking about what to do with all his letters and notebooks for a year, and now I don't have to decide. Because it's all gone. It's just gone, and I'm still here. Maybe I should get them to knock it down,' she adds before I can say anything. 'Build something new.' But even as she speaks, the words fall flat.

'You don't want that.'

'No,' she says. 'But I don't want to live there either. I never have. It's never felt like *mine*. Not without him there. It just feels as though I've borrowed it. As though I'm playing house. It hasn't felt like an actual home in a long time.'

'Are you sure you don't want to sell it?' I ask softly. 'It's okay if you change your mind.'

'I don't know. Maybe. But then no, because even just thinking about doing that makes me feel sick.' She drags a hand down her face. 'I think I'm just confused.'

I stroke her back, trying to ease some of the tension I find there even as I press my lips together, swallowing the words on the tip of my tongue.

Because there's another option. Another option entirely.

But I'm not so tired that I forget the importance of timing. Of knowing my own thoughts before I voice them.

'We'll figure it out,' I say. 'Nothing has to be decided now.'

She seems to relax at that, and laces her fingers with mine, drawing my arm over her body. Ten minutes tick by, and I think she's gone back to sleep, but then her hand drifts down my chest, and she shifts even closer. When the hand doesn't stop, I tilt my chin to look at her, and as if it's what she was waiting for, she pushes up and kisses me.

It's soft at first, gentle and sweet. But that doesn't last long.

We roll so I'm back above her, and she's silent but sure in her movements, guiding my hands to the bottom of her T-shirt. I lift it over her head, baring her to the morning air as she kicks her shorts to the bottom of the bed. Warm fingers trail up my stomach as she removes my own shirt, and then she settles back into the pillows as my briefs go next.

Our first time had been so frantic, a race to devour, but this feels different. Unhurried. Languid. As if we have all the time in the world.

The thought makes me pause because I know we don't. The storm has added a week or two at most to my time here. But I lean down and kiss her before she can notice, sinking my mouth against the side of her neck and then along her collarbone.

Outside, birds sing to the rising sun, and with every press of my lips I try to give her what she needs, to ease her pain, to show her I'm here. I move lower, nudging her legs wider as I settle between them.

She hesitates for only a second, as though not sure what I'm doing, but she catches on quickly, her breath speeding up as I slip her thighs over my shoulders.

The first touch of my tongue sends her hands to my head, her fingers spearing through my hair. Each tug sends a jolt of electricity down my spine, and I stay right where I am until she's arching from the bed, clenching around me.

She rests for only a second before her hands scramble at my shoulders. She urges me up and so up I go, nuzzling her thighs, her hips, the valley between her breasts.

I thank my past self for leaving the backpack right by the bed. It takes only a moment to reach over and grab a condom from inside. Ciara doesn't stop touching me as I do, her hands roving over my body as though to make sure I'm real.

She's more than ready, and within seconds I'm pushing into her, dropping my forehead to her sweat-sheened shoulder.

Pressure mounts between us as I let myself sink into her, get lost in her until there's nothing but the here and now. And as she wraps her legs around my hips I want to tell her how right this is, how perfect *she* is, but she kisses me before I can speak, clenching around me as her release ignites mine, and all coherent thoughts dissolve in my mind as I hold her tight.

For once, we're not focused on the words.

CHAPTER THIRTY-FOUR

Ciara

It takes three days for things to move on. Three days to clean up the mess from the storm. Three days before we're let back into the house to sort out what I need now and what can be put into storage. Three days that feel like an eternity.

The only good thing that happens?

I sleep.

Every night, we return to the room above Delaney's and climb into that tiny bed. Every night, I'm dreaming before I hit the pillow. Sam develops a sixth sense when it comes to me and the internet, miraculously appearing every time I get the urge to Google the book and distracting me with food or a walk or a kiss. It's pretty obvious what he's doing, but I know he's right. The last thing I need right now is a doom scroll. But I also know by all his phone calls and emailing that things are happening, and that it must be difficult trying to deal with it in a completely different time zone. He'll need to go back to New York soon, but for now he barely leaves my side.

One early morning, we sit on a bench outside Delaney's as

Maddie skims through a small list of rentals on her tablet. There's no way I'll be able to move back into the house in the next few months, but I can't live out of a single room above the pub, either.

As predicted, my other options are limited.

'This one looks promising,' Maddie says, pointing to a depressing terraced house. 'It's got a little nook you could write in.'

'That's a fireplace.'

'Yeah, but they've taken the fireplace out. So, it's a nook.'

I peer closer at the photos. 'Is the bathroom outside?'

'You live in rural Ireland in the middle of a housing crisis, Ciara; I don't know what to tell you.' She swipes through a few other listings, only to get distracted when her phone vibrates on the table.

Shane's name flashes up.

'You can get that,' I tell her when she doesn't.

'It's fine,' she mutters, letting it ring out. Barely three seconds pass before it starts again.

'Maddie,' I urge, and she scowls.

'Give me a second.' She passes the tablet to Sam before putting the phone to her ear. 'I'm busy,' she snaps into it, and walks around the side of the pub.

New business partnership is going well, then.

Sam waits until she's out of earshot before pointing at the screen. 'You hate them all.'

'I don't,' I lie. 'I'm just so sick of thinking about the house. And I have to wait for the insurance to kick in and then I'll have to organise repairs and see what else I need to do and it will probably take *years* and I—' I groan, dropping my head into my hands. 'You're going to tell me to sell it, aren't you?'

'No.'

'But you're thinking it.'

'I mean . . . ' He sighs. 'You don't want to live there.'

'I don't know what I want any more. All I know is that he left it to me.'

'As a gift,' Sam reminds me. 'He thought he was making you happy. You think he would have saddled you with it if he'd known it would do the opposite?'

'No,' I admit, looking up. 'But I can't change the past. And if I want to focus on the future, then I need to focus on the book.'

'Casey said he'll give you as much time as you need.'

'I don't want time,' I insist. 'I don't want to lose my rhythm. It's going to be hard enough with you leaving.'

I say the last bit without thinking, and we both tense before I take the tablet from him, pretending to scroll until Maddie sits back down.

'Everything okay?' I ask.

'Everything's perfect,' she says briskly, only to sigh at what she sees on the screen. 'You could just live with me, you know.'

'We'd drive each other nuts.'

'Yeah, but in a sitcom way.' She reaches for the tablet as she shifts in place for the hundredth time. She hasn't been able to sit still all morning.

'You *sure* you're all right?' I ask.

'I'm grand, Ciara. We're focusing on you here.'

'But I'm fine.'

'You're not fine. You've been through a traumatic event.' But she avoids my gaze as she flicks back, landing on a house that doesn't look as if it's been changed since the seventies. 'I think this place could be liveable, with a lick of paint.'

She starts searching again, ignoring her phone even as it lights up with a text from Shane.

Fine.

I turn to Sam, staring at him until he gets the hint and says something about needing refreshment. I wait until he's disappeared into the pub before focusing on Maddie. Then I kick her under the table.

'Did you have sex with Shane McCauley?' I hiss.

'Okay, *ow*,' she says, glaring at me. 'And no! What the hell?'

'You're being so weird.'

'He's just really serious,' she says, dropping her voice. 'Like, more serious than I thought he'd be. I thought he'd back out or lose interest, but he keeps sending me all these plans and asking my opinion and he invited me to dinner next week and—'

'Dinner.'

'A business dinner,' she says. 'To discuss our business.'

'Oh, my God.'

'A *business*—'

'How is this even going to work?' I interrupt. 'Is he moving here?'

'That's the thing,' she says, purposely not looking at me. 'This was always going to be a "next year" opening. So, he suggested we keep going, see out the summer and then, if I want, I can go and work with him in Dublin for a while. Learn the ropes.'

And there it is. She fidgets under my gaze, playing with the bracelet on her wrist.

'Dublin?' I say.

'Yeah.'

'When?'

She shrugs, looking cagey. 'September, maybe.'

'For how long?'

'A few months. And then—'

'*Months*?'

'He's right, Ciara,' she says. 'I've worked in places like that before, but I've never managed them. It's an opportunity I can't turn down.'

'There are cafés closer than Dublin.'

'But none that he owns. And none that he's offered me the chance to run. It means I'll know what I'm doing when we open.'

'So you're leaving.'

'Not forever.'

'For half of the year.'

'You can come and visit me. You like Dublin.'

'But you keep saying you don't like *him*,' I remind her, and she grimaces.

'He's not the worst.'

I shake my head, trying to imagine my days without her. 'I can't believe this.'

'I'm sorry,' she says, reaching over to grasp my hand.

Movement at the corner of my eye catches my attention, and I look over just as Sam steps out of the pub, takes one look at us and goes back inside.

I take a deep breath. 'This is what you want to do?'

'Yes.' She doesn't even hesitate.

'And you're excited?'

'Extremely.'

'Okay.' Another breath. Even though I still feel like pouting. 'To be clear, I'm happy for you but sad for me – that's what's going on here.'

She pats my hand. 'I know.'

'It sounds like a great opportunity.'

'It is.'

'It's just that I love you and you're my best friend.'

'I better be,' she says before rolling her eyes at what is probably a bereft look on my face. 'Oh, Jesus, come here.' She climbs out of the bench and clambers over to my side, where she wraps me in a big Maddie hug. 'For someone who earns a living being inside other people's heads, you're extremely bad at dealing with your own feelings.'

'Hey,' I complain, even though I am.

'You could come too.'

'To Dublin?'

'We could rent together. Complain about the cost of things.'

'I've got to sort out the house first.'

'She said for the millionth time.'

'But this time it's true. I don't know if you heard, but there was this massive storm?'

'Is that what that noise was?' She pulls back, tilting my face to see my bandage. 'Does it hurt?'

'Stings like a bitch,' I say. 'Might get a cool scar, though.'

'We can only hope.' She drops her hand, her face turning serious. 'What do you want to do, Ciara? Anything you want, I'll help you.'

'I want to finish this book,' I say. 'For Dad and for me. After that, I don't know.' I frown. 'You ever feel like you're completely free and yet utterly stuck at the same time?'

'Never,' she says, and okay, great. Just me, then.

Maddie grasps my shoulders, sensing my thoughts. 'You know you're not alone, right? I can be across the country and still only be a phone call away. You have never and will never be in this alone.'

She hugs me again, more tightly than before, and I reluctantly accept the fact that things are changing. That I am not the centre of the universe, no matter how much I'd like to be. That Maddie has a life outside of here. So does Ronan. So does Sam.

And so do I.

I just don't know what that looks like yet.

But maybe that's okay too. Maybe I don't need to know right now. Maybe my story hasn't ended yet.

CHAPTER THIRTY-FIVE

Sam

'Liquid gold. That's what it is.'

Ronan sets a glass before me and casts a critical eye over its contents.

'Mad to think about, isn't it? Malt. Hops. Yeast. Water. Four simple ingredients.' He heaves a sigh. 'And I still manage to mess it up.'

'You're getting there,' I protest as he knocks back his latest brew. 'Really.'

'You're too nice to me, Sam,' he says, wincing from the taste. 'I can no longer trust you as my tester.'

'I am . . . sorry to hear that.'

'Oh, I bet.' He reaches for a glass of water. It's just us two in the pub. It's too late for other customers, and we've been talking about everything and nothing for the last hour as he prepares to close up.

'How is she, then?' he asks, tipping his head to the ceiling.

'Better. Or getting better, at least.' Her cuts and bruises were healing normally, but I know she's heartbroken at the damage. Daunted by all the work it's going to take.

'She tells me you'll be heading off soon,' Ronan continues. 'Back to New York.'

'That's right.'

'Well, you'll be sure to come back and visit. I've grown too used to having you around to never see you again.'

'Is that your way of saying you'll miss me?'

'It is. You're a good lad.' He gives me a sly look. 'Even if you can't hold your liquor.'

Twenty minutes later, he makes a show of kicking me out, but I'm not ready to turn in yet.

A glance up at the window tells me Ciara's asleep anyway, so I don't worry about her wondering where I am as I start along the road the same way we walked that first weekend. It's just as dark as it was then, too.

I walk all the way to her house.

I would have viewed this trip as a pilgrimage for most of my teenage years, and I still haven't gotten used to seeing it. Sometimes, I still can't believe that I've been in it.

Now, I stay behind the yellow warning tape, keeping my distance as I gaze at the gaping, ragged hole along the side.

If it's hard for me to see it like this, I can't imagine how Ciara must feel. And I know she's strong, I know she's surrounded by friends and by people who love her, but I selfishly want her to need *me* too. I want to be the one to comfort her. To make her days better and her smiles brighter. I want to see her through every other thing life throws her way, and knowing I might not be able to leaves a bitter taste in my mouth.

This summer has been like a dream. One that I think I'm ready to wake up from. Maybe not exactly to the life I've had, but something close to it.

Hopefully, something better.

But for that to happen I need something else.

Someone else.

I stay there for a long time, trying to commit every inch of the place to memory before heading back to Delaney's.

I let myself back in as quietly as I can, climbing the stairs slowly so as not to wake Ciara, but I'm only halfway up when I see that the door at the top is open, soft light spilling out.

A second later, I hear the soft murmur of voices. Ciara is talking on the phone. As soon as I realise it, I step back, ready to give her some privacy before the person she's talking to gives a short laugh, and I pause, recognising it.

My sister.

'Is he always like that?'

'Always,' Lizzie says. 'And I have a feeling he always will be. *Billy*. Go to bed. *Now*.' There's a scuffle and then the sound of a door slamming on her end. A second later, Lizzie sighs. 'I shouldn't complain.'

'I'd complain.'

'All right, then, I will.'

I step into the room to find Ciara sitting cross-legged on the bed. Her laptop sits open beside her, and she's holding my phone in her lap.

'How long do you think the repairs will take?' Lizzie asks.

'I don't know,' Ciara replies. 'A lot of different people have told me a lot of different things, but all I keep hearing is *money*. I know I should just be grateful that no one got hurt, but ...'

'It's still a massive shock,' Lizzie says quietly.

'Yeah.' She looks up to acknowledge me, but Lizzie speaks before I can.

'I'm sorry about what happened,' she says. I don't think I've ever heard her sound so serious. 'I never meant to make things so hard for you.'

'You couldn't have known.'

'Doesn't matter. I shouldn't have run my big mouth off. If I could take it back, I would.'

'Thank you.'

'You know,' Lizzie continues, sounding hopeful, 'the next time you're in New York, and you've got the time, I'd love to get lunch. I feel like I know you already, seeing as how Sam hasn't shut up about you.'

'I'd like that,' Ciara says. 'And same. He hasn't shut up about you either.'

'Oh, yeah? What did he say?'

I roll my eyes at the suspicion in her voice, but Ciara just smiles at me.

'All good things,' she says, and they talk for a few more seconds before my nephew forces Lizzie off the call.

'Sorry for answering your phone,' she says, when I join her on the bed. 'She wouldn't stop calling and I got worried it might be an emergency, so I answered and then we... I don't know. We just kept talking.'

'I'm glad you did. Thank you for accepting her apology.'

Ciara shrugs. 'She meant it. Plus, she's kind of hard to stay mad at.'

'I don't know,' I say drily. 'I've managed many times before.' I nod at her laptop. 'You're writing?'

'Yeah. Can't seem to stay away from it.' She pulls her shoulders back, stretching them out.

'Tired?'

'Not really.'

I look out at the starry sky. 'Want to go for a swim?'

*

The beach is empty again.

But then again, I guess it is almost five in the morning.

There's no full moon this time, and we keep the headlights on as we strip down to our bathing suits.

Ciara holds my hand as we walk into the ocean, but when her grip tightens I think it's more to make sure I don't change my mind as opposed to a source of comfort. She doesn't go as far out this time. Only halfway up to her chest before she pauses on a sand bank and turns to face me.

'One second,' she tells me, disappearing under the freezing water before bobbing back up with a gasp. 'Now you.'

'I really don't— Yep, okay,' I say when she glares at me. It's just as cold as last time, and I rise as quickly as I can, already shivering.

Ciara shakes her head, but she can't hide her smile. 'You're so dramatic sometimes.'

'Says the woman who ran into a half-collapsed house.'

'Says the man who went chasing in after me.' She says it like a challenge but there's a hint of doubt there that I'm not used to seeing on her. A question she won't ask even though she has to know the answer by now.

God knows I do.

'I'm going to tell you something,' I begin. 'And I can't tell if it's good or bad timing, but not telling you would be the biggest mistake of my life.' I pause, waiting for nerves or a knot in my throat. But there's nothing. Only the truth. 'I'm in love with you,' I tell her. 'And I know we work together and live on separate continents and have completely different sleep schedules to the point where I don't know how you manage to function half the time, but I love you. I love your voice and your words and your brain, and I love how all your friends and family love you too. I think you're stubborn and funny and that you try and you care, and I think, if we wanted to, we could really make something of this. Something spectacular.'

Her eyes take on a sheen, and she sniffs, but whether that's her overwhelming emotion or the salt water up her nose, I can't tell.

'Spectacular, huh?'

And if I'm baring my soul, I might as well go all the way. 'Sometimes, when you look at me, I feel like I can't breathe.'

'Sam—'

'I want you to come back with me to New York.'

She stares up at me, stunned. 'What?'

'I don't want to end this.'

'I need you to be serious right now,' she says shakily. 'I need you to be completely one hundred per cent serious, because I can't handle it if you're not.'

'I've never been more serious about anything in my life.'

She laughs a little, as if she can't believe what I'm saying, and then looks towards the light dawning over the dunes behind us, then back out at the vast ocean to the west.

'New York?' she asks, but I don't think she expects an answer. 'What if it doesn't work out?'

'What if it does?'

Her gaze lifts to mine, her eyes impossibly wide and open, letting me see every vulnerable part of her. 'Can I think about it?'

'Of course,' I say instantly, relieved it's not a no. 'You can have all the time in the world.'

'I'll give you a proper answer,' she says. 'I just . . . with the house. I can't leave it, but I know I can't—'

'Hey.' I wipe my thumb across her cheek as tears start to fall, and she gives me a watery smile.

'I'll think about it. I promise I will.'

'That's all I ask.'

We fall quiet, watching each other as the world around us lightens, a slow seeping of pale blue drifting up from the horizon.

'I love you too,' she says. 'More than I ever thought was possible. And I think I have for a while.'

Her hand finds mine under the water, and I clasp it tight as goosebumps appear on her arms. 'Are you cold?'

She shakes her head. 'Can we stay here a little longer?'

'We can stay here as long as you like.'

She moves even closer, vanquishing the final inch of space between us as she wraps her arms around my waist. Above us, the sun begins its ascent and as she rests her head against my chest, listening to my heart, I know without a doubt that from now on, every time it beats, it will beat for her.

CHAPTER THIRTY-SIX

Ciara

It's another beautiful afternoon the day I drive Sam to the graveyard. It does not put me in a good mood. It's been a week since the storm, and we've been promised a break in the weather, but, so far, it hasn't happened. No winds come from the ocean, no clouds drift in the sky. Nothing to give us a break from the heat and the humidity and the increasing underboob sweat.

'I'm getting real sick of this shit,' I say as we get out of the car. 'It's August. I'm supposed to start wearing my coats soon. That's the whole point of coat season.'

'You have more than one coat?'

'Of course I have more than one coat. You only have one coat?'

'I think so.'

'I have three coats,' I tell him. 'I have my raincoat, my fancy coat and my day-to-day coat. And I'll have you know I look great in all of them.'

'I don't doubt it.'

'I can't believe you've never seen me in my day-to-day coat,' I mutter, kicking the tire of my car. We're the only people around, which should give me a sense of space but only hammers home the solitary feeling I get whenever I come here. 'Want to go to the beach instead?'

'What?'

'Maddie always needs help these days.'

Sam just gives me a look. 'You're procrastinating again.'

'Yes,' I say. 'Obviously.'

'Come on.' He takes my hand and all but drags me through the gates, ignoring my grumbling.

To be honest, Carrigwest's graveyard has never looked so good. The sunlight's streaming. The birds are chirping. Someone's cut the grass recently, and the gravel paths crunch pleasantly under our steps. I feel places like this shouldn't be so cheerful, but here we are.

Despite rarely coming here, I could walk to my dad's resting place with my eyes closed, and I lead Sam over to the shadow of a small yew tree, where I said my final goodbye to him.

The grave is simple, just like he requested. A modest headstone with his name and date engraved in neat, clear lettering. No one but his family and friends know he's buried here, so the place is left untouched except for a simple bouquet. They look fresh, not dried out from the sun, and a glance at the note tells me Ronan left them there.

My previous sarcastic chipperness falters at the sight, and I turn to Sam, suddenly nervous.

'I'm not really a grave person.'

'Okay . . . ' he says slowly.

'Like, I don't believe he's in there,' I say, trying to explain. 'Or anywhere. I just believe he's . . . ' I wave my arms around. 'Energy or something.' Ugh. 'This was a bad idea. Let's go.'

He grabs my arm before I can leave, tugging me firmly back into position. 'You wanted to do this,' he reminds me.

'And now I don't.'

'I'll give you a minute.'

'No.' I grasp his hand so quickly that he looks at me in surprise, but he doesn't move. 'I want you to meet him.'

'Then I'll follow your lead,' is all he says, and he turns back to the grave expectantly.

I take a breath, feeling like an idiot. If Sam so much as looks at me weirdly, I'm abandoning this thing altogether. But he doesn't. He just waits. His hand in mine.

'This is Sam,' I announce. 'He's a big fan of yours. The biggest, actually. And secretly a giant nerd.' I nudge him. 'Say hello.'

'It's nice to meet you,' Sam says to the headstone. He somehow makes it sound not stupid, for which I am eternally grateful. 'I sent you a letter when I was fourteen. You probably don't remember it, but Ciara tells me that you read every single one you got. Knowing you saw mine means the world to me.'

Oh, God. There's a burning in the back of my nose that won't go away no matter how much I tell it to, and see? This is why I don't come here. This is why I am not a grave person. I am not—

Sam clears his throat.

'Sam's a workaholic,' I say abruptly. 'And an early riser. He's also a brilliant editor and a cheap drunk. He makes me laugh, and he's kind, and I'm in love with him. And I think you would have really, really liked him. I think you two would have been friends and I wish you could have met him. But you should know that it was your books that brought us together. It was because of you that we met. So thank you for that.'

I pause, and Sam squeezes my hand.

'So yeah,' I add. 'I love you. And I miss you. I miss you every single day and I don't know if that's ever going to stop, but I'm okay. I've got lots of people to look after me and we're going to fix the house and I'm going to write your book and it's all going to be fine. I promise.'

I fall silent, letting the words hang in the air. I feel as if I'm expected to say more, talk about how much he's missed in the last year and how much I wish he'd seen, but when I search my soul for more, nothing more comes.

'You all right?' Sam murmurs.

'Yeah.' The word comes out like a sigh of relief, and I lean against him, exhausted. 'All done.'

'That was nice, Ciara.'

'I'm actually extremely sentimental.' I fold my arms across my chest, hugging them in tight. 'He'd probably laugh if he heard that.'

'I don't think so,' Sam says. 'I think, if he could, he'd tell you he was proud of you.'

'Yeah?'

'Yeah.'

And then, in a moment of such perfect timing that it could never, ever be repeated, my phone starts to ring.

Both of us freeze.

'Do you think that's him?' I whisper, and Sam frowns. 'Oh, who are you, the graveyard police? I'm allowed to make jokes.'

'Will you just see who it is?'

'You're going to look so stupid if it's my dad,' I warn, digging it out of my pocket.

I'm expecting Maddie, so I'm surprised when Casey's name flashes up.

Sam just shrugs when I show him the screen. 'Answer it,' he says, but I hesitate.

'What if he asks for an update about the book?'

'Then pretend you're going through a tunnel.'

'Oh, now who's making— Hey!'

Sam taps the accept button on my screen, and I hit him on the shoulder as I answer it. He doesn't so much as flinch.

'Hi, Casey.'

'Ciara.' He pauses. 'I'll admit, I didn't expect you to pick up.'

'Yeah, well, I like to keep people on their toes.' I squint at the sky as a lone bird soars by. 'How are you?'

'Busy,' he says. 'Busy chasing you. Frank's solicitor has been trying to get in touch. He's sent you several emails over the past few days.'

'I've been a little distracted.'

'Which is what I told him. I said I'd pass his message along.' As he talks, I put him on speaker so Sam can hear. 'Have you been online recently?'

'As in, have I logged on to the World Wide Web? Your editorial director won't let me.'

'Then I'll get straight to it,' he says. 'Some of Frank's readers want to contribute to rebuilding the house. They launched a crowdfund in your name when news of the storm hit, and they want to help.'

'They don't have to do that,' I say awkwardly.

'And I'm sure they know that, but they'd like to. They've written you an open letter explaining why.'

'Oh. All right.' I look at Sam, but he shakes his head. He didn't know anything about this either. 'That's nice of them. How many fans?'

'Twelve—'

'Okay, great. I—'

'Thousand.'

I blink. 'Pardon?'

'Twelve thousand or so,' Casey continues. 'The number keeps going up every few minutes, but that's where they were the last time I checked.'

'I . . . what?'

I must look as helpless as I feel because Sam takes the phone from my hand, holding it between us. 'Casey? It's Sam. Care to elaborate on that?'

'I don't know how much more there is to say,' he answers, and I get the sneaking suspicion he's enjoying himself. 'Amy informed me it started after people found out about the damage. At first they wanted to contribute to the repairs, but the more it grew, the more people talked about what else they could do with it. Those behind the initial fundraising have now approached your solicitor with an offer.'

'Which is?'

'To buy it from you.'

'No.' I shake my head even though he can't see it. 'I'm not selling it to one of his fans. Or to twelve thousand of them or whatever.'

'It's not for them to live in,' he says. 'They want to turn it into a museum. Or a museum slash writing retreat, if I'm reading it correctly.'

'But what does that even mean?'

'Ciara, the money raised is a significant amount. We're talking a couple of million dollars already. Enough to buy it and rebuild it and more. They've proposed turning part of the house into a museum where people can learn about Frank, and the rest into a learning space. They've already approached a few of the colleges taking part in his creative writing scholarships, and they've agreed to contribute to a summer programme, should you agree.'

'Like, a school?'

'Frank loved to teach.'

He did. He loved it almost as much as writing.

'What they're suggesting is pretty sound,' Casey continues carefully. 'I was as surprised as you were when I first heard it, but the more I read the proposal, the more I was convinced. I would give it some thought if I were you.'

'I will,' I say, too baffled to say anything else, and we exchange goodbyes before hanging up. 'Holy shit.'

Sam looks as stumped as me. 'You okay?'

'That was not what I expected that phone call to be about.'

'He said they wrote you an open letter?'

He did.

I fumble with the phone, but my fingers are being weird and trembly and when I hold the thing out to him with a helpless grunt Sam takes it from me and looks up the fundraising site.

The letter is right there on the front page.

Dear Ms Ciara Sheridan,

You do not know me and I do not know you, but as a member of the small group that first launched this crowdfunder, I have been asked to write on behalf of all of us.

I think I must have read every Ravian book at least fifteen times. I read them when I was happy and when I was sad. I read them when I was heartbroken and when I was ill and when I was so homesick I thought I might cry. I took them with me to college and then to my first apartment, my second apartment, my house. I read them while I stayed up nursing my first child and, twelve years later, I got to pass the same copy on to my son so that he could discover their magic as well.

I never had the chance to meet your father, but I never felt I needed to. I met him through his words, and I want you to know that he brought me so much

comfort that it was like he had gifted me a second
world I could escape to.

I cannot tell you how grateful I am to hear that you
are finishing these stories for us. He always spoke so
warmly of you in interviews, and I hope you know just
how excited we are for this book and for you.

When we heard the news of the house, we knew
that we wanted to do something to honour your father
and all that he's given to us. We cannot imagine what
you are going through, and we won't try to, but if we
may, we would like to share our proposal, which you
can read in full below.

On behalf of fans everywhere, for the future of
Ravian,

Angela Baxter

I read it three times before I scroll down, only able to skim through the following documents as my mind starts to spin.

'This is . . . a lot,' I finally say as Sam stands silent by my side.

'You don't have to decide anything right now. Take all the time you need to—'

'I think I should do it.'

'Or that.' The corner of his mouth twitches. 'Are you sure?'

'No. Yes. I think so. I mean I obviously have to read it through and get someone who knows what they're talking about to look at it, but I think . . . it makes the most sense, doesn't it?'

'It's up to you.'

'I know that.' I let my head drop and Sam palms the back of my neck, drawing me into him. 'I think it makes sense,' I say. 'Do you think it makes sense?'

'It doesn't matter what I think.'

'But it does if it means . . . ' I pull back, and his arm falls away. It becomes difficult to meet his eyes, so I stare at the base of his throat instead. 'If it means that I go with you.'

The silence is broken only by the sound of birdsong in the distance, and I feel so nervous that it takes everything in me not to just laugh and pretend I was joking. To take it all back. To run and hide. But I don't. I stay right where I am.

'With me?' Sam asks.

'If the offer's still on the table.'

I lift my gaze to find him staring right at me, his brown eyes as warm as I've ever seen them.

'It's still on the table,' he says, his voice low and serious. 'It's definitely still on the table.'

'Okay,' I say, and the word comes out like a chirp. 'Great. Good to know.'

'Ciara—'

'It might be different living together.'

'We already live together,' he reminds me, and yes, point taken.

'I bet your apartment is smaller than my house.'

'You would bet correctly.'

'And that you live up three flights of stairs.'

'Five. No elevator.'

'Wonderful,' I mutter, but he just smiles. Smiles because he knows he has me.

'Come with me to New York,' he says softly. 'Come be with me.'

'All right,' I say as his hands go to my hips. 'But only because you asked so nicely.'

I rise up to press my lips to his, and when I try to pull away he chases me, kissing me until I'm laughing. Or at least I think I'm laughing. There are tears in my eyes, but they're not sad. There's a tug in my chest, but it's not painful.

Instead, it feels like I'm filling my lungs for the first time. It feels like I can finally breathe.

And when he tucks me into him, resting his chin on my head, it feels like I'm finally home.

EPILOGUE

Sam

EIGHTEEN MONTHS LATER

New York

I've lost my girlfriend.

I'm not sure how. Yes, the world is busy today with shoppers, but she's pretty tall, and the last time I saw her three minutes ago she was wearing a very blue coat, so she shouldn't be that hard to spot in the sea of grey and black. Yet, somehow, I've managed it.

I shift the clutch of shopping bags from my left hand to my right as I gaze down the street, ignoring the buzz of my phone in my pocket. I know it's just Lizzie with her standard 'we're running late' update. We're supposed to meet her, Ben and the kids for lunch, but first: girlfriend.

She told me she was stepping outside for some air. Unless she's gone back inside. Or she's— Ah.

I turn as a bus lumbers forward, revealing the row of buildings opposite and one woman in particular standing in front of a bookstore.

The collar of her coat is pulled up against the wind, and her gloved hands are cradling a cup of coffee. She's stuffed her hat into her pocket, the woolly beanie bulging out at her side, and as a result her hair has come loose from its pins and is now flying around her face. It's longer than it was when I first met her, brushing her shoulders in a way she hates, but she wants to grow it out. I suspect this is purely because she wants to dramatically cut it again, but I keep this to myself so she can have her moment.

I cross the street to join her and follow her gaze to the blown-up photo of Frank smack bang in the middle of the window. A few of his books surround it, and whoever set up the display made an effort, folding swaths of green velvet, the same colour Maeve wears, alongside what looks like homemade miniature swords made of foil.

'That's the first window I've seen,' Ciara says, sounding awed. 'They're early.'

'They're excited. You want to go in?'

Her nose wrinkles, but it's half-hearted. 'Do we have time?'

I check my phone to see that it *was* a text from Lizzie, and they are indeed running late. 'Plenty.'

A bell chimes overhead as I push the door open. It's a small space, made all the smaller by the dozens of boxes pushed up against the walls. They clearly just had a delivery, and an ill-timed one at that, judging by the stacks of books half-taken out and abandoned on the tables.

We're barely a step inside when a harried voice calls from somewhere within the shelves.

'I'll be with you in a minute!' they yell, before there's a muttered curse followed by the sound of books tumbling. 'Maybe two!'

I step over a small pile of travel guides as Ciara winds her way through the room, heading for the large table in the centre. Like the window, it's dedicated to Frank, with various editions of his novels arranged around a small blackboard that counts down the weeks until the next release.

The Last Mountain.

Even with the setback with the storm, she finished it on time as I knew she would. More than that, she handed in her final edit with three days to spare. Three days she spent watching movies in bed and emerging only when I enticed her with takeout.

She knocked it out of the park. A little over the word count, but each one of those words is earned. She managed to put her own mark on the world while still honouring Frank's legacy and storytelling. The casual reader might not be able to tell the difference, but the stakes feel higher, the humour darker. It's a fitting finale to the series. I'd go so far as to say a perfect one. Even if I did have to drag the more romantic scenes from her.

She grew more comfortable once she got going, though.

She just needed a bit of practice.

Casey was over the moon with how it turned out. He wanted to sign her for her own series and spent months trying to convince her to write fantasy, but she was firm that she wanted to work on her own stuff for a while. After all, her long-promised detective series wasn't going to write itself. Or at least, that's what I think she's writing. She hasn't let me read so much as a word, despite me waking up more than once to find her typing in the living room.

We've been living together for just over a year now.

Despite the rush of those last few days in Ireland, it wasn't as simple as her just moving back with me when I left. It took months to get everything sorted with the house, to tie up the loose ends not only in Frank's life but in hers. Not that anyone made it hard for her. They were all thrilled by the news. Ronan threw a going-away party at Delaney's, and, from what I heard, the place was packed. Maddie even came back from Dublin for it. And I know Ciara enjoyed it, because I received thirty-seven texts, photos and voice notes over the course of the night and then absolutely nothing for forty-eight hours besides an *I'm alive* update. I could practically smell the hangover from here.

I won't lie and say I wasn't nervous when it finally happened. When she picked a date and booked her tickets. Even if I did miss her so much it hurt, it was still a big decision. We both knew that. But all those fears had vanished as soon as she strode through the doors in the arrivals hall. When one glimpse of her wiped out every doubt in my mind.

'I guess I'd better get used to this,' she says as I straighten the stacks on the table.

'Just wait until the billboards go up.' I take a step back and frown. They've got books six and seven in the wrong order.

'Sam.'

'Hmm?' I swap the piles and re-straighten them before taking a picture.

'I thought you didn't work on weekends any more.'

'This is for personal use,' I say, and take one of her before she can stop me.

Two months after I returned to New York, Casey called me and Laura into his office and informed us that he was retiring after *The Last Mountain*'s publication. He wanted us to run Richardson Books together. Laura as president and me as vice.

The way he said it, I could tell he was expecting me to push back. Maybe Laura was, too. And maybe, a year ago, I would have. But, if anything, I was relieved. I asked for Amy to be promoted to cover some of my list, logged on to our team's leave spreadsheet for the first time in months and booked two vacation days just for fun.

Or for the *craic*, as Ciara would say.

I thought it would be difficult putting the brakes on things when I'd been going so hard for so long, but it turns out it's much easier leaving at five p.m. when there's someone you want to go home to. Easier not to check your email or reach for your phone when the love of your life is standing right in front of you.

My sister was thrilled with my new world view, and she showed it by filling my calendar with babysitting duties. She and Ciara got on like a house on fire, too, the book leak forgiven and forgotten as Lizzie became Ciara's first friend in New York.

It wasn't all smooth sailing. It couldn't be. Some days are stressful. Some days, we snap at each other. Some days, I don't see her at all because we're busy or moody or both. But it's important to have those moments. Important to be human, and be there for each other's lows as well as the highs.

Because some days, I wake up and see her head on the pillow next to mine, and it's as though I've forgotten how to breathe. Some days, when I do, I let her sleep, content just to lie there with her. Other days, I wake her up, making sure to do it in a way that I know she'll be grateful for.

She's become such a part of my life that it makes me wonder how I ever spent a day without her.

'Look.' Ciara pulls off her glove and points to a set of framed photos hanging above the till. They're like the kind you see in restaurants sometimes, famous people who dined there, except instead of actors and singers these are authors. Some newer and some many decades old, black and white or faded with time.

Including one Polaroid of Frank Sheridan and a little girl by his side.

'I thought this place looked familiar,' Ciara murmurs as I move closer to it.

She can't be more than ten or eleven in it. Dressed in a green sparkly dress and missing a tooth. She doesn't care about that, though, not yet grown into self-consciousness, and she grins with her whole mouth, thrilled to be standing next to her father.

'Stop looking at it,' she says when I smile. 'You're not allowed to see any more pictures of me before the age of twenty-two.'

'Was that your glow-up?'

'That was my haircut. Something you wouldn't know about.'

I laugh, catching sight of myself in a nearby mirror. I haven't shaved in a few days. 'Message received.'

'I'm only kidding,' she says, reaching up to touch my jaw.

'You like me scruffy?'

'I like you all ways.' She drops her arm, looking decisive. 'You can kiss me now.'

'Oh, I can, can I?'

'Not if you're going to have an attitude about—'

I press my lips to hers, and she grabs the front of my jacket with one hand, holding me there as if I might try to move away. The syrup from her coffee makes her mouth taste sweet, and when she breaks the kiss she just laughs when I protest.

'I love you,' I tell her.

'You'd better.'

'Hi, there!' a voice chimes. 'Sorry about that.'

Ciara's hair tickles my nose as she turns her head before I do, and we glance up to find the mysterious bookseller emerging from the shelves. She looks as if she's still in college, with bleached blonde hair and a septum piercing. A pile of poetry books is balanced in her hands.

'Just browsing, or need some help?'

'Where's your crime section?' Ciara asks, and I wander after them as she takes her time choosing two for me and two for her, using me as her own personal book butler as she stacks them in my arms.

'I feel like if you're spending this much money, you should at least get a bookmark,' the shop assistant says when we finally make it to the till. She grabs two from beside the register, both Ravian-themed. 'Are you fans?' she asks, catching our look. 'The author loved this spot. My boss said he used to come in here all the time. We've got some signed books if you want to take a look.'

'We're good,' Ciara says. 'Thank you.' And the assistant's professionalism falters as she hands over the bag. I don't know if she picked up on her accent or just guessed, but her eyes go wide as the penny drops.

'Are you— Sorry,' she says, her cheeks going bright pink. 'It's just you look so much like . . . are you Ciara Sheridan?'

'I am.' Ciara smiles, and I step back, leaving them to it.

A little while later, we leave the store and I reach for my pocket out of pure habit, one I've developed in the past two weeks, ever since I snuck away during one of her writing days. But instead of finding what I should, my hand meets nothing but my keys and air.

Ciara pauses, noticing my sudden panic. 'You okay?'

'I'm grand.' The words slip out before I can stop myself and she latches on to them as she always does when it happens.

'It's so cute when you say that.'

'Words are for everyone, Ciara.'

'Not when you can't pull them off.'

'I can pull them off.'

'*Grand*,' she says in a terrible American accent, and I let her make fun of me because at least she's distracted. 'Which way are we—'

'Left,' I say, and she spins on her heel, striding off.

I follow a step behind, still having a mini-heart attack as I rifle through the bags and double-check my front pockets, my anxiety mounting until I shove a receipt aside and my fingers close around a small velvet box. Relief surges through me so strongly that, when I jog to catch up with her, I'm grinning like an idiot.

'Now what?' she asks, exasperated.

'Nothing. Just thought I'd lost something.'

'Besides your sense of direction?'

I'm confused for an instant before she tugs me sharply to the left and down the block we're supposed to go.

'Did you find it, then?' she asks, slipping her hand into mine.

'Yeah.' I duck down to kiss her temple, and she pretends to dig her elbow into my side even as she looks up with a smile. 'I did.'

ACKNOWLEDGEMENTS

As always, the biggest thank you to me. I wrote this book and, therefore, did the most work. Well done, me.

The second biggest thank you to my agent, Hannah Schofield, who took one look at this story and my career and went, 'Hold my beer'. Thank you for your hard work, your passion, and your patience when it's time for my monthly emotional breakdown.

Every publication is a team effort, but this was an international one, too. In the US, I owe so much to my editor, Cassidy Sachs, who was the first person to say yes to this book. Thank you also to John Parsley, Maya Ziv, Stephanie Cooper, Amanda Walker, LeeAnn Pemberton, Melissa Solis, Clare Shearer, and the entire team at Dutton. Traveling north, Deborah Sun de la Cruz is my number one person at Penguin Canada, with an extended thanks to Marion Garner, Bonnie Maitland, Catherine Knowles, Alanna McMullen, Brittany Larkin, and the whole crew there.

On the UK side, a massive thank you to Molly Walker-Sharp

at Sphere for feeding me pasta and wooing me with a Taylor Swift-inspired PowerPoint. Shout out also to Frances Rooney, Charlotte Stroomer, Tom Webster, Louise Harvey, and the sales, marketing and publicity teams.

Thank you as well to all my publishers worldwide for bringing these books to so many new readers.

On the more personal side, I'm immensely grateful to Tilda for looking me dead in the eye (again, over pasta) and telling me firmly and repeatedly to send this book in. To Luiza, Karisa, Danielle, and Áine for reading through and gently asking, 'Did you mean this, or is it a giant, obvious mistake?' and to all my friends and family who have to put up with cancelled plans, laptops on the beach and long, rambling voice notes. I know I am dramatic and stressed all the time, but I'm also so pretty? And you love me. So.

Finally, thank you to my readers, especially if you've been waiting for this one. Thank you for your messages, your creativity, and your kindness. It's a privilege to get to share these stories, and I think of you every time I sit down to write. Thank you for reading. Thank you for sticking with me. Thank you. Thank you. Thank you.

RAISING READERS
Books Build Bright Futures

Dear Reader,

We'd love your attention for one more page to tell you about the crisis in children's reading, and what we can all do.

Studies have shown that reading for fun is the **single biggest predictor of a child's future life chances** – more than family circumstance, parents' educational background or income. It improves academic results, mental health, wealth, communication skills, ambition and happiness.[1]

The number of children reading for fun is in rapid decline. Young people have a lot of competition for their time. In 2024, 1 in 10 children and young people in the UK aged 5 to 18 did not own a single book at home.[2]

Hachette works extensively with schools, libraries and literacy charities, but here are some ways we can all raise more readers:

- Reading to children for just 10 minutes a day makes a difference
- Don't give up if children aren't regular readers – there will be books for them!
- Visit bookshops and libraries to get recommendations
- Encourage them to listen to audiobooks
- Support school libraries
- Give books as gifts

There's a lot more information about how to encourage children to read on our website: **www.RaisingReaders.co.uk**

Thank you for reading.

hachette UK

---

[1] OECD, '21st-Century Readers: Developing Literacy Skills in a Digital World', 2021, https://www.oecd.org/en/publications/21st-century-readers_a83d84cb-en.html

[2] National Literacy Trust, 'Book Ownership in 2024', November 2024, https://literacytrust.org.uk/research-services/research-reports/book-ownership-in-2024